### Rave reviews for *In Plain Sight*

"Gayle Wilson is one of the best
romantic suspense writers in the business."
—*Chronicle Herald* (Halifax, Nova Scotia)

"*In Plain Sight* sizzles from start to finish.
I couldn't put it down."
—*New York Times* bestselling author Carla Neggers

"Wilson's novel mesmerizes from first page to the last,
with chilling twists and a compelling plot."
—*Romantic Times*

"Gayle Wilson pulls out all the stops
to give her readers a thrilling, chilling read
that will give you goose bumps in the night."
—*ReadertoReader.com*

### More praise for Gayle Wilson

"Gayle Wilson is one of the Divine Ones,
a writer who combines impeccable craft with
unsurpassed storytelling skills. Her books are dark, sexy
and totally involving. I can't recommend her enough."
—bestselling novelist Anne Stuart

"Gayle Wilson will go far in romantic suspense.
Her books have that special 'edge' that lifts them out of
the ordinary. They're always tautly written, a treasure
trove of action, suspense and richly drawn characters."
—*New York Times* bestselling author Linda Howard

"Rich historical detail, intriguing mystery,
romance that touches the heart and lingers in the mind.
These are the elements which keep me waiting
impatiently for Gayle Wilson's next book."
—*USA TODAY* bestselling author BJ James

"Writing like this is a rare treat."
—*Gothic Journal*

MAY     2005

**Also by Gayle Wilson**

IN PLAIN SIGHT

**And coming soon from HQN Books**

DOUBLE BLIND

# GAYLE WILSON

## WEDNESDAY'S CHILD

HQN™

ISBN 0-373-77039-1

WEDNESDAY'S CHILD

Copyright © 2005 by Mona Gay Thomas

This edition published by arrangement with Harlequin Books S.A.

® and TM are trademarks of the publisher. Trademarks indicated with ® are registered in the United States Patent and Trademark Office, the Canadian Trade Marks Office and in other countries.

www.HQNBooks.com

Printed in U.S.A.

Monday's child is fair of face.

Tuesday's child is full of grace.

Wednesday child is full of woe.

Thursday's child has far to go.

Friday's child is loving and giving.

Saturday's child works hard for its living.

But the child that's born on the Sabbath day
Is bonny and blithe, and good and gay.

# WEDNESDAY'S CHILD

# *PROLOGUE*

WORKING FOR an almost artistic perfection, he draped the body over the steering wheel, carefully aligning the top of the head with the starred crack he'd created in the windshield. He was almost finished. And as soon as he was—

There was a rustling from the bushes behind him. He backed out of the car so quickly he slammed his head into the top of the door frame. Stifling a curse, he peered into the darkness, hardly daring to breathe. For endless seconds he waited, but there was no repetition of whatever he'd heard.

Coon, he thought. Or maybe a beaver, although he hadn't heard the distinctive slap and glide into the river. Something that wasn't human, in any case. And humans were the only witnesses he cared about.

He eased back through the open door of the SUV, being careful this time to duck below its frame. He tried to position the corpse higher over the wheel, but its dead weight and the angle he was working from made that impossible.

It doesn't matter, he told himself. This body wasn't going to be found. Trying to place it so the location of the head wound made some kind of sense was simply a precaution.

But then, he was a careful man by nature. Nothing left to chance. Nothing forgotten.

He took one last look around the interior of the car, his eyes searching with the aid of the bright moonlight for anything he might have overlooked. That, too, was unnecessary. He'd gone over the car with a fine-tooth comb. And he'd found what he'd been sent to retrieve. The river would take care of any other evidence. Just as it would take care of the marks on the body. And even if it were found—

But it wouldn't be. He intended to make sure of that.

He reached across the driver's seat, leaning in behind the corpse, to locate by feel the lever of the emergency brake. His fingers closed around it as his thumb depressed the release. Despite the angle at which it was parked, the car didn't move.

His cheeks puffed slightly with the breath of relief he released. *So far so good.*

Satisfied that everything was going as planned, he withdrew his torso from the vehicle to take one more slow survey of his surroundings, evaluating the stillness. He'd been out here long enough that the normal night sounds along the river had resumed. Tree frogs and crickets. The occasional plop of a fish jumping. From the distance came the throaty call of an owl.

Satisfied, he eased the door closed, pushing hard enough at the last to make sure the latch caught. Again he listened, but other than a slight hesitation in the nocturnal symphony, there had been no reaction to the noise.

He'd driven the SUV off the bridge entrance and parked it on the reinforced slope leading down to the river. If he had left the headlights on—as he'd thought about doing in order to monitor its descent—they would now be shining down into the swift, rain-swollen current. All he needed was a little luck. And if he got it, the car would never be seen again.

As he walked up the incline toward the rear of the vehicle, his eyes once more searched the woods and the two-lane blacktop that led to the bridge. It was an automatic precaution. There was no traffic. Not here. And especially not now. Nobody was going to be out in Linton at 3:00 a.m. on a Sunday morning.

Taking a deep breath, he put his hands against the back of the SUV and pushed as hard as he could. Despite the incline and the fact that he had left the car out of gear, nothing happened.

He fought the urge to open the door and check that the brake was off and that it was indeed in neutral. Instead, he put his shoulder against the rear door, trying to rock the heavy vehicle to get it started. Still it didn't move.

The first curl of panic fluttered in his stomach. In desperation he bent his knees, trying to bring the muscles of his buttocks and thighs to bear on the task. The soles of his shoes slipped against the concrete, making it hard to get traction. And then, like a miracle, he felt the SUV shift.

That small indication of success was enough to intensify his efforts. With a grunt of exertion, he threw his body against the metal again, feet churning, as they had when he'd butted the practice dummy on the high-school football field.

Just as that seemingly immovable object had eventually given in to his determination, this one did, too. The car moved so suddenly that he fell to his hands and knees as it slowly rolled away from him.

He scrambled up, slipping and sliding down the incline in time to watch the front tires enter the water. Eyes straining to follow the car's path through the darkness, he felt a sense of vindication as the current caught it.

As he'd anticipated, the car was too heavy to be carried downriver, but the rushing water turned the SUV as it began to sink, aligning it so it was parallel to the base of the bridge.

Then, as if on command, the car began to nose downward into the exact resting place he'd designed for it, directly beneath the old concrete supports. Exhilaration filled his chest.

Suddenly, by a bizarre trick of moonlight, the rear window seemed to be illuminated. He could see straight through it and into the back seat of the car that was by now more than half submerged. He watched, unable to pull his eyes away, as water covered the infant seat that had been strapped into the back. He didn't look away until the SUV and all it contained had disappeared forever beneath the surface of the river.

# CHAPTER ONE

*Seven Years Later*

"MRS. KAISER?" The masculine voice on the other end of the phone sounded hesitant. Almost uncertain.

Wrong number, Susan Chandler thought as she considered how to respond. A telemarketer. Some kind of survey. Nothing to get excited about, despite how he'd addressed her.

"Who is this, please?"

"Wayne Adams with the Johnson County Sheriff's Department, ma'am. I'm trying to get in touch with a Mrs. Richard Kaiser."

Despite the fact that by now she had realized this might be the call she'd waited for for so long, Susan knew she still couldn't afford to let down the emotional barriers she'd struggled so hard to put into place. Not yet. Not until she was sure this was somehow connected to Emma.

She closed her eyes, taking a deep breath before she repeated, her voice sounding remarkably steady, "Johnson County? And where is that, please?"

"Mississippi. Johnson County, Mississippi. Sorry, ma'am. You get used to folks you're calling knowing that, I guess." A hint of amusement, clearly self-directed, colored the words.

*Amusement.* Then in all probability…

"What's your call in relation to, Mr. Adams?"

"Sheriff Adams," the caller corrected a little pompously. "You *are* Mrs. Kaiser, then? Mrs. Richard Kaiser?"

"That's right."

She didn't bother to explain the divorce she had finally obtained four years ago, granted on the grounds of desertion. If she mentioned she was no longer Mrs. Kaiser, there was always the possibility he might hang up without giving her whatever information he had.

She needed to hear what he had to say, but she also needed to maintain a tight rein on her emotions until she had. Too many times in the past she'd anticipated being told something positive, only to be devastated when that didn't occur.

"Then…I'm afraid I have some bad news, ma'am."

"Bad news" wasn't one of the phrases she'd been preparing for. Not after his previous tone. Her heart rate accelerated, its too-rapid beating filling her throat and sending blood rushing to her brain until she was almost light-headed.

"What kind of bad news?"

"There's been an accident."

When she had first walked into that eerily empty house seven years ago and gone from room to room, calling their names, that had been one of the first things she'd thought of. *There's been an accident. Something terrible has happened to them….*

Even later, during the long, sleepless nights after

they'd told her what Richard had done, she had paced the floor, trying to work out some other explanation. Something that would explain the nightmare she was living.

She licked her lips, which had suddenly gone dry. "What kind of accident?"

"It's your husband, ma'am. We found his car submerged in the Escatawpa River. Looks like he must have run past the entrance to the bridge in the dark. It's a tricky turn if you don't know the road."

"Richard?"

"I'm sorry, ma'am. His body was *in* the car. I should have told you that at the first."

"He's dead."

Her voice was too flat. Unemotional. She could imagine what the sheriff in Mississippi must be thinking. Even so, she was unable to summon up any regret that Richard's life had ended. After all he'd put her through—

With that thought came another. A terrifying one.

"Was there anyone in the car with him?" Her heart now hesitated, refusing to beat again as she waited for the answer.

"No, ma'am, there wasn't. There was no one else inside."

He probably thought she was concerned about another woman. And at one time she might have been. Long before she understood there were anxieties far more compelling than those.

"As a courtesy, we asked the Atlanta PD to go to the address on his license," the sheriff went on. "The folks living there now didn't recognize the name, so we ran it through the national databases and found… Well, I expect you know what we found. I wasn't sure this number would still be active after all these years. There hadn't been any updates since the initial report was filed, but I figured it was worth a shot."

She'd had to sell the house almost immediately, but due to the circumstances, the phone company had allowed her to keep this number. It wasn't as if Emma had known it, but they told her it was customary with cases involving missing children.

Only then, in thinking back to those first terrible weeks, did she realize the significance of what the sheriff had just said. "Are you saying Richard had identification on him? That his driver's license gave that name and address?"

She had long believed Richard was living somewhere under an assumed name. That's why they hadn't been able to locate him. How could he have escaped those countless inquiries if he'd kept his real name? Especially if he were still in the South?

"His wallet was in the car. Surprisingly, despite all the time it had been in the water, most of the things it contained were in pretty good shape. Of course, his license was the easiest to read since it was laminated."

There was a disconnect between the sheriff's words and what she'd been thinking. It wasn't until she allowed them to replay in her mind that their import began to dawn.

"I don't understand. You said it was an accident."

"Yes, ma'am." The uncertainty was back in his voice.

From what Adams had said, she'd been operating

under the assumption that the accident he referred to had just occurred. Obviously, that assumption was wrong.

"Just how long do you believe my husband's body has been in the water?"

There was a long beat of silence.

"Actually, the coroner can't tell us that for sure—not yet. Given the condition of the car and the body... We're guessing shortly after you notified law enforcement he was missing."

*Shortly after you notified law enforcement...*

The words seemed to exist in some parallel universe. All the months she'd spent searching for him—and for Emma—Richard had already been dead, his car submerged, his body slowly decomposing.

Images of the black SUV sinking into the murky water of some Mississippi river were suddenly in her head, despite her near desperation to keep them out. Refusing to allow herself to entertain those kinds of thoughts was an art she had believed she'd perfected. She'd been wrong.

Despite the endless number of times she had attempted to imagine what Emma would look like now, it was always her daughter's face the last time she'd seen her that was forever in her mind's eye. A picture as clear as the August morning she'd left for the airport and the children's literature conference. She'd had an appointment with an editor who had shown an interest in her illustrations—an appointment which had led to her first freelance assignment with the publisher she still worked for.

Emma had been fourteen months old then. Her hair

slightly curling and dark blond. Her eyes, almost the same clear, dark blue as her father's, were surrounded by impossibly long lashes that spiked, jeweled with tears, whenever she cried.

She had cried that morning. She had held up her arms to Susan, begging to be taken. Laughing, Richard had swooped her up and begun dancing her around the kitchen to allow Susan to escape. That was the last time she had seen either of them.

She had long ago accepted that unless something extraordinary happened or unless Richard decided to contact her, she would probably never see Emma again. And now...

"My daughter," she managed, pushing the words past the constriction in her throat.

"Ma'am?"

"My daughter was with my husband when he disappeared. I was away for the weekend, and when I got back—" There was no need to give him those details. All she wanted was what he knew about Emma. "He took her with him when he disappeared."

Unable to afford two, they had swapped the toddler seat between their cars. It had been in Richard's SUV that morning. And when she'd returned...

"Her safety seat was in his car," she finished. The images of the dark water closing over the top of the SUV were back in her head, no matter how hard she tried to block them.

The sheriff's hesitation lasted so long this time her knees went weak. She sagged against the kitchen counter, closing her eyes against the burn of her tears.

"There *was* an infant seat in the car, ma'am, but

there was no baby in it. I told you. There was nobody else inside your husband's SUV when it was found. Are you sure she was—"

Her strangled sob interrupted his question. It wasn't as if she hadn't been over this a dozen times with the police. Richard, the SUV, the infant seat and Emma had all been missing when she'd returned to Atlanta the following Monday.

"Is there someone there with you, Mrs. Kaiser? Or someone you could call?"

It was concern she heard in the deep voice this time. In spite of the emotional stoicism she'd adopted to deal with the law enforcement community through the years, his sympathy was her undoing. Still holding the phone, Susan slid down the side of the kitchen cabinets until she was on the floor. Sobs, finally unleashed again after all these years, shook her body.

Richard was dead. He had been dead for seven years, making a lie of all the times she had told herself that no matter what else he might be guilty of, Richard had genuinely loved Emma. Loved her enough to give up his life for her. The thought that, no matter what happened, he would take care of their baby was all that had kept her sane.

Now she knew that wherever Emma was, there was no one of her own to look after her. And there *had* been no one during all those long years she had prayed and longed for her daughter.

WHEN SUSAN MET Sheriff Adams the following day, she realized immediately that he was older than she had pictured him during their conversation. She estimated now that he must be in his mid or maybe even late forties.

His face bore the perpetual tan of someone who virtually lived outdoors, however, so her guess could be off by several years. His skin's darkness was unrelieved except for the pale green eyes and the delicate web of small white lines radiating from their corners. Even now, despite the bright sunshine of the October afternoon, he wore neither hat nor sunglasses.

His features were angular, matching the rangy body. The slight paunch around his midsection gave additional evidence for her estimate of his age, although he wore his fading blond hair longer than she would have expected from the sheriff of such a rural community. Or maybe that was because it was still the style here rather than any attempt to appear younger.

As soon as she'd arrived in Linton, he had taken her in his squad car out to the site where the SUV had been found. The old two-lane bridge across the narrow river stood side by side with a wood-and-metal railroad trestle.

According to the sheriff, it had been a train derailment that had led to the discovery of Richard's body. During their efforts to recover the railcars that had gone into the river, the salvage company had stumbled across the submerged SUV.

"Gave that crew a shock, I can tell you." His eyes were focused on the cranes, still parked on the riverbank below. Since it was Friday afternoon, they were idle.

"And they're the ones who pulled the car out?"

"Thought it was a junker. Some folks just as soon

roll 'em into the river or push 'em over a ravine as take 'em to the junkyard. You know how people are."

Apparently realizing how far off the subject of her husband's death that had taken him, the sheriff turned from his contemplation of the equipment to look at her.

"Sorry. That ain't got nothing to do with why we're here."

"And that's when they discovered his body?" she asked, ignoring his attempted apology.

"They called the office, and we notified the coroner."

"And no one found any evidence Emma had been in the car?"

"Nothing but that infant seat. Like I told you, there was no second body, Ms. Chandler."

Almost without her conscious volition Susan's eyes returned to the slowly moving water below. There were questions she didn't want to ask right now because she was afraid of the answers. Since Adams's phone call, she had managed to regain control of the emotions that had momentarily escaped the long restraint she'd forced on them. She didn't want to do anything that might put that fragile containment into jeopardy.

"Were the windows rolled up when the car was found?"

"All I can tell you is they were when I got here. The driver's-side door was open, however."

The men would have had to open it to find the body, she supposed, but the information made her wonder if Richard might have tried to get out. He was a good swimmer, and the current didn't look strong enough to keep him from reaching shore. Unless he'd been too badly injured to try.

"But was it open when they pulled it out of the river?"

Adams's mouth pursed slightly as if he were thinking about that. After a moment he shook his head.

"Don't know. Have to confess I didn't ask. We all knew what had happened. If you live around these parts, you know all about this place. More cars than I can count have missed that turn in the dark. No guardrail. Nothing to keep you from driving right off into the river if you misjudge the entrance. State ain't gonna do nothing about it since they built the new bridge up on 84. Now this road don't get enough traffic to make fixing this worth their while. It could even have been raining that night. Slick pavement. Poor visibility. Your husband a drinker?"

"I beg your pardon?"

"A lot of folks who miss that turn have had a few too many, if you know what I mean."

"Richard didn't drink. Not to excess."

How confident she sounded. Almost smug. And how ironic that was coming from a woman who'd had no idea her husband was planning to disappear, taking everything they owned with him. Everything including their daughter.

"The current doesn't look very powerful." She was still thinking about the terrible possibilities of that opened door.

The sheriff's lips pursed again as he looked over the water. "Can be. Depends on the rain upriver. And if you're out in the middle of the channel, it runs a lot faster. Could have been what happened that night."

"I'm sorry?" She turned, her eyes questioning as they focused on his weathered face.

"If the door was open, I mean. Maybe the current just took her out of his hands."

*Emma. He means Emma,* she realized, sickness stirring the pit of her stomach.

But if Emma *had* been in the car when it had gone off the bridge, she knew Richard well enough to know Emma would have been strapped into her seat. Open door or not, there was no way the current could have washed her out of those restraints.

"She would have been strapped in."

The sheriff shrugged. "Maybe when your husband realized what was happening, he tried to get her out. Maybe he had her free and the current just took her—"

"No," Susan said.

The single syllable was loud in the afternoon stillness. The scenario he had just suggested wasn't an idea she was willing to entertain. Not yet.

Adams had already admitted that he didn't know if the door had been open when the car was pulled from the water. And if it *had* been, then why hadn't Richard, an experienced swimmer, gotten out of the car and swum to safety.

*Because he was trying to locate his baby in that dark, rushing water? Struggling to unfasten straps he couldn't see? Trying desperately to get them both to safety?*

"I didn't mean to upset you, Ms. Chandler. I'll be glad to find out about the doors *and* the windows. Did you ever think that maybe your husband left your daughter in the care of a relative or some friends? Maybe she wasn't with him at all when he come down here."

*Did you ever think...*

There was literally *no one* she hadn't questioned about that possibility. No relative or mutual acquaintance that she had been aware of—and some she hadn't been aware of until after Richard's disappearance—that she hadn't asked about Emma. And about Richard, of course.

None of them had professed any knowledge of their whereabouts. And despite her desperate need for information, there had not been one of them she'd doubted. Now she *knew* they'd been telling the truth. Richard had contacted no one in the weeks after his disappearance because he had been here, hidden by the waters of this narrow, marshy river.

"When will they be back?"

"Ma'am?"

"The people those belong to." She tilted her chin toward the cranes on the bank below. "Will they be back out here on Monday?"

"I'm not sure what their schedule is. I can call the main office of Southern Georgia first thing Monday morning. See if I can talk to the men who were here that day. I'll let you know what they say as soon as I find out. You *do* understand that nobody had any idea at the time that we ought to be looking for your daughter."

There should have been a cross-reference to Emma in the national database of missing persons the sheriff had searched for Richard's name. Apparently that had been another bureaucratic screwup. There had been plenty of those.

Emma had always been listed as an abducted child. Susan had been advised that was the best way to draw attention to her case. Not that she had ever been able to tell it had made any difference. After all, Emma was with her father. And Susan, unaware at that time of how the system worked, had admitted that Richard had no history of mistreating their daughter.

That was the truth, of course, as well as what had kept her sane through the years. But it had lowered the urgency with which the various agencies had responded to her pleas for help.

"I'd like to talk to those men myself, if you don't mind," she said, thinking of all the other "comforting" platitudes she'd listened to during those first few months.

There was too much at stake to trust that another set of law enforcement officials would do everything in their power to find her baby. She was no longer as naive as she had once been.

She had been given another chance to find Emma. A chance to right all the things she had done wrong seven years ago.

"In all honesty, ma'am, I don't think that's such a good idea," Adams said. "First place, it's bound to be upsetting. And those men might not tell you everything they'd be willing to say to somebody who's not as…emotionally involved in this."

"Is there a motel nearby?" she asked, ignoring his advice.

That was something else she had done the first time. Listened to all the people who were supposed to know the best thing to do. And look where it had gotten her.

"A motel?"

She couldn't remember seeing any near the exit to

Linton. It seemed there had been only miles and miles of trees along both sides of the interstate, their leaves just beginning to be tinged with color from the fall nights.

"Somewhere I can stay while I'm in town."

The green eyes widened in surprise, exposing the network of lines at their corners. "Plenty of motels in Pascagoula."

Which was more than sixty miles away. Despite the fact that most of the distance was state highway and interstate, she didn't want to make that commute every day. And until she found out what had happened to Emma...

"I mean here. Somewhere I can stay in Linton."

Somewhere close enough that she could talk to anyone who might have encountered Richard—and please, dear God, encountered Emma—while they were here.

"No motels around here. We had a hotel at one time, but—" The sheriff stopped abruptly, his lips still slightly parted.

"What is it?"

"I was gonna say that the hotel closed due to lack of business once the state highway opened up, but then I remembered Miz Lorena's."

"Miz Lorena?" The title the sheriff had used was the old-fashioned Southern one that had nothing to do with women's rights and a great deal to do with age and respect.

"Miz Lorena Bedford. Got a big ole house a few miles outside the city limits. Tried to make it into one of those bed-and-breakfast places, aiming to get the Yankees heading to the Gulf and the casinos. Once that stretch of the four-lane opened, there wasn't enough traffic on the Linton cutoff for her to make a go of it. Same thing that happened to the hotel. That's what made me think of her place."

"And you think she might rent me a room?"

The sheriff shrugged, looking back down on the river. "Got no idea how she'd take to the idea, but she's got the space *and* the bathrooms. Had 'em put in special for all those guests that didn't show up. It's worth a try. I can tell you how to get out there. You tell Miz Lorena what you're here for, and I doubt she's gonna turn you down."

Susan nodded, taking a last look at the sluggish current below. She wasn't going to leave Linton until she had some answers. Maybe that determination was simply a recognition that this place represented her last chance of finding Emma, but in her heart—the one that had been frozen for the last seven years—there was again a delicate flame of hope.

## CHAPTER TWO

DESPITE THE SHERIFF'S repeated reference to Lorena Bedford's "big ole house," Susan's first sight of it through the trees was a shock. Classic Greek Revival in style, its graceful columns soared from the porch to the roof of the second story. The structure was situated at the end of a long, unpaved driveway, bordered by two perfectly spaced rows of oaks, strands of picturesque Spanish moss hanging from their low branches.

She slowed the car as she made the turn onto the property. The rays of the dying sun touched the white paint with gold and shimmered off the glass of the front windows. The house looked like some Hollywood producer's fantasy of the antebellum South.

As she approached, reality was less kind. There were areas of flecked paint on the Doric columns, and the side veranda was devoid of furniture. The foundation plantings were neatly trimmed, however, and the grass, although not closely mown, was still, despite the season, thick and green.

The driveway circled around a garden, which had been planted directly in front of the steps leading up to the front door. A few of the small old-fashioned roses that comprised most of it were, surprisingly, still in bloom.

She pulled her car parallel to the steps and shut off the engine. Before she got out, she sat a moment in the twilight stillness. The murmur of insects could be heard from the surrounding woods. There were no other sounds. No traffic out on the two-lane she'd followed here. Not even the small-town noises she'd been aware of in the hours she'd spent in Linton.

She opened her door, stepping out again into the heat and humidity. She had discarded the jacket to her navy linen suit before she and Adams had gone down to the river. She thought about retrieving it from the back seat and then decided the temperature should preclude any such attempt at formality.

She brushed her hands over the wrinkles on the front of her skirt, deciding that, too, was a lost cause. Miz Lorena would just have to take her—or leave her—as she was.

Her keys still in the ignition, she walked around the front of the car and climbed the steps. Her heels echoed as she crossed the wooden boards of the porch.

The front door was open, probably as a concession to the late-afternoon heat. She tapped on the molding of the screen door, the sound echoing down the inside hallway she could see only dimly. She waited, politely looking at the roses beyond her car rather than watching for someone to answer her knock.

After a few moments without any response, she turned back to the door. She could hear no movement from inside the house. She cupped the outside of her hand against the screen, peering in under her arched palm.

Was it possible no one was home, despite the open door? Of course, the screen might be latched. Maybe this far out of town that was considered protection enough against intruders. She touched its frame, pulling the door toward her just enough to determine that it wasn't fastened.

She let the screen slip back into place and again tapped on its molding. Although she tried to apply more force than before, the resulting sound didn't seem appreciably louder.

This time she watched the hallway as she waited. Again there was no response.

She should have phoned before she drove out. The sheriff hadn't suggested that, and, as he apparently had, she'd assumed the old woman would be home.

Despite the fact that the hotel in town had closed, she had noticed a café on the square. She could drive back into Linton, look up the Bedford number and place a call from there. Actually, she would probably be wise to have dinner in town, she realized. Even if Miz Lorena agreed to rent her a room, the sheriff hadn't said she would also be willing to provide meals.

Decision made, Susan crossed the porch and descended the front steps. Her hand had already closed around the handle to the car door when a creak announced the opening of the screen.

Her eyes were drawn back to the porch. Since her arrival the daylight had faded enough that, under the overhang of the second-floor balcony, the area was now as dark as the interior hallway had been. She could see a figure in the open doorway, but little else.

"Mrs. Bedford?"

"She's not here." The voice was masculine, its accent not local, and its tone decidedly unwelcoming.

"Could you tell me when she'll be back?"

The pause after her question stretched far past politeness. So much for Southern hospitality.

"That depends on who wants to know."

Susan controlled a spurt of anger at the man's rudeness, acknowledging most of that was due to emotional exhaustion rather than his treatment of her request. After all, she'd shown up here without so much as a phone call asking permission.

Mrs. Bedford's house was no longer a commercial establishment. It was someone's home. And she needed a favor from the owner. Whoever this was, he might be able to exert some influence in that direction.

"My name is Susan Chandler." She tried to make her voice as pleasant as possible, considering the circumstances. As she talked, she walked back around the front of the car and headed toward the steps. "I had hoped Mrs. Bedford might rent me a room for a few days. I'm aware she's no longer in business—"

"Then why ask to rent a room?"

He had apparently turned on a light in the front of the house as he'd come to the door. His body was silhouetted against its glow, wide shoulders almost filling the frame.

Looking up at him from the foot of the steps, Susan's impression was that he was also taller than average. In spite of the width of his shoulders, his torso narrowed to a lean waist and slim hips. She could still see nothing of his face.

"Because Sheriff Adams *suggested* I ask her. It's…"

She let the sentence trail. She might have been willing to try and explain her compulsion to stay in town to another woman, but something about this man's attitude made her doubt he would sympathize with anything she might say.

"It's what?"

"Are you a relative of Mrs. Bedford's? Or..."

*A guest? The yardman?* As she tried to settle on a second option, he made the process unnecessary.

"You seem to have a proclivity for unfinished sentences."

Obviously *not* the hired help. Not unless handymen were better educated down here than she was accustomed to. And just as obviously determined to be rude.

"My husband's body was pulled from the river here two days ago," she said, deciding she had nothing to lose by a matching bluntness. "I need a place to stay until the coroner can tell me how he ended up there."

The silence stretched longer this time. In the few minutes she'd been here, the night creatures had joined the insect chorus, the combined noises the only sound for several seconds.

"I'm Jeb Bedford. Lorena is my great-aunt," he said. "At the moment I'm also her guest—a paying one, in case you were wondering."

She hadn't been. She didn't give a damn about whatever arrangements he had with Lorena Bedford.

Actually, she was beginning not to give a damn about any of this. The commute back and forth to Pascagoula was becoming more appealing by the second.

"Lorena's gone to the monthly fellowship supper at the church. Judging by previous ones, she should be back in less than an hour." His tone had changed. Still not welcoming, it didn't contain the edge of sarcasm. "*If* you'd like to wait."

Would she? A better question might be whether there would be any point. After all, she still didn't know that Mrs. Bedford would rent her a room.

"Actually..." she began, and then hesitated, unwilling to burn any bridges. Of course, she also didn't want to be reminded of her so-called proclivity for unfinished sentences. "I'd rather *not* wait if she's likely to turn me down. If I'm going to have to try to find a room in Pascagoula on a Friday night, I should probably get started in that direction now."

"Lorena's not going to turn you down. Not...under the circumstances. However, you might want to see the accommodations before you decide. What some people consider quaintly charming, others view as not having all the modern conveniences. All the rooms have private baths. And despite the area's reputation, those are *inside* the house." There was a hint of amusement or self-deprecation in that, but no sarcasm. "No coffeepots or microwaves, but with Lorena around you aren't likely to need either. She enjoys waiting on people."

Which sounded more inviting right now than he could probably imagine.

"The beds have feather mattresses," he went on. "Not orthopedically sound perhaps, but you soon get used to them."

He certainly seemed to have changed his tune. She hadn't intended to play the grieving widow, but he'd driven her to it. Given the results, right now she couldn't regret that she had.

"She should hire you for PR. You're quite a salesman."

"I couldn't sell ice in hell, but frankly Lorena can use the money. If you're going to spend it somewhere, it might as well be with her. Do you want the grand tour or not?"

The abrasiveness was back. For some reason her remark, intended to be humorous, hadn't had the desired effect. *So much for trying to mend fences.*

"With you as guide?" she couldn't refrain from asking.

Something of her irritation must have come through in the question. He responded in kind.

"Since I'm all that's available. Take it or leave it."

Her inclination was to tell this arrogant jackass what he could do with his aunt's room. Only the knowledge that she would be cutting off her own nose prevented her from getting back into her car and heading toward the interstate.

"Lead the way," she said, stepping onto the bottom step.

The screen door creaked again. She glanced up in time to watch him step back into the hallway. Although she was aware there was something awkward about the movement, it was not until he was inside and illuminated by the overhead chandelier that she understood what. He moved a couple of steps back in order to allow her to enter, heavily favoring his left leg.

Despite the fact she had continued to climb the steps as if nothing had happened, an unfamiliar emotion stirred in the pit of her stomach. Guilt, perhaps, that she'd returned his rudeness with her own? Embarrassment? Pity?

As he held the screen door for her to enter, she kept her eyes averted, examining the hallway instead of looking directly at him. The floor was of some dark wood that had been fashioned into narrow, irregular planks. It was probably a dozen feet wide and stretched into the darkness at the back of the house.

Pocket doors opened onto a formal parlor on one side and a dining room on the other. Both were furnished in keeping with the age of the house. In the sitting room an old pianoforte sat in the corner. Several pieces of sheet music were scattered on its stand and on the upholstered bench.

"When Lorena operated the house as a bed-and-breakfast, all the downstairs rooms were available for the use of the guests," her guide said. "I'm sure that will still be the case."

With his comment, there was no way Susan could avoid looking at him. She turned, prepared to make some politely conventional reply. All of them, instilled in her brain since childhood, flew out of her head.

She wasn't sure what she had expected Mrs. Bedford's great-nephew to look like, but certainly nothing like this. His close-cropped hair was so black the chandelier over their heads created no highlights in its midnight depths. In contrast, his eyes were a deep, clear blue. Black Irish, her grandmother would have said. Given the strong Celtic heritage of most of the South's population, in this case she would probably have been right.

His skin was almost as darkly tanned as the sheriff's. It didn't have the same weathered texture, but then this man was probably a decade or so younger. Although

Jeb Bedford wasn't handsome in any conventional sense of the word, no woman would ever have overlooked him in a crowd.

She suddenly became aware that her lips had parted to reply to what he'd said, but no words had yet emerged. She was simply staring at him, stupidly openmouthed.

"That's nice," she managed.

He was probably used to having this effect on women, she thought with a trace of disgust. She, however, wasn't accustomed to reacting to a man in this way. Not to any man. And certainly not in this situation.

She owed no loyalty to Richard, of course. He was the one who had walked away from their marriage. The sense of guilt her attraction to this man's rugged good looks produced was because she had something far more important to concentrate on right now—her desperate need to find out what had happened to Emma.

"The guest rooms are upstairs."

He tilted his head down the hall to where a narrow staircase climbed to the second floor. It was uncarpeted, its wooden treads visibly worn from the passage of thousands of feet going up and down them through the years.

"How old is the house?" she asked, more as an attempt to get back on some normal footing with him than because she had any real interest in its history.

He had already taken a step forward, but at her question he turned, looking back at her over his shoulder. "It was built in 1852. It's been in the hands of the family ever since. When Lorena dies..." He shrugged a dismissal.

"But surely there's *someone*—"

"My grandfather and Lorena were joint heirs to the property. Now that he's dead, there is no one else."

"Perhaps *your* father..." He was right, she realized. She *did* have a proclivity for not finishing sentences, maybe because she always seemed to be stating the obvious.

"My father died two years ago. He and my mother were divorced several years before that. Believe me, she wouldn't have anything to do with this place. Or with the Bedfords."

This time she avoided the obvious reply. Whether or not he chose to sell the house or to let it go to rack and ruin when his great-aunt died was none of her business. She wasn't even sure why she had bothered to pursue what he'd said. Maybe to postpone the moment she would have to follow his limping progress up the stairs.

"I...I really don't need to see the room," she stammered. "I'm sure it's fine. After all, from what the sheriff told me, there isn't any other accommodation near town."

The blue eyes told her that he knew exactly what she was thinking. They held on her face long enough that she felt color rise along her throat.

"You have a bag?" he asked, finally breaking the standoff.

Ridiculously, for a second or two she didn't know what he was talking about. "It's in the car."

"Then if you're going to take the room, I might as well get it before I show you up. Keys?"

Whatever she had seen in his eyes when she'd attempted to keep him from having to climb those stairs was back. In force. Challenging her to make another excuse.

That wasn't a mistake she would make again. Whatever was wrong with his leg, he obviously didn't want her concern.

And in all honesty, despite the limp, he looked like someone who was well able to take care of himself. Someone who was accustomed to doing that.

"They're in the ignition. My suitcase is in the trunk."

For an instant there was a gleam of something that looked like approval in his eyes. Whatever the emotion, it was quickly masked by a downward sweep of coal-black lashes. They weren't long, but both their thickness and their proximity to the blue irises made them noticeable.

Without another word, he started down the hall toward the front door. As he passed her, Susan pretended to look up the stairs as if the bit of the second story she could see from this vantage point was so interesting she couldn't pull her eyes away. Then, drawn by a compulsion she didn't pretend to understand, she turned, watching him limp toward the door.

She'd been right about the breadth of his shoulders. The damp material of the olive-drab T-shirt he wore stretched tautly across them, revealing the contoured muscles of his upper back. The shirt was tucked into a pair of faded black sweatpants.

Despite whatever was wrong with his leg, he looked like an athlete. She wondered if he might even have been working out when she'd disturbed him. That would explain the V of moisture at the neck of his shirt as well as the slight color along his cheekbone and dew of perspiration she'd put down to the heat.

"Only one?"

Startled, she looked up from her contemplation of the play of muscle in his back to find him looking at her over his shoulder, waiting for an answer before he opened the screen door. It must have been obvious that she'd been watching him.

He seemed amused by her scrutiny rather than annoyed. For the first time the hard line of his mouth was relaxed.

"Just the one."

"First room on the right," he said. "I'll bring the suitcase up, but you don't have to wait."

She wasn't sure why, but the instructions felt like a reprieve. At least a concession. As if she had just passed some kind of test and earned a grudging acceptance.

"Thank you."

"You want me to move your car around back?"

She hesitated, wondering if she'd missed a sign indicating that's where guests were supposed to park.

"Don't worry," he said when she didn't answer immediately. "As long as it's an automatic, I shouldn't be able to do too much damage."

"I'd be very grateful," she said, ignoring the attempt to intimidate her with the blatant reminder of his disability. "And it *is* an automatic. I never learned to drive a stick."

There was a slight upward movement at one corner of his mouth. "Somehow I was sure you hadn't."

She didn't know what that meant, but it didn't matter. Without giving her a chance at a parting shot, he allowed the screen door to slam behind him, leaving her alone in the wide hall. She drew an unsteady breath, wondering if she had made a mistake in coming out here.

She had sworn she would never trust officialdom again, and yet, because of what the sheriff had told her, she was in an isolated house with a rude stranger who carried an outsized chip on his shoulder. And she had just agreed to rent, sight unseen, a room in that house, never having met her hostess.

If the accommodations were truly awful, she could always leave in the morning. She'd been vague enough about her intentions to allow for that.

At least then she wouldn't have to pretend she wasn't aware of the absolute masculinity of the man who had gone out to retrieve her luggage. Sexual awareness this potent was a feeling she'd almost forgotten. And one she wasn't sure she was ready to experience again. Especially not now.

She turned, looking up the narrow stairs once more. Whatever the room at the top of them was like, it was hers for the night. Everything would probably look different in the morning. As for right now...

Right now she needed a hot shower and a bed with clean sheets, even if it had a feather mattress. If Lorena Bedford's house could provide either of those, she'd deal with everything else. Including Miz Lorena's arrogant nephew.

# CHAPTER THREE

"MY GOODNESS," Lorena said. "I'd been thinking about that poor man's family. Wondering how they must feel to finally know what happened to him. I knew some of them would come to Linton, but I never dreamed they might end up staying here. I'll have to thank Wayne the next time I'm in town. What's she like?"

Jeb wasn't sure his impression would be the kind of information his aunt was looking for. Since he'd been wounded, his reaction to people was too frequently measured by their response to his physical condition. It was a fault he was aware of, but unable to entirely suppress.

When he had turned around tonight and found Susan Chandler watching him, resentment that his limp now seemed to be the most interesting thing about him had resurfaced. In the past, before Iraq, his relationships with women had been based on any number of things: mutual sexual attraction, shared interests, even simple proximity. Now he seemed to be defined by only one thing.

He wasn't sure at what point during the course of his rehabilitation he'd become aware of that. Certainly not in the beginning. He'd been too focused on his own adjustment to his new physical limitations to notice how others reacted to them.

Maybe it had been coming back to Linton, where he'd spent a large part of his adolescence, that had made him aware of how differently the people he'd known then treated him now. Some were openly curious, which he'd been surprised to discover didn't bother him. Others pretended not to notice, as Mrs. Chandler had done tonight when he'd opened the door for her.

Some—and those were the ones he detested—were determined to be "helpful." There was nothing more certain to set his teeth on edge than solicitude. Especially from a woman to whom he was physically attracted.

In that respect, he would have to give his great-aunt's guest credit. In a matter of minutes, she had been able to conceal, if not destroy, any tendency to try to protect him. She hadn't wanted him to climb the stairs to show her the room, which had been a strike against her. She hadn't tried to circumvent his determination to retrieve her suitcase or move her car, however, and thank God she hadn't met him halfway up the stairs to take her bag from him. Despite that ridiculous announcement that she didn't need to see the room she was about to rent, he grudgingly gave her full marks for the rest.

"Exhausted," he said aloud in answer to Lorena's question. "And obviously still stunned."

"Why, I should say so. Bless her heart. What a thing to have happened. I swear they ought to close that bridge, as many people as have gone off into the river through the years."

"Maybe between the train wreck and this, they will."

He was leaning against the kitchen counter watching Lorena take things out of the refrigerator. Although she was almost ninety, she moved exactly as she had when he'd spent those long-ago summers down here. Her motions were quick, almost birdlike, an impression that was magnified by her size and her thinness.

"I didn't promise her supper," he said when she pulled a loaf of homemade bread out of the bread box and began unwrapping it. "Actually, I didn't promise her anything but the use of the room. You don't *have* to fix her a meal."

"You think she's already eaten?" Gnarled fingers paused over the loaf she had baked this morning, she looked up at him, faded blue eyes questioning.

"I doubt it," he said, reluctant to add hunger to the many problems Susan Chandler faced. "She's probably used to eating later than we do."

Most nights Lorena had supper on the table by six. Of course, since they both began the day shortly after five, Jeb wasn't complaining. The timing had been an adjustment, however. As he imagined it would be for Mrs. Chandler.

"From Atlanta, you say?"

"That's what her tag says."

"That poor woman." Lorena's eyes and hands had returned to her task. "I can't even imagine what she must be feeling."

"According to the paper, her husband's car had been submerged for years. She's had a long time to come to terms with his disappearance."

Maybe this was only a welcome closure for something she had dealt with long ago.

"Still…" Lorena said. "I mean she was married to the man. She must have loved him. And then…I guess he just disappeared, and she never knew what happened to him. It breaks my heart to think about that."

Jeb watched as she laid the two thick slices she'd cut off the loaf on a plate she had taken from the cabinet. After she'd spread mayonnaise thickly on both, she began piling ham on one.

"Did you like her?"

His great-aunt's question caught him off guard. For one thing, he wasn't sure whether he had or not. There was no denying that he'd found her attractive. And he had also admired her. Despite the day she'd had, she hadn't backed down when he'd challenged her about the car. And even as much as she obviously wanted the room, she hadn't been willing to cater to his rudeness. *More pluses than minuses.*

"Well enough to offer her a room."

"You *knew* I'd want you to do that," Lorena said.

"Still, I wouldn't have. Not unless I thought she was someone we could share the place with. At least for the night."

"Is that all she's staying?" Lorena looked up from the act of slipping a slice of tomato onto the ham. "Seems like it would take longer than that to work out the arrangements."

"Actually, I don't know how long she'll be in town. We didn't discuss it in detail. And she may decide she wants something more modern after tonight."

"Maybe I can convince her to stay," Lorena said, fitting the second piece of bread on top. "I think hot tea, don't you? I've got some chamomile. That should help her sleep."

"Judging by her eyes—" Jeb began and then stopped.

He'd been about to say that she would be tired enough to sleep without any of his aunt's herbal remedies. When he remembered what Susan Chandler had been through today, he thought she might appreciate something to help remove the images that must be in her mind.

"What about her eyes?"

"Like I said. She looked exhausted. More emotionally than anything else, maybe, but…I think she'd like that tea."

His great-aunt reached over and turned the gas on beneath the kettle that always sat in the exact same place on the back of the stove. "Did you show her where the extra quilts are? There's supposed to be a cold snap, either tomorrow or Sunday."

"Why don't you wait until you find out whether she'll be staying that long before you go worrying about extra cover. She'll be fine tonight."

"Maybe I should spoon up some of that peach cobbler."

"You don't even know if she's eaten, Lorena. Why don't you ask her about dessert before you carry it up?"

The kettle began to whistle, putting an end to his attempt to rein in his great-aunt's innate hospitality. There was some part of him that welcomed the idea that Susan Chandler's stay in the house would end after tonight. Another part admitted a degree of interest in her plans that went beyond casual curiosity. She was an extremely attractive woman. *Woman* being the operative word. At thirty-five, Jeb wasn't interested in someone who thought JFK referred only to an airport.

Susan Chandler was probably a few years younger than he. Late twenties, early thirties, maybe. Her fair skin showed little signs of aging, but with that dark auburn hair, she would have had no choice but to stay out of the sun.

Physically, she wasn't the type he was normally attracted to, both taller and thinner than he preferred. Even as that negative assessment formed, he rejected it.

Given his profession, he'd never been interested in long-term relationships. He had judged women he became involved with on their willingness to accept that. As well as on their physical attributes, he admitted. Something he wasn't particularly proud of. Not considering his present situation.

Despite Susan Chandler's ability to mask her initial feeling of pity, he'd been aware of it. And the look in her eyes wasn't one he wanted to see in a woman he was attracted to.

"There now," Lorena said, stepping back to admire the tray she'd prepared. "What do you think?"

"I think she's damn lucky Wayne Adams sent her here."

"Don't you curse, Jubal Bedford," Lorena scolded, although it was obvious the compliment pleased her. "Remember, you're an officer *and* a gentleman."

So far, he thought. So far.

"IT'S A BED-AND-BREAKFAST on the outskirts of Linton," Susan said into her cell phone. "There isn't a motel around here, but this will do for the time being."

"Are you sure you don't want Dave to come down?" her sister asked. "You know he's more than willing."

"Dave's place is there with you, taking care of my very precious nephew."

After years of trying, including more expensive in vitro attempts than they could afford, Charlotte had finally conceived. Although the pregnancy had been difficult, she was only a couple of weeks away from delivery now. And no one, including her doctor, believed she would go that long.

"I just hate to think of you doing all that by yourself."

"I'm fine. Just tired. A little overwhelmed with the thought of the possibilities."

Although she and Charlotte had already discussed the fact that Emma had not been in the car when it was found, Susan hadn't shared the information about the open door. She had decided there was no point in doing that until the sheriff had had time to confirm whether it had been open when the crane had pulled the SUV from the river.

"And you really think Emma might still be in that town?"

"All I know is that for some reason Richard was here. I need to know what he was doing in such an out-of-the-way area. That's one thing I need to find out. And maybe then…" She hesitated. "Maybe if someone here remembers seeing him, then—"

"They might have seen Emma, too," Charlotte said softly.

"She has to be somewhere. God knows I've already asked everyone any of us ever knew and gotten nowhere."

"Well, you keep us informed, you hear? If you don't call me every day, I swear I'm going to send Dave down there whether you like it or not. And you take care of yourself."

"I will. You, too. Take care of you and my sweet Davey."

"He's fine. We're both going to be fine. I can feel it," Charlotte said with a laugh. "Everybody's so uptight about all this, and I swear, Suz, I'm gonna breeze right through this delivery and pop this baby out quicker than anyone ever has before. Maybe I don't get them or carry them worth a damn, but I'm gonna be spectacular at birthing them."

At the joy and confidence in her sister's voice, tears welled in Susan's eyes. "I know you will. I'm counting on you, sweetie. We all are."

"You call me, you hear?"

"I will. Don't worry."

"Any news, good or bad, I want to know. Don't you two try to protect me. I need to know everything."

"No, I won't," Susan promised, "but…" She hesitated again, wondering if this was something she could share, even with someone she was so close to.

"Suz? You still there?"

"You know how you said you knew the delivery would go well?"

"Yeah?"

"That's the way I feel, Charlotte. She's here. I *know* it. I couldn't tell you how I know that to save my life, but I do."

There was a long silence on the other end of the line before her sister's voice, filled with love and concern, came across it. "Honey, don't you let this break your heart. You can't. Not again. You just take care of *you*. Try not to get your hopes up too much. There's always the possibility…"

Her sister's warning faded, but the unspoken message was clear. Just because Richard's body had been found didn't mean Emma was here. Or even that she was still alive. Most people would argue that the discovery of her father's body would indicate exactly the opposite.

"I know, but…I have to try."

"I know. Just remember that all kinds of things could have happened. Seven years is a very long time."

An eternity in the life of a child. In Emma's case, the only part of it that she would remember. Whatever had happened during those first fourteen months would have been long forgotten. All the scraps of memory Susan had cherished would mean nothing to her daughter.

"I'll call you tomorrow," Susan said, unwilling to let her sister's warning interfere with her surety. "Sleep tight."

"Don't let the bedbugs bite."

They must have said the same silly rhyme thousands of nights, lying side by side in their twin beds. Tonight, with so much riding on the events of the next few days— for both of them—the familiar words were comforting, providing the same web of love and protection Charlotte and David would give their son from the instant of his birth. The kind that unless Susan found her, she could never be sure that Emma had ever known at all.

"I HOPE JEB MADE YOU welcome. He can sometimes be…a little off-putting."

Susan wasn't sure she'd ever heard the term before, but it was appropriate. Lorena, however, had proved to be as warm and welcoming as her great-nephew had been "off-putting."

"Jeb? Is that your nephew?"

"Great-nephew. And it's not really Jeb. It's Jubal. Jubal Early Bedford the Fourth. We'd run out of nicknames by then, so they just used his initials."

However he'd acquired the name Jeb, Susan thought, it fit. As hard and totally masculine as he had been.

"I know I should have called before I came out."

Susan smiled her thanks as she accepted the tray the old woman had brought up to her. Although it contained only a sandwich and a cup of tea, the bread was obviously homemade and the piece of ham large enough to droop out over the bottom crust. At the sight, Susan's mouth watered, reminding her that she hadn't eaten anything since the cereal bar she'd grabbed from her pantry this morning.

"You want some cobbler to go with that?" Lorena asked as she bustled over to turn back the covers on the bed. "I canned the peaches myself. Not as good as they were this summer, of course, but pretty good for October, I promise you."

"This is fine, Mrs. Bedford. I don't expect you to feed me, too."

"Lorena. You call me Lorena. Everybody does. And as far out as we are, you'll find it convenient to take your meals with us. I have to cook for Jeb anyway. There's always plenty."

The house was less than five miles from town, but apparently to Lorena that seemed a distance one should find onerous to travel for meals. Susan suspected she *would* find it convenient to eat some of her meals here.

The thought of sharing a table with Jeb Bedford was a bit intimidating, however. That was the second time she had used that word in conjunction with Mrs. Bedford's great-nephew. Apparently his tactics tonight had been successful. He would probably be pleased to know that.

"Has he been living with you long?"

"Jeb? Since he was released from Walter Reed. I'm glad to have him, of course. Even if some days we don't say two words to one another, it's nice to know there's another soul in the house. You know what they say about having a man about the house? All those things I used to have to find someone in town to do for me, the yard work and such, Jeb does without me even having to ask him. Not that I would have asked him—"

The old woman stopped, putting the arthritis-twisted fingers of both hands over her lips. When she removed them, she smiled at Susan.

"You'd think I'd learn, wouldn't you. That's the one topic of conversation that's forbidden around here. What Jeb *can't* do. *He* admits to no limitations, of course. And he can't understand why I find it so hard to see him struggle to do things. I guess it's his training. Some kind of secret unit. Special Forces, but I'm not supposed to tell that either. Anyway, that's where he got that never-admit-defeat and all, but sometimes…" She shook her head, her smile fading.

"I think it's always hard to watch those we love struggle," Susan said. "No matter what it's with."

"He was just always so adept at anything physical. Not that he's not plenty bright, too, you understand, but Jeb could *do* anything. I remember when he was a little boy, he was as rough-and-tumble as a child could be. Into every sport known to man. Far more than my brother, Jubal, or his father ever were."

It was slightly disconcerting for Susan to think about the man who had answered the door tonight as a little boy. The persona he'd projected had been too blatantly masculine, even to his determination not to allow her to make any of the normal concessions because of his limp.

"Here I am, babbling on while your tea's getting cold," Lorena said. "It's just so nice to have a guest again. You go on now and eat up. I didn't mean to keep you from your meal. Folks always like to just settle in their first night."

Susan smiled, unable to resist either the kindness or the food. She picked up the sandwich, bringing it to her mouth as the old woman crossed the suite and closed the door to the hall. As soon as she disappeared, Susan lowered the food, hunger forgotten.

Special Forces, Lorena had said. And the information fit her initial impressions of Jeb Bedford. The military-style haircut. The olive-drab T-shirt. Even his arrogance.

He was old enough, maybe midthirties, that he must have been a career soldier. And an officer, of course. There was no logical reason for her certainty about that, nothing except the indefinable air of being in command that had been obvious even in the few minutes she'd spent with him.

And it *had* been only minutes. She had no idea why Jeb Bedford had made such an impression. He had been outright rude, at least until she had told him why she was here. Apparently, although he clearly rejected any sympathy for himself, he wasn't incapable of feeling it for others.

She attempted to put Lorena's great-nephew from her mind, lifting the sandwich again. This time she took a bite, savoring the salt-smoke flavor of country ham, perfectly complemented by mayonnaise and the yeasty bread.

She ate half of it before she stopped to taste her tea and realized she hadn't asked if it was decaf. Tonight it wouldn't matter. Once she lay down on that feather mattress, she'd be asleep in a matter of minutes. Something devotedly to be wished for, given the events of the last few days.

This afternoon she had seen the river that had taken Richard's life. No longer were the images of his death imaginary as they had been during the last forty-eight hours. She had been to the place where he'd died. Smelled the miasma of that muddy, slow-moving water. And she would never be able to forget any of it.

She banished those images, determined not to think about them anymore. Tonight she would finish her sandwich and drink her tea and then climb between the lavender-scented sheets her hostess had already turned back.

And then tomorrow she would set about finding Emma.

# CHAPTER FOUR

JEB UNSTRAPPED the weighted belt from his ankle and tossed it on the stone floor, waiting for the familiar agony to subside. Damaged muscles still trembling in the aftermath of exertion, he picked up the towel that he'd draped across his waist and used it to wipe sweat from his eyes.

Despite the warnings of Dr. Duncan McKey, the rehabilitation genius at Southeastern Rehab whom he'd come down here to work with, he had increased all the weights this morning as he'd gone through the routine he did twice a day. And he knew he would pay for that senseless bit of bravado.

In spite of McKey's continued encouragement, however, Jeb hadn't been able to detect any improvement either in strength or flexibility during his last few sessions. With the medical board's reevaluation in a few days, he desperately needed to believe there would be.

Although McKey had warned him that overdoing could be as harmful to his progress as slacking off, Jeb had taken matters into his own hands. If he wasn't able to demonstrate progress this time, he wasn't sure the Army would give him another shot. After all, he had just about used up the special leave he'd been granted.

And the military experts had been skeptical from the first, given the extent of his injuries, that he could get back into the kind of shape necessary to resume his duties with Combat Applications Group, the elite Delta Force team he'd been part of for over ten years.

Actually, he was the only one who had ever believed that was possible. With encouragement from McKey, however, he had given it his all during the six months he'd been in Mississippi.

He'd known from the first time he walked into the surgeon's office that he'd found a kindred spirit. Between the framed degrees and awards had been an old poem Jeb had remembered reading as a child. It hadn't made much of an impression then, but the final lines "I am the master of my fate. I am the captain of my soul" had, at the time, seemed to reflect his own determination. And obviously McKey's philosophy as well.

The problem was determination apparently wasn't going to be good enough, he acknowledged bitterly, running his palm down the scar that bisected his thigh. Although that was now the most visible of the injuries he'd sustained when the land mine had exploded under his Humvee, it was the mangled foot and ankle that had defied his attempts—and those of his doctors—to regain the mobility he'd had before the injury. That was what the Army was demanding before they would consider returning him to CAG.

It wasn't that he didn't understand their insistence. Or accept it. He did. After all, the lives of others might one day depend on how well he was able to perform. What he *couldn't* seem to accept was that no matter how hard he worked, he might not be able to change what he feared was going to happen during the up-coming review at Walter Reed.

Disgusted with how skewed his thinking had become this morning, he put the evaluation out of his mind. He wiped perspiration from his neck before he ran the towel across his hair.

From upstairs came the familiar sounds of Lorena fixing breakfast. The soft clink of china. Water churning through the ancient pipes. *And no voices.*

He glanced at his watch. It was only a little after six. Probably too early for their guest to be up. Which meant that if he didn't want any further disruption to the routine he'd established since he'd been here, he should go up now and have his breakfast before she came downstairs.

He didn't bother to analyze why he wanted to avoid Susan Chandler. All he knew was that even after he'd cut out his bedside lamp last night, certain things about their meeting had replayed over and over, stuck in his mind like the notes of some half-forgotten melody. The way the dim light of the old-fashioned chandelier had put threads of gold in her hair. The way her eyes, their irises an unusual blue-gray, held on his, determined not to look at his damaged leg.

He was doing it again, he realized. Dwelling on those few awkward minutes they'd been thrown together last night. It had been a long time since he'd been this conscious of a woman. Actually, Susan Chandler was the first woman he had reacted to this way since he'd been wounded.

*Just horny,* he assured himself, his mouth relaxing into a grin. And a good sign. An indication of returning normality.

In truth, she was a damn fine-looking woman. He should be worried if he *wasn't* aware of her sexually—and therefore aware of how long it had been since he'd been with a woman.

There was another sound from upstairs, one he couldn't quite identify. Head cocked, he listened with a mixture of apprehension and anticipation, but again there were no voices.

He dropped the towel, running his left hand across the top of his hair as if to groom it. Then, balancing on his right leg, he pulled his sweatpants up over the gym shorts he wore.

He could smell the biscuits as he climbed the basement stairs, his muscles still trembling from the routine. The area where he'd set up his equipment had at one time served as cold storage for things like apples and potatoes. It was always ten or fifteen degrees cooler than the rest of the house.

Lorena's age and the steepness of the stone steps prevented her from using it anymore. Since he'd been here, the basement under the kitchen had become his domain. One he would probably retreat to more often than before if their guest spent many more nights in the house, he acknowledged.

He opened the door at the top of the stairs and stepped into the light and warmth of the kitchen. His great-aunt was standing at the stove, brushing melted butter over the tops of the biscuits she had just taken out of the oven.

"Morning," she said without turning. Whatever frailties of aging she suffered from, Lorena's hearing was excellent.

Despite his belief their guest wouldn't be up yet, Jeb took time to check out the small table that stood before one of the windows. It was set, as usual, with only two places. Relief he couldn't quite explain washed over him in a flood.

"Those smell good." He limped over to kiss Lorena's cheek.

"I thought this morning we'd have some of that home-cured ham Isaac brought with the eggs yesterday rather than bacon. You can't get ham like this at the store."

Several slices of it lay sizzling in a cast-iron skillet, its scent mingling with that of the biscuits. Underlying both was the inviting smell of coffee, which perked gently on the back of the stove. In the months he'd lived here, he had become accustomed to having it prepared this way, so that he'd finally packed away the electric coffeemaker he'd brought with him.

Using a hot pad, he picked up the pot and poured a stream of black coffee into his mug, which Lorena had already set out on the counter by the stove. He stood sipping it, watching as his aunt broke eggs into the same pan from which she'd just taken the steaming slices of ham. The bits that had stuck to the bottom were churned into the eggs as she scrambled them.

"You go on and sit down," she ordered as she did every morning. "Drink your coffee in peace."

They had come to an unspoken understanding shortly after he'd arrived, one that satisfied them both. Lorena had desperately wanted to wait on him. At mealtimes he let her. She would bring the platter over when everything was ready, and then she would sit down opposite him, bowing her head as she invoked the Lord to bless their food.

The first few weeks he had waited through her prayer, eyes defiantly open. After a while he'd given in to her devotion and his own upbringing, bowing his head now as a matter of course.

Carrying his coffee, he made his way to the sunlit table. It was going to be another warm day, despite the calendar.

For some reason, that reminded him of Susan Chandler. Maybe it was the memory of her crushed linen skirt. Or the sleeveless silk blouse she had worn with it. Or how damp tendrils of hair had curled at her temples and against the back of her neck.

"I thought I'd go into town," Lorena said right beside him, startling him out of those memories. She set the platter of eggs, ham and biscuits down and then slipped into her place. "I can't feed a guest what we eat."

"Why not?" he asked, putting a biscuit onto his plate.

"Not fancy enough. That was one thing the bed-and-breakfast association told me. Folks that pay good money to stay in a home expect something special when it comes to food."

"There's nothing more special than what you fix every day," Jeb said, smiling up at her. The crease between her brows smoothed with the compliment. "I mean it, Lorena. You serve Mrs. Chandler what you serve me, and I guarantee you she'll be happy as a pig in mud." His great-aunt wouldn't have put up with the usual description in that phrase. "Besides, she isn't a guest in the strictest sense of the word. I don't think she expects you to go out of your way to cater to her every whim."

"She certainly does *not*."

Hearing Susan Chandler's voice produced a jolt of sheer physical reaction. Jeb raised his eyes to find her standing in the door of the kitchen. She was dressed less formally today in a pair of brown knit slacks and a brown-and-white striped top.

"I hope I'm not intruding," she said apologetically. "I smelled the coffee and hoped there might be enough for me."

"Of course you're not intruding." Lorena pushed her chair back to stand. "You come right over here and sit down. The eggs are still hot. I'll pour you a fresh cup of coffee."

"I can't take your place," Susan protested.

"Yes, ma'am, you sure can. I just sit here to keep Jeb company. I ate a while ago."

It was a lie. And since he was already dreading the unpleasant meal this was apt to turn into if their guest did sit down opposite him, Jeb was tempted to call his great-aunt on it, despite knowing how much that would embarrass her.

"You go on, now," Lorena urged, starting toward the stove where coffee still occasionally perked up into the glass button on top of the pot, although it had been re-moved from the burner.

"I don't normally eat breakfast."

Still hesitating in the doorway, Susan seemed no more eager to join him at the table than he was to have her there. In spite of his own sense of dread, Jeb was suddenly—and bitterly—conscious of the probable rea-son for her reluctance.

"Have a biscuit," Lorena went on, oblivious to the

tension between them. "I made that apple butter myself. Or if you'd rather have it, there's peach preserves in the icebox. I always put the other out because that's what Jeb likes…"

The sentence trailed as she poured a stream of steaming coffee into a cup she took from the cabinet. Finally the lack of a response made the old woman turn to face her guest, brows raised questioningly.

Jeb looked down at the breakfast he had been anticipating only minutes before. He knew he would have a hard time forcing a bite of it through the angry tightness in his throat. And that was a reaction he again couldn't quite explain.

"Apple butter's fine," Susan said, bringing his gaze up.

She had started toward the chair Lorena had deserted. Her eyes touched on his for the first time this morning. Again, the same heat of sexual awareness he'd felt last night roiled through his lower body, tightening his groin.

As if she were conscious of what had just happened, Susan quickly looked away, her gaze fastening on Lorena. The old woman crossed the kitchen and set the cup at the side of the plate she had intended to eat from herself.

"There now," she said, beaming at Susan and then at him.

For an instant, Jeb wondered if his great-aunt could possibly be matchmaking. Even Lorena, die-hard romantic that she was, must realize any effort in that direction would be highly inappropriate. Although, according to the local paper, the body they'd found in the river had been there for years, that man *had been* Susan Chandler's husband.

She was again looking at him, he realized, obviously as uncomfortable with the situation as he was, but for far different reasons. Angered by that as well, he mockingly inclined his head toward his aunt's empty chair. Susan's eyes held his a heartbeat before, lips tight, she slipped into it.

She picked up the linen napkin and unfolded it across her lap. Lorena dipped eggs onto her plate and then a slice of ham from the platter. When she reached toward the covered basket of hot biscuits, Susan again attempted to protest.

"I'm really not very hungry."

. Jeb had tried the same argument when he'd first arrived. It was probable that the first bite of Lorena's cooking would convince her, as it had him, that she was mistaken.

"And a biscuit," Lorena said, continuing to draw the basket closer. "Jeb, if you'll pass that apple butter…"

He obeyed, watching as his great-aunt placed the apple-shaped glass dish near Susan's plate.

"Now then," Lorena said again, stepping back, her hands crossed in front of her apron as if she had performed some sleight of hand and was waiting for her audience to respond with the proper amount of awe.

Susan looked as if she wasn't sure what had just happened. She took a breath, deep enough that it lifted her shoulders. Then she put a biscuit on her plate, split it deftly, and began filling it with the apple butter. She glanced up, finding his eyes on her.

"My aunt and I were wondering how long you plan to be in town, Mrs. Chandler."

Not only did he really want to know the answer to

that, Jeb also knew the question would constitute polite conversation in Lorena's eyes. Never let it be said that he hadn't done his part to make their guest feel welcome, he thought dryly.

"I'm not sure. I suppose it depends on how long it takes for certain things to happen."

Like getting the autopsy results? Or the accident report? If they even did one of those for something like this.

"Like what?" Lorena asked, her eyes bright with curiosity.

"Lorena," he warned softly.

"Did I say something wrong, dear? Don't mind me. I'm just a nosey old woman who never knows when to keep her mouth shut."

"It's all right. I want the medical examiner's report, of course, but… Actually, I need to stay until I can find out what Richard was doing here."

"In Linton?"

Susan nodded, looking from one of them to the other.

"You don't know?" Jeb asked.

"I have no idea. I can't imagine why he would come somewhere like this—" She stopped, conscious of how that must sound. "I don't mean to be insulting. It's just that Richard was very much a big-city person. He'd take the freeway even if a local route were much quicker. It was just the way he was."

"Maybe he was visiting someone," Lorena suggested.

"If so, I need to find out who. As far as I know, he didn't know anyone around here."

What the hell difference could it make why he was here? Jeb wondered. The guy had been dead for seven years.

"In the circumstances," he said aloud, "I understand your being curious about what brought him to Linton, but…" He lifted his hands, the right still holding a biscuit, in a gesture that questioned why it could possibly matter.

"He took my baby with him that morning."

Into the *river?* If that's what she meant, her phrasing was macabre. It also didn't make any sense, he realized quickly. The papers had mentioned only one body.

"When he left home," Susan clarified, as if sensing his confusion. "I was out of town for the weekend, and Richard was keeping Emma. When I got back, they were both gone."

"And you think he brought her down here?" Lorena's tone expressed her puzzlement.

"I don't know. All I know is the authorities have been looking for her for seven years. I've questioned everyone either of us ever knew. No one saw them after that weekend. So if she *was* with Richard…"

Then she must also have been with him when the car went off the entrance to the bridge. Jeb looked down at the cooling breakfast on his plate, trying to imagine how a mother could deal with something like that.

"Her body should have been in the car," she went on after a moment. "And apparently, it wasn't. So…it's possible she's still alive. Maybe even right here in Linton."

It was understandable that she didn't want to accept

the death of her daughter. But after this length of time, and especially after her husband's body had been found, it must be very hard to cling to any kind of hope.

"And you think you'll be able to find her?" Despite Jeb's attempt to keep the skepticism out of his question, it obviously came through.

"All I want right now," Susan said, her voice steadier, "is to know whether or not she was with him when he got to Linton. I just want to talk to someone here who saw them."

Without a body, maybe a witness that the child was in the car with her father would help her find closure. There didn't seem to be any other way for that to happen now, given the time that had passed and the ultimate destination of the river.

"I can't imagine that coming to Linton was in Richard's plans when he left that weekend," she went on. "Something—or someone—sent him here. If I can figure out what that was…"

The soft voice faltered. Jeb looked up to find that she was looking at him. Hoping he could supply some kind of answer? He couldn't. After all this time, there probably was no answer.

"Truck stop, maybe," Lorena offered. "Maybe somebody there sent him into town."

"For what?"

"I don't know. Maybe he had car trouble. Maybe he needed a part for the car."

Susan nodded as if that made sense. Maybe it did, but to Jeb there was something wrong with his aunt helping her with this hopeless quest. It was also macabre, just as he'd thought before.

The reality, whether either of them wanted to accept it or not, was that her daughter's body had probably been washed downriver by the current. All the other what-ifs Susan Chandler wanted to consider seemed to him only attempts to deny the inevitable. A denial he didn't intend to be a party to.

"If you'll excuse me," he said, pushing up from the table.

His leg had stiffened during the few minutes he'd been sitting, which would make his limp more pronounced. *And why the hell should I give a rat's ass if it does?*

"Land's sake, Jeb. You've hardly touched your breakfast."

"Why don't you take my place and keep Ms. Chandler company? I'm not really all that hungry this morning."

"Why don't I leave instead?" Susan began to rise, but Lorena put her hand on her shoulder.

"Nonsense. You stay right there. We haven't thought of half the people you ought to talk to. The truck stop on the interstate like I said. The two mechanics in town, of course. And the drugstore. Maybe he needed something for the baby."

As he crossed the room, Jeb could hear his aunt pull out the chair he'd just vacated to take her place across the table from her guest. He had had too much experience with the brutal finality of death to play this kind of game, however.

Even as he walked away, he knew he was judging both of them too harshly: a mother who wanted to know what had happened to her baby and an old woman who always wanted to right the wrongs of the world. And if what they were doing helped Susan Chandler deal with the loss of her daughter, who was he to begrudge either of them that comfort?

# CHAPTER FIVE

"HELL, LADY, I can't remember who came in here yesterday, and you're asking me about something that happened seven years ago?"

In response to her inquiry, one of the waitresses had called the owner of the truck stop out of his office. His impatience to get back to whatever he'd been doing was obvious.

Thankfully his attitude was in contrast to most of the people she'd talked to in Linton. They'd all known who she was and why she was here, one benefit of an effective small-town grapevine. Their willingness to help had made the process of asking questions easier than she'd expected. The downside was that none of them remembered seeing Richard.

"He was driving a black SUV," she said for at least the tenth time today. "There would have been a toddler in the infant seat in the back."

It was the same information she had given everyone she'd talked to during the last two days. In actuality, it was all she knew. And the part about Emma being with Richard was speculation, of course.

Since the baby hadn't been in the car when it was found, but the car seat had been, that was the scenario that seemed to make the most sense. At least to her. If Richard had left Emma with someone on his way down here, then surely he would have left the safety seat as well.

"I already told you. Too many people come through here for me to try to remember 'em. The casino regulars maybe. Anybody else…" The owner shrugged, his eyes deliberately moving beyond her to whatever was going on at the crowded counter where Sunday supper was being served.

"He might have had car trouble. Or maybe he asked about a place to spend the night."

There had to be some reason Richard had turned off the interstate at this exit. The next one was nearer to Pascagoula. And although the new state highway did eventually go into that city, Richard would have had to turn off that road in order to end up at the bridge in Linton. She couldn't imagine that had been Richard's plan when he left Atlanta.

*Whatever that plan had been.* She knew no more now about where he'd been headed than she had the weekend he'd disappeared.

"If that *had* been what he was asking, I sure as hell wouldn't have sent him to Linton, now would I?" Realizing how abrupt that sounded, the owner attempted to modify his tone to something approaching compassion. "Look, I'm sorry about your husband. I really am, but I got a business to run here. And it seems to me you're about seven years too late in trying to figure out how or why he ended up at that bridge."

After that, there seemed little point in continuing the conversation. Maybe she should value his bluntness. At least he was being honest about the impossibility of what she was asking him to do. If it hadn't been for Emma...

"Thank you for your time," she said, choosing to ignore his advice because she had no choice. "If you remember anything that might be helpful, here's my number." She handed him one of her business cards with the number of her cell, knowing it would probably end up in the trash as soon as she walked out the door.

She had thought about talking to the waitresses, but neither of them looked as if they were old enough to have been working *anywhere* seven years ago. Besides, with the Sunday-night crowd, it was apparent they had no time for conversation. Maybe another day when they weren't so busy.

As she stepped out the front door and into the halogen-lighted parking lot, she realized that while she'd been inside, the rain that had been falling off and on all day had gotten much heavier. Although the day had been warm, there was a definite chill in the night air.

Holding her purse over her head, she made a run for the car, unlocking the driver's-side door and slipping quickly behind the wheel. She sat for a moment, listening to the rain beat down on the roof of the Toyota, trying to think if there was anything else she could do tonight.

During the two days she'd spent in Linton, she had talked to everyone Lorena had mentioned who might have seen Richard. Then she had followed up on any other possibilities the people she'd talked to had suggested. The owner of the busy truck stop, farther from town, had been the last name on her list.

Not only had she run out of people to ask about Richard and Emma, she was also tired, damp, cold and hungry. The thought of her hostess's solicitude and the comforts of the room she'd been given offered more temptation than she could resist. She'd done all she could today. She would start again in the morning.

Maybe with Sheriff Adams, she decided. Surely there was some way he could speed up the coroner's report. How long could an autopsy take, given what she'd been led to believe about the condition of Richard's body? She shivered, deliberately destroying that unwanted image.

She turned the key in the ignition and then pulled out of the parking lot and onto the narrow two-lane that led back into Linton. There were no streetlights this far out, of course, and with the rain, visibility was poor. Although she had driven the same route this afternoon, she found it was a very different prospect under these conditions.

She concentrated on the centerline, the only marking on the blacktop. She leaned forward, peering over the steering wheel and through the windshield, which was beginning to fog. Keeping her eyes on the road, she felt for the defrost switch with her right hand. After a couple of attempts she located it, and in a matter of seconds, the windows began to clear.

She tried to relax her shoulders, which had tensed with the effort of following the winding, unfamiliar road. The sign just off the interstate had said it was twenty miles into Linton. This afternoon, she hadn't been conscious of that distance at all. Tonight it seemed as if she had already been traveling forever.

For the first time since she'd left the truck stop, a vehicle approached in the other lane. Either the driver had his high beams on or the headlights reflecting off the wet asphalt made them seem brighter. She squinted to shield her eyes from the glare as she blinked her own lights from low to high a couple of times. The signal had no effect on the oncoming car.

*Pickup,* she realized as it flew by with a swish of tires. Judging by the way her car responded to the wind force created by its passage, it had been a big one. And making no concession in speed, despite the conditions.

*Idiot,* she thought before she put the pickup out of her mind, forcing herself to concentrate again on the centerline.

She had gone perhaps two miles when she became aware of headlights in her rearview mirror. She kept her eyes on the car coming up behind her long enough to determine it was traveling at a much higher rate of speed than she was. Obviously someone who was familiar with this road and who would undoubtedly want to pass because of the snail's pace she was forced to maintain.

Although the line was double, indicating a no-passing zone, she eased as far to the right as she dared, considering there were no markings along the shoulder. She maintained her speed, fighting the urge to accelerate as the headlights behind her loomed larger in her review mirror.

There was a straightaway just ahead. She could see the double yellow lines change to a single one. Under her direction the Toyota hugged the edge of the road, giving the automobile behind her as much room as possible to pass.

As it did, the driver blew his horn. Not a quick honk to warn her he was coming around, but a long sustained blast that grew louder as the vehicle pulled alongside her car and then whipped by with the same noise she'd heard before.

*Exactly* the same, she realized. Through the rain and darkness, she caught only a glimpse as it sped by, but the size was right. As was the color, either black or a dark blue.

She would have sworn it was the same pickup that had been traveling in the opposite direction only moments before, its headlights on high. She watched until the red of the oval-shaped taillights disappeared around the curve ahead.

Only then did she draw a deep, relieved breath. The first one she'd taken in a while, she realized. Even if it was the same truck, she told herself, there were dozens of explanations. A couple of kids out joyriding. Or maybe the driver had forgotten something and had needed to go back to town for it.

Just because the same vehicle passed her twice on a relatively deserted stretch of highway didn't mean she should get paranoid. Despite those attempts at self-assurance, she automatically slowed the car. *Let whoever is in such a hurry get far ahead. Let him get to Linton long before I do. Let him arrive, take care of his business and get out of my way.*

After a few minutes, that ridiculous sense of threat began to fade. She even managed to relax the grip her hands had taken on the wheel and to sit back in the seat. Despite the poor markings, the centerline was proving to be a reliable guide. Only a few more miles to the town limits, and then she could look for the turnoff that would take her to the Bedford house.

Daring to glance away from the road a moment, she adjusted the heater, feeling better as the warm air began to fill the car. She pushed the button on the CD player, letting the familiar, relaxing sound of Norah Jones's voice wash over her.

She looked up at the rearview mirror to find the road behind her still deserted. There would probably be very few people out on a night like this. Even as the thought formed, headlights appeared in front of her at the top of the next rise. Her hands automatically tensed around the wheel again.

Ridiculous, she chided herself as she loosened them. Even if this were the same pickup, that was no reason to act as if its driver were targeting her. He probably hadn't thought twice about her car, except to bemoan her lack of speed.

She tried to decide if the truck would have had time to return to town and then make it back here. Since she had no reference points along the unfamiliar stretch of highway, and since she'd failed to look at the odometer when she'd left the truck stop, she had no idea how far from town she was.

She tried to ignore the approaching lights, again keeping the car as near the shoulder as she dared. This attack of nerves wasn't like her. And she hated it. All she could do was put the unaccustomed anxiety down to her exhaustion and the emotional toll of the last few days. After all, her husband had died on one of the roads in this area.

She raised her eyes from the yellow line, watching

as the approaching lights grew larger. And they were still on high, she had time to think before she realized that they were not only blindingly bright, they were also headed directly at her.

She blinked, attempting to see through the driving rain. In the split second she had to evaluate the path of the oncoming car, she knew she hadn't been mistaken. It was headed straight for her car.

She swerved to the right, that reaction unthinking. The right tires left the road with a jolt as the headlights shone into her eyes, their glare terrifying.

At the last second before collision, she jerked the steering wheel, plunging the Toyota completely off the road. It bounced over some unseen obstacle as the pickup roared by, so close she couldn't believe it hadn't struck her car.

She had automatically slammed on the brakes, but as the car began to fishtail, she released them, trying to steer back up onto the road. The back right tire seemed to be slipping in the roadside mud. All she accomplished was to turn the car so that it continued to slide sideways along the shoulder for a few more feet until the right front fender struck a telephone pole.

Her rate of speed had been slowed enough by then that the impact was minimal. Restrained by her seat belt, her head jerked forward, slamming back into the headrest as the car came to an abrupt stop.

Stunned, she sat without moving as the wipers continued to clear the rain off the windshield, revealing the twin beams of her own headlights shining across the two-lane at an upward angle. She looked to her left, but there was no sign of the pickup that had run her off the road.

She tried to analyze her impressions of its make or model, but everything about the last few seconds had been a blur. She'd been too busy trying to avoid a collision to get a clear picture of anything about it except those glaring lights.

After a few seconds, she reached over and punched the off button on the CD player. In the sudden silence, the drumming of the rain and the noise from the back-and-forth movement of the wipers seemed to intensify. As did her feeling of isolation.

Someone had just run her off the road. She was out in the middle of nowhere with a possibly disabled car.

That was the first thing she needed to find out, she realized. Whether the car could be driven back into town.

Her knees were shaking so badly with delayed reaction that it was difficult to get her foot back on the gas pedal. She eased the accelerator down, but the back tires spun, unable to get any traction in the mud. After a couple of careful attempts, she shut off the engine and then killed the lights.

Now there was only the sound of the rain, but she felt safer in the darkness. If he came back again—

Despite the fact that her body was vibrating as if she had a chill, she had enough presence of mind to realize that thought had slipped over the line. Someone had forced her off the road, but the idea that the driver had made a couple of preliminary passes at her before he'd done so was ridiculous.

This couldn't have been deliberate. A drunk driver. Or, as she had speculated before, teenage joyriders.

The arguments presented by her rational mind had no effect on the surety of its more primitive, instinctive part. Someone had deliberately caused her to wreck her car. The same someone who had sped by her with his lights on bright. The same someone who had passed her with an angry wail of his horn.

Who might even now be turning his truck around to come back and finish the job he'd begun. She could sit here and wait for him to return, or—

Put in those terms, the decision was simple. She reached across and grabbed her purse off the passenger seat. Even as she climbed out of the car, her fingers fumbled her cell phone out of the bottom of her bag.

She could call 911, although they probably wouldn't consider a car in a ditch an emergency. Better to dial information and get the name of the nearest wrecker service. It would probably be out of Pascagoula, but there might be something local. In any case, it didn't seem she had a choice.

And then she needed to call Mrs. Bedford. She had already missed supper, and if she were a couple of hours later getting home, as she suspected she would be, she knew Lorena would imagine the worst.

Wrecker first, and then the Bedford house. Even as she dialed information, the image of a pair of mocking blue eyes was in her head. She could imagine Jeb Bedford's reaction if she told him what she believed had happened tonight. The same one anyone in this sleepy little Southern town would have.

That didn't mean she was wrong, of course. It only meant that she would be alone in her opinion. Being alone, however, was something with which she was now very familiar. Something with which she had long ago made her peace.

## CHAPTER SIX

IF IT HADN'T BEEN for Lorena, there was no way in hell he'd be out here in the rain looking for a car that had gone off the road. Or for the woman who had been driving it.

*And who do you think you're kidding?*

Jeb had known who was on the other end of the line as soon as his aunt picked up the phone. Just as she had, he, too, had been listening for it to ring as soon as it had gotten dark.

He slowed as the headlights of his Avalanche illuminated a vehicle on the side of the road. It was sitting perpendicular to the two-lane, the right front panel crushed against a telephone pole. He had no doubt the car belonged to Susan Chandler.

He drove past the small silver car, evaluating the damage as well as he could through the fogged driver's-side window. Then he made a U-turn in the middle of the deserted highway and guided the big sport utility truck onto the shoulder a few feet from the sedan. He was careful not to pull off the road far enough to get stuck in the ditch where the rear wheels of the Toyota were mired.

Although his headlights were directed at the driver's

side of the car, there was no sign of the driver. Just as it had when the phone rang, a knot of unaccustomed anxiety began to form in the pit of his stomach. If Susan Chandler wasn't in her car, then where could she be?

She'd told Lorena on the phone that she'd already called a tow truck and was going to wait here until it arrived. Clearly, since the car was still in the ditch, that hadn't yet happened.

He rolled down his window, sticking his head out despite the downpour. "Mrs. Chandler?"

He waited, but the only sound was the rain pelting the roof of his car. Muttering profanities, he opened his door.

After the cocoon of warmth the heater had created inside the cab, the wet chill immediately assaulted him. He knew from experience it would seep into the shattered ankle, aching along all the pins and wires and screws that held it together.

Given the situation, however, it didn't seem he had any option other than to go look for his aunt's guest. He eased down from the high cab, holding on to the handgrip until the undamaged right leg was solidly on the ground beside the left.

"Mrs. Chandler?" Again he waited, rain pouring down on his bare head and shoulders. Surely she wouldn't be stupid enough to start walking back into town. But, of course, he would have passed her on the way if she had.

Maybe someone driving back into town had spotted the wreck and stopped to help. It was the kind of thing he'd expect almost anyone around here to do. Whether or not Ms. Chandler would be trusting enough to accept a ride from a stranger was another question. If she had, maybe she'd left a note with instructions for the wrecker service on the dash.

Mindful of the treacherous footing, Jeb began to limp over to the Toyota. As he approached, he realized that she'd been right to call a tow truck.

Any idea he might have had that he could maneuver the Camry out of the ditch himself was discarded as he surveyed the situation. It was obvious someone had tried to drive it out, causing the wheels to sink even farther into the mud.

Still looking down at the back tires, now buried up to their rims, Jeb opened the driver's door. The overhead light came on, making it obvious there was no note on the dash or in the seat. And no sign of Susan Chandler.

He blew out an exasperated breath before he straightened to look over the top of her car. He had left his headlights on, and the twin beams cut a swath through the rain and darkness into the area beyond the telephone pole. As he watched, a figure materialized out of the bushes along the side of the road, stepping forward into their illumination.

He recognized Susan immediately, despite her bedraggled appearance. Her clothing was soaked, making her cotton blouse cling revealingly to her body. The strap of her leather purse still hung over her shoulder, however, as if nothing out of the ordinary was going on.

He refrained from asking any of the obvious questions as she approached, shoes sloshing with each step. When she rounded the car, he could see that her eyes were wide and dark in a face that was far too pale. Strands of hair were plastered to her cheeks and neck, water streaming from them.

He couldn't imagine why she'd gotten out in the rain rather than waiting inside the Toyota for the wrecker. Not unless—

The thought was sudden and disturbing. A concussion might create enough disorientation to cause that kind of behavior. He'd seen men with head wounds do some bizarre things.

"You hurt?" he asked as she stopped in front of him.

Wordlessly she shook her head.

"Didn't you hear me calling you?"

"I didn't know who it was."

Not the most rational answer, he decided, considering that she was supposed to be waiting for the wrecker. There was no way she could have been certain he wasn't the tow-truck driver, considering the poor visibility. Or had she been planning to hide in the bushes even after they'd arrived?

*Hide.* That was exactly what she'd been doing, he realized. For some reason, Susan Chandler had been hiding.

"Who did you *think* would be out here in a downpour calling you by name?"

She pressed her lips together as if deliberately refusing to respond to his sarcasm. With as much dignity as she could manage, considering that water was dripping off her chin, she pushed a piece of hair off her cheek before she shook her head.

"What's wrong?" he demanded, knowing there was something else going on here. It would have taken more than a minor accident on a rain-slick road to rattle her this badly.

"Nothing. I…" Again she closed her mouth, cutting off whatever explanation she'd been about to make. "Nothing."

"You *did* call a wrecker, didn't you?"

She nodded, her eyes holding on his face. Seeing what was in them, something that looked very much like fear, he found that he had to resist the urge to put his arm out to draw her to him. He would have done that to Lorena or almost any other woman of his acquaintance. Susan Chandler, however, had given no indication she would welcome that kind of comfort.

Not from him or anyone else. The aura that surrounded her was one of unapproachability. Even now.

"They said it would be about an hour."

Obviously not local. "They're coming from Pascagoula?"

She nodded, pushing her dripping hair out of her eyes with the spread fingers of her right hand. Through her thin cotton shirt, he could see the outline of lace on the top of her bra. And under it, the too-rapid rise and fall of her breasts. As if suddenly aware of how revealing the wet fabric might be, she put that hand on its opposite arm, running her palm up and down.

Despite the Indian-summer temperatures of the morning, this rain felt winter cold, and she was soaked to the skin. He needed to get her somewhere warm and dry, or she was liable to end up with pneumonia. If she did, he'd never hear the end of it from Lorena.

"Come on," he said, turning to head back to the pickup. The cab should still be fairly warm.

"Where?"

"To Lorena's." As he looked back at her, he raised his voice to make sure she could hear him over the downpour.

"What about the wrecker?"

"Leave them a note. Tell them they can take the car to Reynolds."

"Reynolds?"

"It's the service station on the square. He'll pay them tonight. You can pay him tomorrow."

"But...will he be open on a Sunday night?" she asked as she walked over to where he had stopped.

Probably not, Jeb realized. Like it or not, they were stuck here until the tow truck from Pascagoula showed up.

"I don't know. What I *do* know is that it's a lot dryer *inside* my truck than it is out here."

He automatically put his hand in the small of her back, urging her toward his vehicle. This time she cooperated, walking ahead of him as he made his slow and careful way over the uneven ground. As he neared the passenger side, he looked up to find she'd been watching him as she waited. Without meeting her eyes, he reached out and opened the passenger door.

"There's a handgrip," he said, gesturing toward it.

Although she was tall for a woman, probably five-seven or five-eight, she used it to climb up into the high cab. As soon as she was settled, he slammed the door and started around the back. Now that he knew she couldn't see him, he held on to the enclosed bed of the truck for balance.

The dull, familiar ache in his leg had already started.

Susan wasn't the only one who needed to get in out of the cold.

He opened the driver's-side door and, gritting his teeth against the pain, climbed into the seat. As soon as he closed the door, killing the interior light, he became aware of the intimacy of their situation.

The intensity of the rain would hold them prisoner as they waited for the arrival of the wrecker. Something over which they had no control.

"Did Lorena send you to find me?"

He debated telling her the truth. His great-aunt's anxiety had been a factor, of course, but she would never have asked him to go out in this, no matter how worried she was. That had been his decision. Given what he'd discovered, it was one he couldn't regret, even knowing what it would cost him tomorrow.

"Lorena takes her responsibilities seriously," he said. "You're her guest. That makes you hers to look after."

Her laughter was a breath of sound. "I was thinking on the way home how unaccustomed I am to having someone worry about me. And how welcome her solicitude would be," she added softly. "I didn't expect it to extend to rescue missions, however."

"Did you need rescuing?" He hadn't forgotten that she'd been hiding when he'd arrived.

"A figure of speech. I didn't mean to sound melodramatic."

"It's obvious you weren't trying to avoid the tow truck by hiding in those bushes, Ms. Chandler, so I'm curious as to who you *were* avoiding."

The rain seemed to beat down with renewed force as he waited for her answer. Or maybe in the sudden silence after his question he was simply more aware of it.

"Someone in an outsized pickup," she said finally.

Since the description was a little too apt, he turned to look at her. She was staring out the windshield, so that he could see only her profile. Despite the darkness, he could discern the delicate shape of her nose and the slight upward angle of her chin. Its tilt was almost challenging.

"Are you talking about...*my* truck?"

Despite the fact that he hadn't been particularly welcoming last night, he didn't believe that anything he'd said would be grounds for trying to avoid him. Besides, she couldn't have had any idea he would embark on this knight-errant foolishness.

Susan turned at the question, meeting his eye. "I'm talking about the truck that ran me off the road."

*The truck that ran me off the road....* There was only one possible interpretation of that.

"Are you saying someone *forced* you off the road?"

"I know it sounds ridiculous, but...that's what he did."

"He?"

"I guess I just assumed it was a man, maybe because of the size of the truck. I didn't actually see the driver."

"But you're sure he *deliberately* ran you off the road?" Jeb made no attempt to hide his skepticism. That kind of thing didn't happen around here.

"Yes." She offered no explanation for her certainty. And made no defense of it.

"Why would someone run you off the road?"

"I don't know. Maybe he was impatient because I

was being careful. Or because I blinked my lights to get him to turn his down. All I know is he headed directly toward me, and that he was flying."

When she'd mentioned the driver being impatient, he had pictured someone coming up behind her as she was negotiating an unfamiliar highway in the rain. The part about blinking her lights didn't seem to fit that scenario.

"He was behind you? Or approaching you?"

"Both. Actually…" She took a breath, seeming to gather control. "He approached a couple of times. During the last one it was obvious that if I didn't move over he would ram my car. Since he had a distinct size advantage…"

"You're telling me someone went past you and then turned around and came back in order to force you off the road."

"Or maybe he just made a U-turn," she said.

As he had done. Which meant she'd been watching his arrival from her hiding place. And if what she had just claimed happened really did take place, it was no wonder she hadn't wanted to be waiting inside her car when…

"You thought *I* was the person who ran you off the road."

"I thought it was a distinct possibility. He'd already made a couple of passes at me."

"*After* you went off the road?"

"I didn't mean that. He passed me coming from town and then turned around and came up behind me. When he went around my car, he sat on his horn. Then the next time… That's when he came at me. When I saw you go by, all I knew was that the size and color of your truck were the same as the other."

He couldn't tell from her tone if she still suspected he might have been its driver. Of course, she *had* responded to his call once she'd recognized him.

"I can't believe anybody around here would do that."

"I thought it might be kids. Showing off. Terrorizing the tourists."

He thought about the possibility. His few encounters with the local population during the months he'd spent here hadn't extended to any of the teenage population. Judging by the acts of violence the papers reported in other places, he supposed it wasn't outside the realm of possibility that some local kids, drunk or stoned, might have pulled this kind of stunt.

"You *are* going to report what happened to the sheriff?"

"I don't have a lot to tell him. I doubt big, dark pickups are all that rare in this area."

They weren't, of course, as evidenced by the one they were sitting in. His was perhaps bigger than most, but a lot of the local farmers used their trucks for hauling supplies and produce and even for towing trailers filled with livestock. All of which called for heavy-duty vehicles.

"Besides, I get the feeling Sheriff Adams thinks I should just go back home and wait for someone else to figure out what happened to my daughter. The problem is, if I do that, I don't think anyone ever will."

He knew from town gossip Lorena had repeated to him today that most people believed the baby's body must have been washed downriver. Under certain conditions the currents in the Escatawpa could certainly be strong enough to take a child out of a father's hands, which according to Lorena was Wayne Adams's explanation of what had happened.

"She would be eight years old now," Susan went on, the anger he'd heard before no longer in her voice, leaving it flat and hard. "Everyone said she looked like Richard, but…with babies that age, it's so hard to tell. And now…"

He waited through the silence, knowing there was nothing he could say that would temper the pain of her loss. Despite the passage of time, it was all still there in her voice.

Her chin lifted again as she swallowed the emotion that had threatened her control. Slowly she shook her head.

"I know what you're thinking, but I'd know if she were dead. I'd *know*." The declaration was almost fierce, brooking no argument. "She isn't. She's out there somewhere. Without anyone of her own."

"Ms. Chandler—"

"That was the one thought I clung to all those years. That she was with Richard. I hated him for taking her away from me. I cursed him for not telling me where she was or why he'd taken her, but…no matter how bitter I was toward him, there was no doubt in my mind that he loved her. And I *knew* he'd take care of her."

The rain pounding on the roof was the only sound in the cab after her last impassioned sentence. Even their breathing seemed suspended.

"Now…" she said again, turning to face him. "Don't you see? Now I'm all she has. I just can't let her go on thinking that no one has been looking for her."

# CHAPTER SEVEN

"I'M NOT EXACTLY SURE about what you want me to do, Ms. Chandler."

Susan had known this would be an exercise in futility. She couldn't believe she'd let the Bedfords talk her into calling the sheriff's office. There was nothing he could do about what had happened last night. Reporting it only made her appear the hysterical type.

"I didn't think there was anything you could or necessarily should do. I simply wanted to make you aware of the situation. It *did* occur in your jurisdiction."

"Yes, ma'am. And I can tell you that things like that don't normally happen around here."

She wasn't certain if he were doubting her word or defending his constituents. Not until he went on.

"Probably kids. There's a bunch of wild-as-bucks young'uns across the county line. Sheriff over there's had a lot of trouble out of them. I'll give him a call and see if he recognizes that pickup as belonging to one of them. They may have seen your out-of-state tags and decided to make a little mischief. And I'll make sure there's a deputy on that stretch of road after sundown tonight. Don't you worry about traveling around here. Now that we know what's been going on, we can keep a closer eye on things. What about your car? Any damage?"

"Some. I'm not sure yet how extensive it is. I had it towed into Reynolds last night. It was probably still drivable, but I had to get the wrecker to pull it out of the ditch, so I decided to let them bring it on into town and check it out."

"You ride in with them?"

She wasn't sure what business that was of his, but small towns probably worked differently than somewhere like Atlanta. Maybe that came from everyone knowing what everyone else was doing. Maybe they eventually considered it to be a right.

"Actually, Mr. Bedford came out to get me."

"Jeb Bedford?"

"That's right."

"Well, that's good. Must mean he's a lot better than the last time I saw him."

There was no way she could comment on that, not with both Jeb and Lorena listening. Besides, she had no idea what Jeb's condition had been the last time the sheriff saw him.

"As I indicated," she went on, ignoring what Adams had said, "I just wanted to make you aware of the incident."

"You think of anything else that might help Sheriff Tate out in identifying the kids involved, you let me know."

Tate must be the sheriff of the adjoining county. It was apparent that Adams didn't intend to pursue any investigation of the citizens of this one, having apparently already made up his mind about who had run her off the road last night.

Since she had also speculated that it could be kids, she didn't know why having the sheriff jump to that conclusion bothered her. To be fair, Adams knew these people far better than she did. And judging by Lorena's shock when she'd told her what had happened, things like this really *weren't* common occurrences around here. *Thank God.*

"I will," she promised. "And thank you."

"You bet. You take care now, you hear?"

"About the medical examiner's report," she managed to say before he could hang up. "You think I can expect it today?"

"I doubt that, Ms. Chandler, with the weekend and all."

"Could you ask?"

"Be glad to. I'll give you a call if the M.E.'s done."

The click on the other end of the line signified the connection had been rather abruptly broken. So that she couldn't ask more questions? Or prompt him to do more checking for her? Her suspicions about the sheriff's motives made her as guilty of jumping to conclusions as he'd been, she conceded.

She hung up and turned to face her hostess, who had been listening to every word with avid interest. Susan shrugged to indicate that Adams had offered little in the way of solutions.

"What did he say?" Lorena prodded.

"He thinks it might have been kids from the next county. He suggested that when they saw the out-of-state tag, they decided to harass the driver. Apparently they're notorious for that kind of wildness. He said he'd contact the sheriff over there and report the incident."

Jeb Bedford made some sound. Although soft, it had clearly been derisive.

"You hush now," his aunt chided. "Somebody over there vandalized the high school. You remember that."

"What I remember is that Wayne Adams is never going to do any more than he has to."

"I didn't give him a lot to work with," Susan said.

"You really think it would have mattered if you had?"

Jeb was probably right. It seemed to her that the sheriff had made up his mind even before she'd given him the few details she had. Still, there was nothing else she could do. She had made a report of the incident, as the Bedfords had urged her to. Whether the sheriff pursued it was out of her control.

"Do you think I should call the service station and ask about the car?" she asked, deliberately changing the subject. "Or do you think they've had time yet to look at it?"

Jeb glanced at his watch. "I don't think they open until eight."

She had forgotten how early it was. And besides, she had exhausted the avenues of investigation Mrs. Bedford had given her. Unless her hostess or Jeb had others to offer, it really didn't matter that she was temporarily without transportation.

"I guess I'm anxious to have it in working order again. I'm not accustomed to being without a car."

"You're welcome to use my truck."

She looked up to find Jeb's eyes on her, their sky-blue again startling against the darkly tanned skin and black lashes.

"Thank you, but it's quite a bit larger than I'm used to."

"It drives the same as your car. It just takes more room to park. *And* it's an automatic."

He had asked that question before he'd agreed to move her car to the back. She was surprised to detect a hint of amusement in his reminder of their conversation that night.

"I don't think I'd feel comfortable borrowing it, as much as I appreciate the offer."

"It's insured. If someone runs you off the road again, it's covered."

"Nobody's gonna run her off the road," Lorena said sharply. "It's like Wayne said. Just some kids on a tear."

"Why would you think someone might try to do that again?" Susan challenged, sensing more in Jeb's comment than the subtle teasing of the previous one.

"You said that the first time you saw them, they were approaching your car."

"That's right."

"Then how would they see your tag?"

He was right, Susan realized. There was only a dealership plate on the front of the Toyota. Of course, they could have seen the Georgia tag when they'd come flying up behind her, but that would have been their second pass. Made *after* they had turned around and come back to harass her.

Although she told herself there were other possible explanations for their decision, she felt the same dread she'd felt as she'd watched those headlights come closer and closer. In the cold light of day she had dismissed last night's terror as an overreaction. Now Jeb seemed to be suggesting that she *hadn't* been a random victim.

"It didn't have to have anything to do with her tag," Lorena said. "That was just Wayne's get-up. And any reason you come up with for what they did doesn't amount to a hill of beans. There's just some crazy people in this world, and there always will be. That doesn't mean you have to worry about something like that happening again. If you'd feel better, Jeb could drive you around."

Watching his eyes widen in response to his aunt's suggestion, Susan wasn't sure which of them was more shocked. Neither responded for several seconds.

"I'm sure Mr. Bedford has more important things to do," she said, letting him off the hook before he had to come up with a reason to say no. "Besides, I've already talked to everyone you mentioned. Unless you've thought of someone else…"

She let the sentence trail, hoping her diversion would work. In spite of her gratitude for his rescue last night, she didn't want to spend the day in Jeb Bedford's company. And she was certain he was no more eager to be thrust together in the confined space of his truck than she was.

"Who *did* you talk to?" Jeb asked.

"The people Lorena mentioned. And any others they suggested. The deputies. The bank. The lady who runs the café on the square. The grocery stores. I even talked to the people who worked at the hotel before it closed."

"And none of them remembered seeing your husband?"

"I don't think that means too much," she said stiffly, "considering the length of time—"

"A man traveling alone with a baby?" Jeb interrupted. "Maybe that wouldn't be unusual in Atlanta, but here… I would expect someone to remember him here."

"Maybe," Susan said, finally expressing those same doubts that had kept her from sleeping last night. It seemed as if she were going about this all wrong, but she wasn't sure what else she could do. "If he *went* to any of those places. Maybe he just took the wrong turn and got lost. Maybe he didn't talk to anyone before he ended up on the road leading to the bridge. He wasn't much on stopping to ask directions."

"Men aren't," Lorena agreed. "I guess it was wishful thinking on my part that he might have spent any time in town."

"There had to be a reason for him to turn off the interstate here," Jeb said. "Linton isn't exactly on the way to anyplace."

"That's why I drove out there last night. To the truck stop at the exit. I thought maybe Richard had stopped there for some reason, and they'd sent him into town."

"Car trouble seems the most likely explanation. You *did* talk to the garages and service stations?"

"On Saturday. Most of their business is local. One of them said there have been few enough out-of-towners through the years that he would have remembered working on the SUV. I showed him Richard's picture. It didn't ring any bells either."

"I can't think of anybody else," Lorena said.

"What about Caffrey's? Weren't they still open back then?"

"I never even thought about Ed and Gladys. I can't remember when they closed, but it's worth a trip out there."

"Caffrey's?" Susan asked.

"A mom-and-pop operation that used to be on the edge of town," Jeb explained. "It was the first thing you came to before you hit the city limits. Kind of a general store. They carried a little bit of everything. Including things you couldn't get at a truck stop."

"Like what?" Susan wasn't sure what he thought Richard might have needed so much he'd drive almost twenty miles for it.

"I was thinking of diapers. I don't know much about babies, but I doubt they have the same needs that truckers do. And truckers are who Carl Williams caters to."

Taking a supply of diapers with him, beyond what she kept in Emma's bag, was something Richard probably wouldn't have thought of. That had been her job. To make sure the baby had everything she needed whenever they went anywhere.

"If the prevailing theory is that your husband got lost or made a wrong turn and somehow ended up at the bridge," Jeb added, "it would be much more feasible if that had happened at night. Seven years ago, Caffrey's would have been the only game in town if he'd come through here late."

Like his comment about her tag, Jeb's reasoning made sense. Certainly as much as any of the other possibilities.

"And this Mr. Caffrey still lives in town?"

"A few miles outside the city limits," Lorena said. "He's become something of a recluse since his wife got sick. That's why folks stopped going to the store. Ed has the personality of a fish. He always acted like it was a chore to wait on you. Without Gladys he just couldn't make a go of it. Not since the Wal-Mart went up on the highway. I can't remember exactly when she got sick or when he closed down the store. Like I said, it'll be worth it to ask him if he was still open then."

"Maybe instead of needing diapers, the baby was sick," Jeb said. "How about Doc? You talk to him?"

"I asked if there were a clinic here," Susan said, turning to Lorena for confirmation of what she'd been told.

"There's not," the old woman said quickly. "And there wasn't one seven years ago."

"But if her husband had stopped to ask anywhere around this area about a doctor, they might have sent him to Linton," Jeb said to his aunt. "Doc Callaway retired more than a dozen years ago," Jeb explained, "but he still keeps up his license. He'd help anyone in an emergency. Especially if it was a sick baby. Williams would have been aware of that."

"But he said he didn't remember Richard. And I specifically mentioned Emma. I *did* think people might be more apt to remember a man with a baby…"

"Doc certainly would," Jeb said, his voice decisive. "Would you like me to take you to ask him?"

It was the same offer his aunt had made on his behalf. The one Susan thought he'd rejected. One that she, too, had been uncomfortable with.

Now, with a new avenue of investigation that seemed to make more sense than most of the ones she'd pursued yesterday, it was suddenly appealing. Certainly worth spending more time in Jeb Bedford's company.

"I'd be very grateful if you would," she said.

# CHAPTER EIGHT

"THE CALLAWAYS ARE relative newcomers," Jeb said as he pulled the Avalanche up to the curb of a deeply shaded street.

Dr. Callaway's house, very near the heart of Linton, was almost as large as Lorena's. Its Victorian architecture, punctuated by gingerbread detailing and typical turn-of-the-century colors, made it obvious this structure had been built decades later than the Bedford mansion. The fact that it would still be more than a hundred years old, as well as Jeb's tone, let Susan know he appreciated the irony of his statement.

"Maybe we should have called first," she hedged, a little intimidated by the size and condition of the Callaway home.

Jeb had already opened his door. He eased down to the ground, holding on to the handgrip until his right leg could support his weight. She felt a touch of guilt as she remembered the conditions in which he'd come out last night. They'd both been soaked to the skin by the time they'd gotten into his truck. She wondered how much that combination of cold and dampness had exacerbated his injuries.

Ignoring her suggestion, he slammed his door and

started around the truck. Susan had already put her fingers around the latch of her own door, but as Jeb rounded the front, obviously headed toward her side, she hesitated. Apparently chivalry wasn't dead in the modern South.

As he opened her door, he held out his hand to help her down. She debated the wisdom of taking it, but without being outright rude, she had little choice. After all, he had been kind enough to drive her here, despite his initial resistance to Lorena's suggestion. Without his cooperation, she was without transportation. She didn't want to antagonize him.

Reluctantly, she put her fingers into his. As they closed around hers, an unaccustomed sensation shivered through her lower body. This was clearly a man's hand. A man who, despite his limp, engaged in physical activity frequently enough that his fingers were hard and strong.

It was only a matter of seconds until she was standing beside him on the curb. Despite the fact that he had immediately released her hand, it seemed she could still feel his fingers, their texture pleasantly rough and callused.

*A complete contrast to the smooth softness of Richard's.*

The comparison had been unthinking, but it bothered her that she had made it. It put Jeb Bedford into a context in which she wasn't sure she was ready to think about him.

She preceded him up the walk and then climbed the three steps leading to the house's wraparound veranda without looking back. She stopped when she reached the leaded-glass door, waiting to allow Jeb to ring the bell. When he had, they stood side by side without speaking. Several long minutes passed before he reached out and stabbed the button again.

"Hold your horses," a voice called. "I'm coming."

The door opened almost at once, revealing a portly, white-haired man. Half glasses perched on his nose, he carried a book in his right hand, one finger inserted to hold his place.

His frown disappeared as soon as he saw Jeb. He pulled the door wide, looking at him assessingly over his glasses.

"And they told me you were half-dead." His delight was clear and obviously genuine.

"'The reports of my demise—'" Jeb quoted, returning the old man's grin.

"Have *obviously* been exaggerated. Thank you, Lord."

Jeb laughed. The sound was exceptionally pleasant, just as the feel of his fingers wrapped around hers had been.

"And who is this pretty thing? You bringing her here to show her off? Should I offer congratulations?"

The silence that followed was thick enough that the doctor's smile began to fade. Jeb cleared his throat, either as a warning to Callaway or in preparation for denying his suggestion. Before he could do either, Susan offered her hand.

"I'm Susan Chandler, Dr. Callaway. It was my husband's body that was pulled from the river here last week. I'd like to ask you some questions, if you don't mind."

The brown eyes above the half glasses moved from her face to Jeb's and then back again before the doctor took the hand she'd offered, shifting the book he held in order to do so.

"Forgive an old man's romantic foolishness, my dear. It's just that I'd heard such terrible things about Jeb's injuries. Then to find him standing on my stoop with someone like you... I'm afraid my enthusiasm at what I would consider his great good fortune ran away with my common sense. Jeb can tell you that's *not* an uncommon occurrence. My apologies to you both."

"They aren't necessary," Susan said, smiling at him. "It was a natural mistake."

"But with your recent loss, an unforgivably painful one."

"Hardly recent," she said, responding negatively to the sympathy in his voice. It was a sympathy she didn't deserve. "The sheriff believes my husband's body had probably been in the river since shortly after he left home, which was seven years ago. Although I *had* believed he was alive during that time, I can assure you those years were long and painful enough that I'd certainly stopped grieving over his desertion."

The old man's eyes assessed her as closely as they had Jeb. After a moment, he nodded, as if he'd come to some decision.

"Fair enough," he said. "Why don't you come inside to ask your questions? We'll all be more comfortable, I think."

He meant Jeb, she realized. More comfortable where there were chairs. "Thank you."

Callaway nodded again before he turned, leading

the way into the house whose interior decoration was very much in keeping with its exterior design. In contrast to the dark furniture and heavy upholstery of the formal rooms they passed through, the sun porch he took them to was bright and modern.

From the stack of books and a glass of what appeared to be iced tea on the small table next to a wicker chaise, Susan suspected this was where the old man spent most of his time. She couldn't blame him. It would be hard to find a more appealing setting than this, with its view of the back gardens.

"Ms. Chandler," Dr. Callaway said, indicating a high-backed chair constructed of the same material as the chaise. Both were covered with a worn chintz whose predominate color was yellow.

She sat where he'd directed her, watching as Jeb shook off the old man's gesture that he should take his own place on the lounge. Instead, Jeb chose the settee, moving a couple of cushions before he sat down. Although he had said nothing, the sense of strain she'd noticed in his features eased as soon as he took his weight off the damaged leg.

As the old man settled back into his chaise, unconsciously she studied Jeb's fingers, lying relaxed on his jean-covered thighs. Although long, befitting his height, they were square in shape. Entirely masculine. Exactly like the man himself.

After a few seconds, she glanced up to find he was watching her. She couldn't imagine what he thought she was doing. At least she didn't *want* to imagine it.

"Now then," Dr. Callaway said, offering an unexpected rescue, "what can I do for you two?"

Jeb answered before Susan had time to gather her thoughts. And she knew very well why they were scattered. It had been a very long time since she'd been so conscious of a man. Aware of his every move. Of his almost blatant sexuality.

"We're trying to figure out why Susan's husband would have been in the area of the bridge," Jeb said. "Even if he'd come into Linton for something, it seems he should have then headed back to the highway rather than driving on through town."

He had called her Susan, which was surprising. Even more surprising was his use of the plural pronoun. *We're trying to figure out...*

As if they were working together to find Emma. After years of being alone, of having only herself to depend on, his linking of himself with her in that endeavor created almost the same surge of emotion the touch of his hand had earlier.

"Took a wrong turn," the doctor said. "He's not the first to do that. Sign's about as clear as mud."

"You may be right. More importantly, I suppose, we need to try and figure out why he was in Linton at all," Jeb went on. "Which is why we came to see you."

"You think I know something about that?"

"We've been trying to come up with scenarios that would draw him off the interstate, which is where we're assuming he would have been, and into the town. Susan has checked the service stations, most of the stores in town, the café, as well as the truck stop at the exit. Nobody remembers seeing him."

"Or my daughter," Susan added.

She had felt all along that Emma would be the most

important element in tracking Richard's movements. Jeb's agreement with that had simply solidified her thinking.

*"Daughter?"* the doctor repeated.

"When Richard left Atlanta, he took our daughter Emma with him. She was fourteen months old at the time he disappeared. Her car seat was found in the back of his SUV, but…she wasn't." She still found it difficult to even think about the possibility of Emma being in the car when it went off the bridge, much less to articulate it. "The straps on the seat weren't fastened. Whatever failings Richard had, he would never have let her ride in the car unrestrained."

"You think he left her with somebody here in town?"

Susan knew she wasn't explaining this well. The problem was that she had no idea why Emma *wouldn't* be in the car with Richard. Although she was grateful that her daughter's body wasn't there, Richard being alone that night made no sense.

"I have no idea. No one here seems to have seen either of them, but I do know he didn't leave her with anyone we know. No friends or relatives. I questioned all of them when this first happened. I even hired a private investigator. Despite all of that, as well as the publicity surrounding her abduction, no one came forward. Surely if he'd left her with someone we knew—"

"Her *abduction?*" the old man repeated.

"Legally that's what it was. My husband had taken all the money out of both our checking and savings accounts."

She realized as she talked that this was something she hadn't mentioned to Jeb. She glanced at him before she continued, but his expression hadn't changed.

"Because of the amounts involved," she went on, "he'd had to go to the bank personally to do that. He had Emma with him when he did. The teller indicated that was one reason she wasn't overly concerned about him cleaning out the accounts. She thought maybe the family was relocating. And then, after they left the bank, they both just…disappeared."

"That's why the police believed he had left voluntarily?" Jeb asked. "Because he took the money?"

"And because there was no evidence of foul play. The withdrawal certainly argued against that. It appeared that Richard had just decided to leave our marriage, but that he didn't want to go without Emma."

There was a small silence. Susan had become accustomed to that reaction through the years. No one ever knew what to say at this point in her story. Not even the police. After all, husbands walk out on their wives all the time. They usually don't take their toddlers with them.

"I called the police, of course, but when they found out about the bank…" She shook her head, reliving that particular humiliation. "One of the first things they asked me was if Richard was a threat to Emma. Based on everything I knew about my husband at the time, I told them the truth. I said that he wasn't. I realized later that I should have lied, because as soon as I told them that, the sense of urgency to find her suddenly vanished. Emma wasn't a child at risk. She was just a little girl who had been taken away from her mother."

"Are you saying they did *nothing?*" Callaway asked.

"They went through the motions. They added her to the national database of missing children. Her picture was posted on several law enforcement sites, and there were some local newspaper stories. Nothing turned up, so after a while…" She paused, strengthening her voice to tell the part that had always made her most bitter. "After a while everyone just stopped looking for her. Emma was, after all, with her father, who had no history of abusing her."

"So because no one came forward with her during those years," Callaway said, "you believe your husband must have had Emma with him when he came through here."

"It seems the most logical explanation."

"And he didn't even leave you a note?" the old man asked. "No phone call? Nothing?" he reiterated while she shook her head to all of his questions. "He just picked up the baby and walked out the door?"

"Apparently. Along with every cent we owned."

"Then a few days, weeks or months later," Jeb said, "he drives his car into the Escatawpa."

"If your husband was in the water as long as the paper indicated, they aren't going to be able to tell you whether it was days or months," Callaway warned.

"I know. That's why I'm trying to figure out why he came into town and who might have seen him while he was here. And who might have seen Emma, of course."

"We thought maybe she'd gotten sick," Jeb said. "Or maybe he had. Maybe he asked for a hospital or clinic at the truck stop, and they directed him to you."

"I have a picture," Susan offered, opening her purse to remove the photograph she had shown everyone she'd talked to. "It's a newspaper photo, taken to announce Richard's promotion at the accounting firm he worked for, but it's a good likeness."

She handed it over, watching as the old man studied her husband's features.

"And this is Emma," she said after a moment, handing him the second picture. "She was a year old there. At that age they seem to change from month to month, but…it's the last good one I had." She realized she was talking too much, and none of that was relevant. "If Richard *did* bring her here—"

"Would you have treated someone under those circumstances, Doc?" Jeb asked.

"Of course. I've gotten a few patients that way. Folks that were passing through or were involved in an accident. Seven years ago. Let me think," the old man said, still looking from photograph to photograph. "Better yet, let me check."

"Check?" The doctor had swung his legs off the chaise in preparation for getting up, when Jeb's question stopped him.

"If I'm going to treat people out of my home, then I'm gonna keep records of it. They may not be as detailed as the hospital's, but it's something. Come on, and I'll show you."

As she followed the old man down the hall, behind her she could hear Jeb's uneven footsteps on the polished wooden floors. Dr. Callaway opened a door at the end, stepping aside to usher her into what was essentially an examination room, complete with a table and a rolling light. Around the walls were glass-fronted cabinets full of instruments and medical supplies.

"This was my father's office," he explained. "Despite my age, I never practiced this kind of medicine. In his day he saw to the needs of the whole town. Made house calls, too."

Susan wasn't sure what she was supposed to say to that, but luckily the old man didn't seem to expect an answer. He opened one of the cabinets, running his finger over the spines of a set of leather-bound books.

"Seven years, you say?"

"Seven years ago this past August."

She would never forget the heat and the unnatural stillness of the house when she'd arrived home from the airport. Richard had turned the air off before he left. It was something they did when they were going to be away because money was so tight. She had walked from room to room, looking for a note. Searching for some kind of explanation. An explanation she'd never found.

Dr. Callaway pulled one of the books off the shelf, laying it down on the counter. He opened it, flipping pages until he found the place he was looking for. Then, just as he'd done with the spines, he ran his finger slowly down the entries.

Neither she nor Jeb said a word, waiting through the process as the long, silent minutes ticked off. It was so quiet she could hear the grandfather clock in the front hall.

After what seemed an eternity, Callaway turned. His lips pursed as he looked at her face. Again his eyes jumped to Jeb's before they came back to hers. From the compassion in them, she knew what his answer would be before he gave it.

"At my age, I have trouble remembering what I ate for lunch yesterday, but I never forget a patient. I had hoped I was wrong, but…I didn't treat your husband or your daughter, Mrs. Chandler. I'm sorry. I wish I had. I wish I could tell you something that would help."

She didn't know why the sense of disappointment was so strong. She should be used to coming to another dead end. It had been that way for seven long years.

"Are you sure, Doc?" Jeb asked.

Maybe that was why she had expected this to be different. Because someone else now seemed confident there had to be answers out there. Answers to how a baby could just disappear and no one know what had happened to her.

"Believe me, I wish I could tell you something else. Even back then I didn't treat many people here. I looked at everything from the date you gave me until three years later. None of the patients I saw fit the information."

"Maybe he had someone with him. Another woman."

Susan had lived with that idea long enough that she had no hesitation in giving voice to it. Although she'd had no indication anything was wrong with their marriage, Richard's leaving seemed pretty undeniable proof that there had been.

"That possibility *had* occurred to me," Dr. Callaway said gently, smiling at her. "I can't say for sure about your husband, of course, but I didn't treat a child of the right age during any of those years. Not one I didn't know, that is."

"What about those you *do* know?"

The old man turned toward Jeb. "What does that mean?"

"If Susan's daughter is in Linton, she'll be eight years old now?" He turned to Susan for confirmation. "You know any girl here of that age whose origins might be questionable?"

For some reason, Jeb's questions brought home to Susan the reality of the situation. Despite the number of times she had tried to imagine what Emma might look like, despite the computer-generated pictures of her daughter at a variety of ages that had been posted on the Web site, for the first time Susan thought about actually encountering Emma as she was now.

"A child's origins are something I learned a long time ago never to speculate about," Dr. Callaway said. "If you're asking whether there are adopted children in town, then I'll tell you there are. And I've no reason to believe any of them are Mrs. Chandler's daughter. Now, is there anything else I can help you with?"

From the coolness of Callaway's tone, it was obvious Jeb's question had made him uncomfortable. Susan wasn't sure why it would have, unless he felt it was an attempt to circumvent doctor-patient confidentiality.

"Maybe," Jeb said. "Susan's still waiting for the results of the autopsy. I'm not sure it will tell us anything we haven't already assumed, but it's possible it might offer some additional information about why her husband was in Linton."

"And you think I might have connections with the medical examiner." With the change of subject, the teasing gleam she'd noticed when he had opened the door was back in Callaway's eyes.

"I think you know just about everybody in this part of the state who has anything to do with medicine."

"Actually, the M.E. happens to be a old fishing buddy of mine. He's been angling for a trip to the Keys, and I'm about ready to give in and make one. Give me a couple of days, and I'll see what I can find out."

"I thought maybe you might ask some of those questions this morning," Jeb suggested with a smile.

"You forgetting you ain't in command here, boy? You got too used to the weight of those oak leaves on your shoulder."

"I just think Susan has waited long enough for answers to what happened to her little girl."

The old man's lips pursed again, before he nodded. "You all wait here. I don't like anybody watching over my shoulder while I'm trying to bribe a public official."

"Good luck," Jeb said.

As soon as the doctor closed the door to his father's office behind him, Jeb turned to look at her. "If the autopsy's complete, he'll get the information."

"Thank you for asking. I don't want to impose, but…maybe there *will* be something in the autopsy results that can help us. I hadn't thought about that."

Jeb nodded, walking over to the examination table to prop his hip on its paper-covered surface. His eyes briefly examined the framed diplomas on the wall next to it before he warned, "Don't get your hopes up. After all this time, I doubt they'll be able to tell us anything very enlightening."

She nodded. In the silence after the exchange, she realized she could hear Dr. Callaway talking. She was unable to distinguish the words, but the sound of his voice, teasing again, came clearly from down the hallway.

As she waited, her eyes considered the man half sitting on the examination table. Jeb was wearing a pair of worn jeans and a black polo shirt, its short sleeves emphasizing the corded muscles in his arms.

She pulled her gaze away, concentrating on a framed copy of the Hippocratic oath that had been hung beside one of the glass-fronted cabinets. She had read probably half of it, when the door opened again.

The laughter that had been in the old man's face when he'd talked about the fishing trip was no longer there. Jeb looked up, meeting his eyes, his own questioning.

"Was it complete?" he asked, when Callaway didn't speak.

"They haven't written up the formal report. That'll probably take a couple of days, but…"

"What's going on, Doc?" Jeb asked when the old man paused.

"According to the preliminary findings, Mrs. Chandler, your husband died of a particular type of occipital condylar fracture."

For a moment neither of them responded. That hardly seemed the kind of shocking news Callaway's demeanor had led them to expect. After all, Richard had been involved in an automobile accident in which his car had ended up at the bottom of a river.

"So?" Jeb said carefully.

"To put it into layman's terms, the type of skull fracture he suffered isn't consistent with a frontal blow."

"Like…if his head struck the windshield."

Callaway nodded.

"What does that mean?"

"That the injury doesn't match the description of the accident given to the medical examiner," Callaway said.

"I don't understand," Susan said.

She didn't. She felt exactly as she had when they'd told her about Richard's visit to the bank. As if they must be talking about someone else. Something else. Something that bore no relation to the people she had loved.

Again it was Callaway who answered. "In the M.E.'s opinion, the fracture is of a type that would indicate your husband was struck with a blunt object at the base of his skull. Maybe *before* the car went into the water."

*...struck with a blunt object...before the car went into the water...*

"You're saying..." She licked her lips, trying to decide before she asked the question if there was any other possible interpretation. "Are you saying someone *killed* him?"

"I'm saying that as of right now, that's the opinion of the medical examiner."

# CHAPTER NINE

"YOU THINK WE SHOULD check in with Adams?"

Jeb had begun to wonder if Susan could be in shock. She hadn't said two words since they'd left Doc's house.

Of course, the information he'd given them had certainly challenged the prevailing theory of what had happened to Richard Kaiser. Instead of a tragic accident at a notoriously dangerous bridge entrance, the autopsy finding seemed to point to murder, something virtually unheard of in Linton.

"*After* we talk to the Caffreys," Susan said.

She had insisted that they still make the trip out to the Caffrey place. He'd been surprised at her determination after what Callaway had told them, but her entire focus seemed to be on finding her daughter.

He supposed he couldn't blame her. After all, no matter what had happened to her husband, he was definitely dead. And that was something they couldn't definitively know about Emma.

She had told Doc that her husband had cleaned out their accounts, but she hadn't been specific about how much that amounted to. If someone had found out he was carrying a lot of cash when he came through town—and that was assuming he still had been—that would be a motive for murder almost anywhere in this country. He just hated that it had been in Linton.

"Was that the turn that leads to the river?"

He was surprised she recognized the road they'd just passed, having been there only once. "That's right."

She glanced at her watch and then turned to look at him. "Do you think we could go down there? To the bridge, I mean."

"Are you sure you want to?"

"Sheriff Adams thought the men who found Richard's car might be back out there today. I'd like to talk to them."

It was a reasonable request, considering what was involved. Jeb glanced in his rearview mirror and then swung the Avalanche around in the middle of the highway.

"Do you ever get caught doing that?"

"Too few troopers and too much road," he said, glancing over at her again. She seemed composed, but he was conscious of the strain she must be under. "You sure you're up to this?"

"I need to know *exactly* how the car was when they found it. According to the sheriff, when he saw it, the driver's-side door was open. He hadn't asked if it had been that way when they pulled it out, but he said he would."

As he topped the rise before the road dipped toward the bridge and the river, he could see the equipment the railroad company had sent out to clear the debris. The crew was back, and the county cruiser parked alongside the trailer the men had set up down there indicated Adams had kept his promise.

Jeb maneuvered the pickup off the road and parked beside the sheriff's car. Susan was out of the vehicle before he could shut off the engine.

He watched through the windshield as she walked over to where Adams and a deputy were talking to one of the men in hard hats. The worker was gesturing downriver.

The three turned as Susan approached. They waited until she reached them, and then it appeared that the sheriff was making introductions.

Jeb opened his door, swinging down from the cab. The noise of the crane, which was still bringing up twisted pieces of the derailed train cars, drowned out the conversation taking place below. He arrived in time to hear the guy in the hard hat, who must be the foreman, tell Susan what she'd come here to learn.

"One of my men opened that door. I thought afterward that he probably shouldn't have, but when you see something like that you don't think things through. You just react. When he saw that skeleton inside…" He shrugged.

"And the windows? Were they up?" Susan asked.

"Everything closed up tight. Most of the water drained out as we dragged it onto the bank. A lot of mud. After that long on the bottom you'd expect that, but nothing was open."

"What kind of damage did it have?" Jeb asked.

Despite the M.E.'s opinion, the argument was bound to be made that the skull fracture had occurred at some point during the car's descent to the bottom of the river. If there *was* evidence of a collision with something, Jeb would be more apt to buy into that possibility. And if not…

"Sheriff can maybe tell you more about that, but just from looking at it…" The foreman shook his head. "I didn't see much. Looked like it just slid off the road and got caught in the current."

"You think when something like that happens folks would have plenty of time to get out," Adams said, "but they tend to panic. They start trying to open doors before the pressure equalizes. The water shorts out the automatic windows, so they don't work. When they can't get out by the normal means, they panic and start beating at the door until the air's all gone."

Even the foreman seemed to realize that graphic description was inappropriate. He looked down at his muddy boots rather than at the wife of the man whose possible death throes Adams had just detailed.

"I take it then you haven't talked to the medical examiner this morning," Jeb said.

"Are you saying you have?"

"Richard Kaiser died from a fractured skull."

"So it's possible he was unconscious *before* he went into the water." The name badge of the deputy who made that comment read Buck Jemison.

Jeb didn't remember Jemison from the summers he'd spent here, but then he looked to be several years younger than his crowd. And given the guy's size— maybe six-five or six-six—Jeb thought he would have remembered if Jemison had been a teenager back then.

"Seems like a much better way to go to me," the foreman offered. "At least you know he didn't suffer, ma'am."

"That would be comforting," Susan said, "but according to the autopsy, this particular type of injury isn't consistent with what supposedly happened to the SUV."

"I don't understand," Adams said.

"The blow was to the *back* of his head," Jeb explained. "Literally at the base of his skull."

"Your husband wasn't wearing a seat belt, Ms. Chandler," Adams reminded her, "and his car didn't have air bags. The force of the collision could have thrown him around. All kinds of freak things happen in wrecks."

"Except Mr. Evans just indicated he didn't see any evidence of a violent collision," Susan reminded him.

"I don't claim to be an expert," the foreman hurried to add. "I'm just saying that to the layman's eyes, that car didn't appear to be heavily damaged."

"Even if it were," Susan said, "the medical examiner doesn't believe the injury is consistent with the description of the accident."

"I'll talk to the M.E.," Adams said, as if that should make her feel better about the information she'd received.

"I'd like to have my insurance company examine the car and provide an accident report. If you'll tell me where you've taken it…"

Apparently while Jeb had been wondering if she were in shock, Susan had been thinking about what she needed to do. Bringing in her insurance company's experts to assess the damage and provide an analysis of how the accident might have happened was an excellent idea. One he could tell the sheriff hadn't been prepared for her to make.

"That'll have to wait until the department releases the vehicle," he said brusquely.

"And when will that be?"

"When we're finished with it." Although the sheriff's answer had held a scintilla of anger, he couldn't be expected to have a firm timetable since he'd just received new information. "If you're right about the M.E.'s report—and mind you, I haven't heard anything official—then your husband's car could be considered a crime scene."

"*Could* be?" Jeb questioned the wording.

"Like I said, I gotta have something official before I make that determination."

"And as soon as you do?"

"Then we'll get right on it, Mr. Bedford," Adams said, his eyes cold. "Until then, our hands are tied."

"YOU WANT TO CALL it a day?" Jeb asked as soon as they were back in the Avalanche.

She didn't, but she couldn't be sure he hadn't asked because *he* needed to. She was very much aware of what an imposition it was for him to have to drive her around, but things seemed to be happening so quickly that she felt she couldn't quite keep up. At how much more of a disadvantage would she be without transportation.

If the medical examiner was right, then Richard had been murdered. That possibility seemed to make it even more urgent that she find out what had happened to Emma.

"We *were* on the way to the Caffreys'," she reminded him.

She stole a look at Jeb's face as he began to back the big truck up the slope to turn it to head away from the bridge. Judging by his expression, he wasn't annoyed by her need to continue with their mission.

*Their mission...* At some point she realized that she had begun to think of Jeb Bedford as an ally. She couldn't deny that she needed one.

"Adams is right, you know," he said, meeting her eyes before he shifted into drive.

"About what?"

"Even if the fracture isn't consistent with the accident as it was described to the M.E., his finding isn't definitive. I know you said that your husband had cleaned out your bank accounts, but how would someone know he was carrying that much cash? It wouldn't be something he'd want to broadcast."

"Richard wasn't stupid. And letting anyone know he had that much money would be. It wasn't a huge sum, you understand. Like most people, we managed to spend most of what we made. There was only six thousand dollars between the two accounts."

Enough to get someone killed. But Jeb was right. Why would Richard let anyone know he had that money on him?

"I don't know what happened," she went on, thinking out loud, "but the money would provide a motive. I can't think of any other reason someone would hit a complete stranger over the head and push his car into the river."

With the foreman's description of the undamaged vehicle, that now seemed the most likely scenario. And the primary reason she wanted the experts from her insurance company to examine the SUV.

"But I still need to know if Emma was with him

when that occurred. And if so, what happened to her. So if you don't mind…"

She hesitated, again trying to gauge his tiredness and level of pain from his face. Having no success, she decided that he was perfectly capable of saying no. And until he did—

"I'd still like to talk to the Caffreys."

"MR. CAFFREY?"

The old man would be in his seventies by now, Jeb realized. Until he'd come back to Linton and encountered the people who'd been a part of his childhood, they had all been frozen in time. The Caffreys had seemed old to him then, but he realized that they had probably only been in their fifties.

Just as he'd raised his fist to knock again, the door opened. Caught with his hand in midair, Jeb smiled in anticipation of the same kind of welcome he'd gotten from Doc. After all, like most of the kids who'd ridden their bikes around this community all summer, he had made almost daily visits to the Caffreys' store.

"Who is it?" Ed Caffrey asked, peering out from the dimness of the small house's interior.

The smell of stale cooking grease and an odor reminiscent of nursing homes seeped through the open door. Jeb couldn't hear the familiar hum of air-conditioning, something that with the heat and humidity of the area wasn't a luxury.

"It's Jeb Bedford, Mr. Caffrey."

The man at the door squinted as if to bring his features into focus. "Bedford?"

"Jubal's boy."

Caffrey nodded, but until he spoke, Jeb wasn't sure the old man had made the connection. "How's your aunt?"

With the appropriateness of the question, Jeb's tension began to ease. Apparently there was nothing wrong with Ed Caffrey's memory, which was why they were here.

"She's fine. She asked me to say hello for her. And to tell you she's sorry she hasn't been out to see you folks in a while. She doesn't drive anymore, you know."

Caffrey nodded again, his expression expectant. And social niceties handled, Jeb acknowledged it was time to get on to what they'd come here to ask.

"This is Susan Chandler, Mr. Caffrey. She's staying at my aunt's house while…" He couldn't think of an appropriate way to finish that sentence, so he started again. "It was Ms. Chandler's husband whose body was pulled from the river last week. You may have heard about that."

Caffrey nodded, his eyes considering Susan briefly before they came back to Jeb's. "I heard. Maybe now they'll do something about that bridge. I been saying that for years."

"Yes, sir. It's a danger, especially for someone, like Ms. Chandler's husband, who doesn't know the roads."

The rheumy eyes again surveyed Susan, but the old man didn't reply.

"We're trying to figure out what he was doing in Linton that night," Jeb went on. "I wonder if we could come in and talk to you about that."

"Talk to *me?* What for?"

"We were thinking maybe he stopped by the store

on the way into town. Maybe he needed something he couldn't get at the truck stop."

"We ain't had that store in more'n six years. Had to close up 'cause of my wife being sick."

"This would have happened before then," Jeb explained.

"Who is it, Ed?"

The quavering voice came from the room behind the old man. He turned, throwing words over his shoulder. "Ain't nothing for you to worry about, Mother."

*Mother?* Obviously not Caffrey's mother. Not at his age. Which meant the voice must belong to Mrs. Caffrey, who side by side with her husband had run the general store. A lot of older couples still referred to one another by the names their children had called them.

"Is that Mrs. Caffrey?" Jeb asked. "We'd like to speak to her, too, if you don't mind."

"She ain't up to company." There was a definite movement of the door, so that the opening began to narrow.

"We won't take five minutes of your time, Mr. Caffrey," Susan interrupted. "We wouldn't bother you, but it's very important. My little girl was with my husband when he left home. I'm trying to find out if anyone in town saw her."

"They didn't say nothing about a girl in the paper."

"No one knew then she was with him. I just need to know if you or your wife saw them. Could we come in, please?"

"Who is it, Ed?"

Again the old man turned, speaking into the dimness behind him. "Somebody looking for somebody. Ain't nothing for you to worry about." Each word was distinctly enunciated.

"Please," Susan said again as soon as he turned back to the door. "It's very important."

Jeb couldn't tell from Caffrey's face whether her plea had any effect. The question became moot, however, as Gladys Caffrey stepped by him and into the opening.

She was wearing a starched and ironed cotton housedress of a kind that even Lorena had stopped wearing twenty years ago. Her smile was bright, and her eyes flicked quickly from one of them to the other.

"I like company," she said. "Y'all come on in and get out of this heat. I'll fix us some iced tea."

Since it appeared to be much hotter inside the Caffrey home than out here, her comment should have been their first clue that she might not be the most reliable source of information. Susan apparently had no such qualms, quickly taking advantage of the opportunity Mrs. Caffrey offered.

"Thank you," she said, pushing by Jeb and through the doorway. "Tea would be very nice."

Almost reluctantly Jeb followed her. The smells he'd been aware of on the porch were much stronger inside the small, dark room. He was immediately conscious of those and of the heat. The drapes had been pulled across the windows, so it took longer for his eyes to adjust enough to take in the rest.

Judging from both its style and fabric, the furniture had all been purchased as a suite sometime in the fifties. The tops and the arms of the upholstered pieces were covered with crocheted doilies.

Figurines cluttered every available surface. He remembered these same kinds of gewgaws lining the shelves behind the front counter of the Caffreys' store, each bearing a neatly printed yellow price tag on the bottom. As a child, he had once bought one for Lorena for her birthday.

Despite her promise of tea, Gladys Caffrey sat down in an oversized upholstered rocker. Her feet, adorned in white socks and tennis shoes, barely reached the floor, but with her toes she set the chair into motion, rocking back and forth.

Mr. Caffrey seemed at a loss as to what to do with them. Susan walked across to the sofa opposite Gladys' chair. Unsure where the old man had been sitting, Jeb waited for him to indicate a preference. He stood instead, rawboned hands twisting as he watched Susan and his wife.

"I'm trying to find someone who remembers seeing my husband while he was in town. It was seven years ago," Susan said, speaking directly to the woman in the rocker. "He was driving a black SUV. It was probably at night. He might have come into your store for diapers or medicine for the baby."

"Pretty little thing," Gladys said.

For a long moment everything seemed to stop except for the back-and-forth movement of the rocker. Susan's mouth had still been open from what she had just been saying. She closed it, pressing her lips together as she swallowed.

"The baby?" she asked softly. "Do you remember the baby?"

"*You.* You're a pretty little thing."

"Thank you," Susan said, forcing a smile. "My

daughter was with him that night. She was fourteen months old. A little blue-eyed blonde. I have a picture if you'd like to see it."

The vacant eyes brightened. The old woman held out her hands as if she'd been promised a treat. Susan hurriedly took the photograph from her purse and held it out to her.

"That's Emma. That's the little girl I'm trying to find."

"Did she get lost?"

Susan nodded. "She was with my husband. Seven years ago. I thought maybe you saw them. Maybe they came into your store."

"They can get away from you before you know it," Mrs. Caffrey said, looking down on the picture. "They'll be right there one minute. You turn around and they're gone. Happened to me more times than I can count. Their daddy would have to whup 'em for running away. They'd be good for a while, and then they'd be up to their old tricks again."

Her laughter was loud and inappropriately prolonged. Susan turned, looking at Jeb as if asking for advice. He shook his head slightly, knowing she would undoubtedly have come to the same conclusion he had.

"She don't remember so good anymore," Caffrey said, confirming what they were both thinking. "She'll tell you stuff, but it may be something that happened fifty years ago. Something that ain't got nothing to do with what you're asking her about now."

"Do *you* remember them, Mr. Caffrey?" Susan asked. "I have a picture of my husband, too. It was taken for the papers a few months before his death to announce a promotion he'd received."

She stood, walking back across the room to hand the black-and-white photograph of Richard to him. He studied it for a long time before he shook his head.

"Running a store, you see lots of people. Not so many from out of town though. Not after that stretch of highway opened."

"He was driving a black SUV."

"I read that in the paper, but... I'm purely sorry, ma'am. I just plain don't remember him."

"Or the baby," Susan said. It was not a question.

"Wish I could help you. Sure do."

"I appreciate your talking to us," Susan said, taking the picture from his hands.

She turned to glance back at Gladys, who was still looking down at the one of Emma. A knotted, arthritic finger stroked the paper as if she were touching the baby's fair hair.

Susan crossed the room again, kneeling down beside the rocker. Mrs. Caffrey's eyes remained on the photograph.

"I need my picture back so I can show it to other people."

The old woman's eyes came up at that. She looked at Susan as if she had no idea who she was or why she was by her chair.

"May I have it back, please?" Susan reached for the photo.

Gladys Caffrey clasped it to her bosom, crossing her thin arms over it protectively. She shook her head sharply once and then resumed the steady rocking.

Almost helplessly Susan turned to Mr. Caffrey. "It's the only one I have. I can send her another..."

"It don't matter. She'll make a fuss, but five minutes from now, she won't remember a thing about it. Here, Mother. You give this lady her baby's picture back now, you hear?"

As he approached the rocker, Mrs. Caffrey looked up at him with fear in her eyes, but she clutched the photograph more tightly to her chest. Again she shook her head.

"Give it back now, or I'll whup you just like I used to them kids."

As he made the demand, Caffrey began to pry at her crossed arms. The old woman began to cry, slapping at him with one hand as she continued to hold the picture against her body with the other.

"It's all right, Mr. Caffrey," Susan began, but by then Caffrey had retrieved Emma's picture, holding it high above his head as Gladys reached for it.

"I don't really whup her, you know, but she's like a little kid. You gotta make her think you will."

He held the photograph out to Susan, who took it almost reluctantly. The old woman made keening noises, but there were no tears.

"You be good now, and you can have some ice cream. You'll like that," Caffrey promised, soothing his big hand over the disordered white hair.

"I'm sorry we bothered you," Susan said. "I thought it was worth a chance."

"Wish I could help, but I don't remember nobody like that coming in. Been a long time, 'a course. Truth be told, *my* memory ain't what it was. Still, I'd remember that baby, I think."

"Thank you," Susan said. She had already turned,

making eye contact with Jeb, when the old woman spoke again.

"I can tell you she wasn't wearing *that*. What she's got on in that picture. She was wearing pink that night. Them kind of overalls babies wear. He had her all wrapped up in a quilt so she was snug as a bug in a rug." Again the cackle of inappropriate laughter rang out. "Yes, sir, snug as a little old ladybug in her daddy's arms."

## CHAPTER TEN

MOVING ALMOST in slow motion, Susan turned back to the old woman. Jeb could hardly bear to watch the hope in her face as she stooped, putting her hand on Gladys's arm in an attempt to bring her attention to bear on the questions she needed to ask.

"You remember them, Mrs. Caffrey? The man and the little girl? Do you remember why they came into the store?"

"Mother, don't you go making stuff up now," Caffrey said, his tone hard. "You know you don't remember that baby."

"Do too remember her. *You* wasn't there that night. It was just me and Travis."

Travis was the Caffreys' youngest son, who had helped out at the store. He would be in his forties by now, Jeb realized, but he hadn't seen him during these months he'd spent in Linton.

Of course, his social contacts since he'd been back had, by his own choice, been limited. Besides, he and Travis had never moved in the same circles. The youngest Caffrey had been taciturn, almost surly, even in the days when he'd waited on his parents' customers.

"Don't you go getting your hopes up based on what

she's saying to you," Ed warned Susan. "Just 'cause she's telling you something don't mean it happened."

"Is Travis here, Mr. Caffrey?" Jeb asked. "Maybe we could talk to him. Even if Mrs. Caffrey's memory is failing, there may be some shred of truth in what she's saying."

"Travis don't live with us no more."

"Still, I'd like to talk to him," Susan said. "Can you tell us how to contact him?"

"He moved away. He don't keep in touch like he ought."

"Blue and pink. Squares, I think it was," Gladys Caffrey said, "but it's been so long. Not a full-size quilt, mind you, but one of them little-bitty things people piece just for babies. He had it wrapped around her like she was a papoose. Those big blue eyes peeking out over the top of it."

"Don't you go telling no more lies, Mother. You've caused enough trouble. I've told you what happens to liars."

"Liar, liar, pants on fire." The motion of her rocker kept rhythm with the chanted words. "Hellfire and brimstone."

"But if there's a chance your son could provide corroboration—"

"Miz Chandler, you can't pay no mind to what Gladys says. She don't remember your baby any more than she remembers her own name. She just says what she thinks you want to hear. You made it mighty plain you wanted to hear something about your baby."

"Even so, we need to talk to Travis," Jeb insisted. "If we have to, we can get Sheriff Adams to ask you for his address. There may have been foul play involved in the disappearance of Mrs. Chandler's husband and daughter. I'm sure you and Mrs. Caffrey don't want any trouble with the law."

"Don't you come in my house threatening me, Jeb Bedford," Caffrey said, bristling with indignation. "I don't care who your folks are or how high and mighty. Neither you *or* Wayne Adams scare me. I done told y'all all I know."

"Except your son's address," Jeb reminded him.

"I *told* you. That's *all I know*," the old man repeated, emphasizing each of the last three words.

"Are you saying you don't *know* where your son is?"

"I told you. He don't keep in touch like he should."

"But he *was* here seven years ago," Jeb prodded. "And he was working at the store."

"Sometimes."

"And he and Mrs. Caffrey worked the store together sometimes, too, didn't they? Just the two of them?"

The old man's jaw worked. His hesitation made it clear he didn't want to answer in the affirmative, but finally he was forced to. "Sometimes."

"So it *could* have happened like she said," Susan suggested.

"Don't you understand? She don't know what she's telling you. She's sick. You talk to Doc Callaway. He'll tell you. She's got that Alzheimer's." He pronounced each separate syllable carefully, as if he had learned the word by rote. "You can't count on nothing she says being true."

"Except my daughter *did* have a quilt. Very much like the one your wife described. And it was missing from home after that weekend. Even if she's sick, I can't discount what your wife just told me, Mr. Caffrey. Why can't *you* understand that?"

"You must have had some address for your son after he moved away," Jeb said, recognizing that argument was going nowhere. "Even if you haven't heard from him in a long time, maybe we can still locate him. Just give us whatever information you have."

The old man's anger was palpable, as was the tension in the room. Only Gladys seemed immune to it, rocking back and forth in her chair. After a moment Caffrey strode over to the table where an old-fashioned rotary phone sat. He opened a drawer and rummaged around in it, finally pulling out a scrap of paper.

"This is the last address we had for Travis," he said, bringing it across the room to hand to Jeb. "I don't know if he's still there or not."

"If you have something I can copy it down on—"

"Take it. It ain't doing me and Mother no good. He don't answer our letters. You just keep Wayne Adams out of my house, you hear? I don't want no trouble with the law. I done everything you asked me to do."

"I can't promise that the sheriff won't want to talk to Mrs. Caffrey. She has information—"

"Only reason she said all that stuff is 'cause that's what *she* wanted to hear." Caffrey jerked his head toward Susan. "By the time Adams shows up to ask questions, she'll have forgot all about what she told you."

Unfortunately, the old man was probably right. Even if Gladys *had* seen Emma seven years ago, no one could give much credence to her testimony. No one but Susan, Jeb realized. And he still wasn't sure whether that was a good thing or not.

"I THOUGHT YOU MIGHT need this."

Although Susan had recognized Jeb's distinctive footsteps on the wooden boards of Lorena's front porch, she deliberately hadn't reacted to them. Not until he spoke.

She was sitting on the top step, looking over the rose garden as dusk fell. Despite last night's cold rain, the evening was pleasant, neither too hot or too cold.

Even the low symphony of insect noises from the woods that surrounded the old house was soothing. After the events of the day, she had needed the peace and quiet it afforded.

"What is it?" she asked, looking over her shoulder to find Jeb holding out a tumbler to her.

"Bourbon and water."

"I'm not much of a drinker," she said, reaching up to take the glass from his hand.

"That's my grandfather's private stock. You won't have to be 'much of a drinker' to appreciate it."

"Thank you."

She took a tentative sip and discovered Jeb was right. Although there was a predominance of whiskey in the mixture, it was very smooth. She took a larger swallow, deciding he was just as right about her need for it as he had been about the quality of the bourbon.

"May I join you?"

Although she'd wanted an escape from conversation when she'd retreated out here, the combination of the setting and the alcohol, which was beginning to relax the knot of tension in her chest, seemed to have changed her mind. Besides, Jeb already knew everything that had happened today. It might be helpful if he were willing to talk about some of it. Maybe he could help her sort out the important things from the rest. Something she hadn't found the emotional distance to manage.

"Of course," she agreed.

Using the column that flanked the broad steps for support, Jeb eased down beside her, stretching his left leg out in front of him. "It's been a very long day."

Deciding his comment didn't require an answer, Susan took another swallow of her drink. She was conscious of his nearness in a way she hadn't been before, not even when they'd been together in the close confines of the truck today.

It was obvious he had showered after they'd returned to the house. His hair was still slightly damp and the fragrance of soap again clung to his body. She cut her eyes to the side, looking at him through her lashes. He was staring out at the garden and the avenue of oaks that stretched beyond it.

Fireflies were beginning to rise from the lawn and flit through the trees. Although she'd played with them as a child, after her years in the city, she couldn't remember the last time she'd seen one.

"I've been thinking about what Mrs. Caffrey said." Jeb still had not looked at her.

Which was all right. She wasn't sure she was ready to talk about what the old woman had told them. That's why she'd come out here. To get things straight in her own mind before she had to answer Lorena's eager questions at dinner.

She allowed the silence to build, hoping Jeb would let the topic drop. Tomorrow she would have to tell Sheriff Adams about Gladys Caffrey's supposed sight-ing, and she knew exactly how he'd react. He would be no more inclined than her husband to take seriously what the old woman had said.

She realized she had no idea what Jeb thought about Gladys's description. Unless she counted his demand for Travis's address, he hadn't expressed an opinion.

"You can't possibly know what Emma was wearing," he went on finally, his voice low. "You'd been gone all that weekend."

"The bank teller told the police Emma was wearing something pink."

"Overalls? Pink overalls?" Jeb's tone was skeptical.

"I think Mrs. Caffrey meant coveralls. Emma had a pair. Pink cotton rompers that she wore with a white shirt. They, along with several other things, were missing after that weekend."

"And a pink-and-blue quilt," Jeb said, his voice flat.

"Actually…I don't remember that there was any blue. It had bunnies appliquéd on it," she admitted. "Pink bunnies. Richard's grandmother made it for her."

"Not squares."

"No." She took another swallow of her drink. She could feel the liquor beginning to buzz slightly in her head, but then it had been a long time since breakfast.

"That's a very fragile base on which to build your hopes."

She lowered the glass, realizing that he'd turned to look at her, abandoning his contemplation of the trees and the roses. In the fading light, his eyes seemed almost translucent, their gaze brutally direct.

"Emma didn't disappear into thin air," she said. "Richard didn't leave her with anyone we know. She wasn't with him when he died. She has to be *some-where*, Jeb. And Gladys was right about the quilt and right about her being dressed in pink."

She expected him to say that most baby girls were. Or that the old woman had made a lucky guess. Any of the disclaimers she was already too aware of.

He didn't. He held her eyes, his own without the pity she usually saw in the eyes of others when she talked about Emma.

Maybe because he understood that emotion's corrosive effect. He'd probably been on the receiving end of it as often as she had. Maybe that was another thing that drew her to him.

"Help me," she said softly.

Until the plea was on her lips, she hadn't known she was going to make it. She couldn't regret, however, that she had.

Jeb Bedford was one person in this town she could trust. He was bright, and she no longer had only Lorena's comments to base that opinion on. He had asked all the right questions today, even when she hadn't known what they were. More importantly, it was clear he wouldn't let sympathy for her situation keep him from telling her the hard truths.

"I'm afraid I have my own agenda," he said. "Something that, believe it or not, is probably as important to me as your daughter is to you. That sounds cruel, I know, but…I have a medical review board evaluation in exactly three days. If I don't pass it, I don't know if I'll get another chance."

"And if you don't? Get another chance, I mean."

"I won't be allowed to rejoin my unit."

"And that's as important as a little girl's *life?*"

She couldn't believe anyone would seriously argue that. He didn't know Emma, she told herself. She was nothing to him. But she still found it hard to believe anyone of normal sensibilities wouldn't care what had happened to her.

"Of course it's not. But…it is *my* life. It has been for almost ten years. I don't expect you to understand, but CAG is both my job *and* my family. More importantly, what we do means something to this country. I don't expect you to understand this either, but the thought of having to give that up—"

"I'm not asking you to," she said quickly.

"But you're asking me to take time away from my efforts to pass that evaluation. Time that, quite frankly, I don't have. More than that… I'm sorry, but I don't share your faith that your daughter is alive," he said, the words very soft.

"I know. I know you don't, but… Better someone who acknowledges his uncertainty than someone who won't even entertain the possibility. Or someone who will tell me only what he thinks I want to hear."

"What *do* you want to hear?"

"That you'll help me find out what happened here. Even if we don't find Emma…" Her voice betrayed her, faltering over the unthinkable. "Even if we don't find Emma," she began again, "I need to know what happened that night. First, what happened to Richard. And then, if possible, what happened to Emma."

"I'm not a trained investigator. You need a professional."

"Like Wayne Adams? Someone who's already got his mind made up before he's heard the facts."

"The state police, then. Or the FBI. Or someone private, working just for you. Doing nothing but looking for Emma."

"The police and the FBI have been looking for Emma for over seven years. And I *hired* a private investigator. Shortly after I figured out that they weren't looking hard enough. He found no trace of Richard. No credit card transactions. No employment records after he left Atlanta. No records at all."

"None of which means he wasn't competent. Those things didn't exist because Richard was already dead."

"And the investigator didn't find *that* out, either. Look, I know that what you're saying is what anyone would tell me. It *is* what they told me. And I did it. All of it. For seven years I did exactly what I was told, and I was no closer to finding either of them than I was the day they disappeared. I'm not willing to step back and let someone else take charge of this. Don't you understand? This is another chance. A chance to do it right this time. To do what my *heart* tells me."

She knew as soon as she said it, it was the wrong argument to use with a man like Jeb. A man who was accustomed to rules and regulations. To the chain of command. He couldn't possibly understand her instinct that Emma was here, so close she might meet her on any street corner. So close—

"Which is?"

She could detect no sarcasm in the question, so she treated it in the same way she had treated the others he'd asked. As legitimate. Deserving of the truth.

"That she's here. In Linton. Waiting for me to find her."

His eyes didn't change. And he didn't ridicule her conviction, for which she was infinitely grateful.

Instead, he did what she had thought she would value in having him for an ally. He told her the truth.

"If she is here, Susan, she isn't 'waiting' for you. She doesn't even know you exist. And she probably doesn't want to know. All you represent to Emma, if she's alive, is a disruption of everything she's ever known or ever loved.

"That's something you need to be very clear about before you go any further with this. If you find her, you're going to tear her world apart, and neither of you may be able to put it back together again. Not in the way you envision."

"THE PROBLEM IS that no matter how accurate the old woman's information is," Susan said, "no one here will believe her."

"Are you sure *you* can believe her?" her sister asked.

She had needed Charlotte to be as excited about this as she was. She was determined not to let Jeb's doubts infect her optimism. Now, however, with her sister's matching skepticism, she felt the surety she had clung to all afternoon unraveling.

"Richard always wrapped Emma up when he took her out of the car. He thought it was easier than putting her jacket on. If he had to take her in someplace down here, he would have put that quilt around her. I know it. And the bank teller said Emma was wearing pink. It all fits."

"Except the person telling you suffers from Alzheimer's."

"She didn't back then. Not when she saw them. That memory is old enough she hasn't lost it yet. That's how the disease works. Short-term memory goes first, but they remember the rest for a long time."

"Honey, are you sure you aren't just grasping at straws?"

"Of *course* I am. Any damn straw that comes my way. I'm trying to find my *baby*, Charlotte. If you, of all people, can't understand that—" Her voice had risen sharply before she caught back the angry words. Her sister was only saying what everyone else would think.

"I do understand. I didn't mean to sound like I'm trying to discourage you. I just wish I could be there with you. I don't want you to be hurt again."

"I know. I know you don't. And I'm sorry. It's just been…a very emotional day."

"You can't do this by yourself, Suz. You're too close to it. Call the guy you used before. The P.I. What was his name?"

"Harbinson. Nolan Harbinson."

"You want me to call him? He's in Atlanta, isn't he?"

"I have someone helping me. Someone here in Linton."

"An investigator?"

"Someone who lives here. Someone who knows the town and the people. Someone they all know."

There was a beat of silence. "A professional?"

"Not exactly. But he's ex-military. He's been going with me to talk to people."

"And you're paying him?"

"He's… I'm not paying him. He's at loose ends right now, and he's agreed to help me look for Emma."

"To look *where* for Emma?"

"Here. In Linton. If Richard brought her here—and what Mrs. Caffrey said indicates he did—she must still be here."

"But if someone murdered Richard and took the money—"

"Then what?" Susan asked into the sudden silence.

"Then maybe they took Emma, too."

"Took her *where?* And for what?"

"There's always a black market for babies. People will pay almost any amount of money for an infant. Believe me, I know."

It was a scenario that had not occurred to Susan. She had been so convinced that Emma was here, so sure of what her instincts were telling her.

"I'm sorry," Charlotte said when she didn't respond. "I don't know why I said it. Hormones. They make me crazy."

"I know. I shouldn't be telling you all this."

"Oh, yes, you should. You *better* tell me. You better tell me everything, no matter how insignificant it seems."

"I will. I promise. And what you said about Harbinson. I just thought of something I need him to do. If you could look up his number in the Atlanta directory for me…"

"Sure, but what for?"

"The Caffreys have a son who was with Mrs. Caffrey the night she saw Emma. I have his last address.

If Harbinson could track him down, he might be able to confirm her story." *Or not,* but she refused to think about that possibility. "When I call you tomorrow, you can give me his number."

"Give me the son's name and address, and I'll get Harbinson started on it in the morning. There's no reason for you to have to deal with that. You've got enough to worry about."

After Charlotte had taken down the information Ed Caffrey had supplied, she couldn't resist a little sisterly concern. Susan would have been surprised if the questions *hadn't* come.

"This guy who's helping you. The one there in Linton. Are you sure you can trust him? He's not going to try and take advantage of you in some way, is he?"

That was the one thing she was sure of, Susan realized. That she could trust Jeb Bedford and that he wasn't trying to take advantage of her. Okay, two things she was sure of.

"I'm sure. He's the all-American-hero type."

"What does that mean?"

"That he's one of the good guys, I guess. I promise you, Char, you don't need to worry about Jeb."

After she'd finished the call, that phrase kept repeating in her head. *One of the good guys.* And out of all the things she *couldn't* be sure of about this situation, she was surprised at how absolutely certain of that she was.

## CHAPTER ELEVEN

JEB HAD DROPPED her at Reynolds to pick up her car on his way to the airport Friday morning. Despite the fact that she knew how much was riding on these tests, she had been unable to say anything to him about them. Not even to wish him luck. Although Jeb's focus had clearly been directed inward, as soon as the Avalanche pulled away, she had regretted not at least attempting to break through his tight-lipped self-absorption.

Before she headed back to Lorena's, she had planned to do some shopping in the town square, buying toiletries she'd forgotten to pack in her rush to get to Linton after the sheriff's call. She had ended up at the Linton Elementary School instead, the words Jeb said to her on the porch three nights ago echoing in her head.

*If she is here, she isn't waiting for you. She doesn't know you exist. And she probably doesn't want to know.*

Until he'd reminded her of that, Susan admitted she had unconsciously been picturing Emma as the toddler she'd been the last time she'd seen her. *Her* baby, with blond curls, holding up chubby arms and begging to be held. Jeb's words had reinforced the reality that Emma was now eight years old, a child with no memory of her.

And if Susan's instincts were to be trusted, then Emma would be a student at this very school.

She had pulled into an empty space in the row of staff cars that faced the playground. For almost an hour she had sat inside her car, watching as various groups came out of the building for recess. Trying to decide if the children running out to play were the right age.

Some of them had obviously been too old; some, just as obviously too young. Judging from her limited experience with the children in her neighborhood and with those of her friends, the boys and girls who were on the playground now, however, had seemed to be about right.

Almost as soon as she'd reached that conclusion, Susan had opened her door and stepped out into the afternoon heat. A few minutes later, drawn by a compulsion she didn't try to resist, she had been standing at the edge of the playground, her fingers laced into the chain-link fence that surrounded it.

Her gaze had moved over each of the girls in turn, searching their faces, trying to find something of Emma in any of them. And she hadn't. There was no one here who reminded her of the baby she'd lost.

She glanced again at the teacher, an older, heavyset woman. Unlike some of the others Susan had watched, who had organized games and activities for their students, she sat in a folding chair under one of the huge, old trees that dotted the playground, a paperback novel in her hands. Occasionally she would look up at her charges, especially if there was a particularly loud shriek or if she heard the sound of an argument. Otherwise, the children seemed to be on their own.

They had divided into groups almost immediately. Actually, they'd come out of the building already aligned in those, which determined the kind of activities they engaged in.

Most of the boys were playing a game of dodgeball that to Susan's admittedly untutored eyes seemed overly rough. A few girls were playing hopscotch on a set of blocks someone from an earlier class had drawn in the dirt. Several others were jumping rope, while one group had chosen not to play, but sat on the steps of the building laughing and talking.

A couple in that particular set could be classified as blondes, although their hair was obviously lightened by the past summer's sun. According to his mother, Richard had been towheaded as a toddler. Susan knew from his family's photographs, however, that his hair had darkened by the time he started school. She didn't know if Emma's could be expected to follow the same pattern.

Her eyes again scanned the remaining girls. One, whose long curls were a glossy ebony, she felt confident in rejecting as a possibility. And four of the girls playing hopscotch were black. That left eight or nine with hair in varying shades of brown—the color she thought Emma's would probably be by now.

She was too far away to determine the color of their eyes, which might have helped her narrow her options. And from this distance, their features seemed indiscriminate, the unformed faces of little girls not yet on the verge of adolescence.

Despite the inattention of the teacher, Susan knew she couldn't venture any closer, however, certainly not onto the school grounds. She wasn't sure what the laws were here, but no matter the locale, any stranger on the premises of an elementary school would cause concern. Even watching the children, as she was, might be enough to arouse unwanted attention.

She had acknowledged all that intellectually before she'd gotten out of the car, yet she was unable to tear herself away from her vantage point. She wasn't doing anyone any harm. And only a couple of the children seemed to be aware she was here. None were alarmed by her presence. They probably assumed she was someone's mother. *Someone's mother...*

"Are you looking for somebody?"

She looked down to find a little girl staring up at her through the chain link. Her hair was ash brown. A smattering of freckles dusted a turned-up nose below eyes that were light gray and very direct.

"I'm waiting for someone." It wasn't a lie. She *was* waiting for someone. She had been waiting for over seven years.

"What's your name?" the child asked, small fingers closing around the holes in the wire fence like Susan's were.

"Susan. What's yours?"

"Alex."

"Alex?" Susan repeated, unsure she'd heard correctly.

"It's short for Alexandra. A-L-E-X-A-N-D-R-A. It really *is* a girl's name," she said, as if she'd made this argument countless times. "The queen of Russia was named Alexandra."

"Yes, she was. It's a very lovely name."

The little girl ducked her head, but not before Susan had seen the pleased tilt at the corners of her mouth.

She was wearing a black T-shirt and a pair of jeans. Although both were faded from innumerable washings, they were essentially no different from the clothing the other children wore. On her feet were scuffed sneakers.

"Susan what?" the child asked, looking up at her again from under nearly colorless lashes.

"Chandler. Susan Chandler."

"I don't know any Chandlers. Do they go to school here?"

"Who?"

"Whoever you're waiting for."

"I'm not sure."

"You're waiting for them, but you aren't sure they go to school here?"

"It sounds pretty silly when you say it like that," Susan agreed with a smile.

"You better go ask Mrs. Perkins or you might get into trouble. There's a sign that says visitors have to sign in."

"I'm not really a visitor."

"You live here? I haven't seen you before."

"I meant I'm not a visitor to the school. I *am* a visitor to Linton," Susan hedged, deciding it was time to distract the questioner. "What can you tell me about those girls? The ones who aren't playing."

She held her breath, wondering how far she could go in questioning Alex without setting off an alarm. Apparently the child had not taken to heart the probably oft-repeated parental injunction about not talking to strangers, but she couldn't know how trusting Alex would be when asked about her classmates.

The gray eyes focused on the group on the steps. "They don't want to get dirty." Her disdain for that was clear.

"Do you know their names?"

The direct gaze returned to her face, evaluating either her or the request. Apparently Susan passed whatever standard of trust the child had applied.

"Emily, Anna Kate, Haley and Beth. They don't *ever* play."

"And the ones jumping rope?"

"Madison, Patti, Willow and Karen."

After those identifications had been made, the little girl's eyes returned to Susan. They seemed almost challenging.

"And the others?" Susan asked, giving up any pretense that she wasn't vitally interested in learning all the children's names.

"You aren't going to kidnap somebody, are you?"

Despite the gravity of Alex's question, Susan laughed. "I promise I'm not. I'm really not up to anything nefarious."

"I don't know what that means."

"Anything bad."

"You're just looking for somebody."

"That's right, but not to do them harm, I swear to you."

As she said the words, Jeb's warning reverberated in her head. How could she possibly know what effect her quest would have on her daughter? And since she couldn't, how dare she make that kind of promise?

"Cross your heart," the child commanded.

"And hope to die." Despite that moment of self-awareness, Susan's oath was as heartfelt as Alex's demand.

"Tamika, Caroline, Lakeisha, Bethany and Mandy."

Susan wanted to ask which group she usually played with, but some instinct prevented her. She hadn't seen the girl mingling with any of the other children since she'd been here. Alex had come out of the building alone and spent most of the recess watching the boys' game of dodgeball. That's why she'd been able to approach the fence without Susan being aware of her.

"Are any of them particular friends of yours?" she asked casually, her gaze moving from the small freckled face back to the group on the steps.

"Not really. Did you recognize her name?"

"I'm sorry?"

"Whoever you're looking for. Did you recognize her name?"

"No, but… Maybe this isn't the right class."

"Third grade?"

"Is that what you're in? Third grade? How old is that?"

"I'm eight. A couple of the kids are already nine."

Exactly right, Susan thought, her heart starting to beat a little faster. Her eyes again searched the faces of the girls Alex had identified, trying to find something—an expression or a mannerism—that sparked a memory.

Everyone had said Emma looked just like Richard, but it was impossible to see his distinctly masculine features reflected in any of those faces. They looked exactly like what they were. Little girls. None of them reminded her of Richard or of the baby she had said goodbye to that bright August morning.

"Is that the right age?" Alex asked.

Before Susan could reply, the child turned, responding to her teacher's call. "Time to go in now, children."

The boys ignored her, continuing to throw the ball at the victim. The girls with the jump rope allowed it to swing to a stop, giggling in response to a comment one of them had made.

"I have to go," Alex said, quickly bringing Susan's attention back to her. "I hope you find her."

"Thank you."

"You never told me her name. Maybe I know her."

"Emma," Susan said. "Her name is Emma."

"Are you sure it isn't Emily?"

"I'm sure."

"I don't know anybody named Emma. Maybe you've got the wrong school."

"Is there another school here?"

"Not another elementary school. Not in Linton. I meant maybe you've got the wrong town. Maybe in Moss Point—"

"No, this is the right place. I'm sure."

"Come on, children!" The demand was louder this time. More strident.

"I have to go, or I'll get in trouble."

"I know. You go on. I think I'll just watch a little while. Is there another third grade?"

"Only us. Only Miz Perkins's class."

"Then maybe I was wrong about the grade," Susan said. "It's okay. You go on before you're late. I'll find her."

"I could ask my teacher," Alex offered.

"No, I think you were right before. They probably don't want me to be here looking for her."

"You could say you're somebody's aunt or something. A lot of the kids have aunts."

Susan smiled, both appreciative of and amused by the child's efforts to help her create an acceptable story. "Maybe I'll do that. Thank you."

"Good luck," Alex said, and then she turned, running to catch up with the others, who had finally begun to form a ragged line at the bottom of the steps leading into the building.

When she joined them, she looked back at Susan and waved. Raising her hand, Susan returned the gesture. As she did, Mrs. Perkins turned, too, obviously looking for the person Alexandra was waving to.

Susan let her hand fall. The teacher stared at her for several seconds before she turned back to her students, pulling Alex from the line by her elbow to ask her something.

Realizing that she had crossed the boundary of acceptable behavior, especially here, Susan began to walk back to where she had parked the car, taking care not to appear to be in a hurry. She climbed into the driver's seat, immediately putting on the sunglasses she had left hanging over the visor.

Their darkness provided a sense of anonymity, but she knew it was too late. She had told Alex her name. Even now it was probably being reported to the principal or the security officer, if the school had one.

Still, unable to tear herself away, she sat in the car a long moment, looking out over the deserted playground. Since that first day down by the river, she had believed that Emma was here. Her instinct had been both sure and persistent.

Why then had she been unable to feel a connection to any of the children she'd watched today? She had been so sure that if she could only see Emma again...

*She isn't waiting for you. She doesn't know you exist. And she probably doesn't want to know.*

Her fingers closed over the key she had left in the ignition, turning it with an anger that was uncharacteristic. This was not how it was supposed to be. After all those hopeless years, she had finally discovered the place where Richard had brought her daughter. Everything she'd learned since being in Linton told her that Emma must be here, too.

So close that if she had known which of those children she was, she could have reached out and touched her this afternoon. One of the little blondes on the steps? Or one of the girls playing hopscotch? The self-possessed Alex?

The notion surprised her. Even as they'd talked, she hadn't once considered the possibility that Alex could be Emma.

*I'd know her. Surely to God, I'd know her.*

She took a deep breath, trying to calm the tumult of emotion that threatened to overwhelm her. She was here, and with all her heart, she believed Emma must be here, too.

And yet it seemed they were as far apart as they had ever been. The gap of seven long years loomed between them, not only threatening her ability to identify her daughter, but also, if she believed Jeb, her right to claim her when she did.

## CHAPTER TWELVE

"THERE'S A FEW THINGS I thought I should touch base with you about before we go any further," Wayne Adams said.

This was the first time the sheriff had called her since she'd been in Linton. Susan had immediately thought when she heard his voice that he had somehow learned of her visit to the schoolyard two days ago.

She'd been expecting someone to contact her with a formal complaint since she'd backed her car out of the teachers' parking lot. Every time her cell phone or the phone at Lorena's had rung, her stomach knotted.

That hadn't prevented her from driving by the school today at the same time the third-graders had been at recess the afternoon she'd gotten out of her car. The misting rain had apparently kept the children inside, because the playground had been deserted. Its emptiness had produced a sense of loss Susan couldn't begin to explain.

"What kind of things?" she asked, trying to keep her dread of a lecture from coming through.

"I got the final autopsy report today. And it isn't quite as clear-cut as you all led me to believe. Despite the location of that skull fracture, Dr. Crandall isn't ready to classify your husband's death as anything other than an accident."

That didn't make sense. According to Dr. Callaway there had been no equivocation in the M.E.'s findings. Now, at least according to the sheriff, his opinion had completely changed.

"Then how does he explain the blow to the base of Richard's skull?"

"Like I told you. All kinds of injuries can happen in an accident. I don't mean to distress you, Ms. Chandler, but without the presence of soft tissue, there's no way to say definitively whether your husband was struck on the head with some kind of object or if he suffered that blunt-force trauma during the car's descent into the river."

"I don't understand. What does the lack of soft tissue have to do with it?"

"Because of the condition of the body, all we've got to go on is a fractured skull. If someone delivered a blow to the back of the head with a rock or a two-by-four, say, there might have been particles embedded in the scalp that would verify a weapon was used. We've got none of that in this case."

The river and the passage of time had taken care of those clues. Had that been the intent of the murderer all along?

"Is it possible someone pushed the car into the river in an attempt to do away with that kind of evidence?"

"Anything's *possible*. Are you asking if I think someone could manipulate your husband's car into the river so it would lodge under that bridge? I think that's highly unlikely."

"But you have to admit it's the perfect location. If the car *were* ever found, everyone would assume exactly what you did at first. That Richard was simply another victim of that treacherous turn."

"That's still my assumption," Adams corrected.

And he was unlikely to budge from it unless he had to. After all, it made his job so much easier.

"I'd like to read the final autopsy report."

There was a hesitation before he grudgingly agreed. "I guess you got the right to do that. You can come by the office and look it over."

"No, I'd like a photocopy, please. I'll be glad to pay the cost of having one made," she added before he could refuse.

There was another, less prolonged silence before the sheriff gave in. "I can arrange that."

"Thank you." Susan had already taken the phone away from her ear in preparation for hanging up, when Adams spoke again.

"There's another thing. Something that may be related to the M.E.'s report or not."

Although she had experienced a surge of anxiety when he'd mentioned something else he needed to talk about, the second sentence didn't sound as if this had any connection to her visits to the school. "What is it?"

"If your husband's death was an accident, and that's the conclusion I'm leaning to, then I think it's possible…"

The sentence trailed. Susan waited for him to go on. When he didn't she began to wonder if the connection had been broken.

"Sheriff Adams?"

"I think I may have discovered what happened to your baby."

"I don't understand."

She seemed to be saying that over and over, but nothing about this conversation had gone as she'd anticipated. She had been expecting to be told to stay away from the school. Instead, she'd been given information that contradicted almost every conclusion she'd reached since she'd been in Linton.

"Four years ago they found the body of a Baby Doe up in Randolph County. It's the right age and sex for your daughter, according to the coroner there. I didn't remember the details, but when I talked to him this morning, I asked about the body."

As it had during the first call Adams had made to her, Susan's heart had begun to hammer until it seemed to fill her chest, leaving her no room to breathe. This was *not* Emma, she told herself. Whoever they'd found, it wasn't Emma.

"But four years ago—" she began, only to be cut off.

"It was only a skeleton at that point. The body had been buried in a shallow grave, but some animal had dug it up. A hunter stumbled over the remains."

Bile crawled into her throat, making it impossible to respond, even if she had known how.

"They never were able to match those remains to any child who'd gone missing in that area—"

"And what makes you think this might be my daughter?" she interrupted, cutting to the heart of his allegation.

"As I understand it, nobody was looking for your

husband down here, and yet here he was. In Linton. And that baby was found less than a hundred miles away."

"Downstream from the bridge?"

That was her greatest fear. That the scenario Adams had painted that day at the river might somehow be what had happened. That Richard had removed Emma from the infant seat and then had been unable to make it to shore with her.

But if the current had taken her out of his hands, why would he have gotten back into the car? It made no more sense now than it had then.

"No, ma'am. Randolph's due north of here."

She closed her eyes, breathing a prayer of thanks before she demanded an answer to what she'd asked before. "Then how do you explain how my daughter's body could have ended up there?"

The silence on the other end went on longer than before, but she didn't interrupt it. Adams didn't have an answer, and she wanted him to admit it.

"Maybe the same thing that caused your husband to withdraw all the money from his accounts and come down here in the first place. I'm thinking maybe he decided he didn't need the complication of a toddler."

He meant another woman, Susan realized.

"So he just killed her? Is that what you're suggesting? Richard decided Emma was an inconvenience, so he murdered his own baby and left her in a hole for some animal to dig up?"

She could hear the hysteria building in her voice as she posed those ridiculous questions, but she didn't try to do anything about it. Of all the things Adams had suggested to explain why Emma wasn't in the car with her father, this was the most terrible. And the most inconceivable.

"I expect you found it just as hard to believe your husband would take all your money and then disappear," the sheriff said. "The fact is, despite whatever you think he was or wasn't capable of, he certainly did that."

"He didn't kill Emma."

*But maybe whoever murdered Richard had...*

She didn't want the thought in her head, but it was better than the other. Whatever else Richard was guilty of, she refused to believe he could have done anything to harm Emma.

That was something she had denied from the beginning of this nightmare. A denial that had insured the authorities had never made finding Emma a top priority. For Adams to suggest now that she'd been wrong about that—

"We may never know what really happened," the sheriff began, his tone more conciliatory.

"I know damn well *that* didn't."

"Nevertheless," he said, effectively negating her objections, "that Baby Doe is something we have to investigate."

As much as she wanted to disagree, she knew he was right. If that unidentified body was a match in age and sex, the authorities would have to consider the possibility it was Emma.

"So how do I go about proving that isn't my daughter?"

Another beat of silence.

"I can give you the name of the coroner up there. Actually, why don't I set up an appointment for you. You tell me when it's convenient for you to go up, and I'll arrange it."

"As soon as possible."

"Tomorrow?"

"If he can see me."

"I'll talk to him, and then I'll call you back."

"Thank you," Susan said, following the polite conventions she had been taught all her life.

In reality, the information the sheriff had just provided was nothing she was grateful for. Not the autopsy report or the news about the Baby Doe. Neither fit into the almost comforting scenario she had devised to explain what had happened here. And neither seemed to indicate that she would ever find Emma alive.

"YOU CAN'T POSSIBLY GO up there alone," Charlotte said. "Even if that baby isn't Emma…"

The sentence trailed, but Susan knew what her sister meant. At this point, even if she was certain the unidentified body wasn't her daughter's, it would still be an emotionally wrenching experience. That baby had belonged to someone. Any living creature deserved a better fate.

"I'm sending Dave down there tomorrow," Charlotte went on. "Don't you do a thing until he gets there."

Susan deliberately hadn't called her sister tonight because she didn't want anything to upset Charlotte during these last few difficult days of her pregnancy. Yet when she had picked up her cell and heard the concern in Charlotte's voice, she'd been unable to keep the news to herself. She desperately needed someone to confide in. Maybe if Jeb had been here…

*Jeb.*

"No, you aren't," she said briskly, wiping the emotion from her voice. "We've been through that already. Dave isn't going to be anywhere but with you."

"Suz, you can't possibly go up there and try to identify that baby's body. Not by yourself."

"I don't think it will come to that. As I understand it, the town raised funds and buried her. They put up a monument and everything. No one's mentioned exhuming the body."

She had found all that out at the local library this afternoon. She'd fed the information the sheriff had given her into the computer and found a couple of references to the Baby Doe story immediately. Then, with the help of the librarian, she had read on microfiche the back copies of the *Randolph County Ledger,* which had carried many more details.

One of those had been the measurements of the skeleton. According to the coroner's report, Baby Doe had been almost an inch shorter than Emma at her last checkup.

"Besides, I told you," she continued, "the description doesn't fit."

The resulting silence reminded her of those awkward pauses during her conversation with the sheriff. Enough so that she felt betrayed by her sister's willingness to even entertain the idea that the body could be Emma's.

"Even if they *aren't* asking you to view the body, you can't go up there alone. It's crazy to even think about doing that."

"I'll get somebody to go with me."

"The sheriff?"

Asking Adams to accompany her was something that had never crossed her mind. She couldn't imagine making that kind of journey, with its emotional pitfalls, with someone who would describe the discovery of that baby in the way he had to the person he believed might be her mother.

"Not the sheriff. A friend. I think I told you about him. Jeb Bedford. He's the great-nephew of the woman I'm boarding with. He's already been very helpful."

"Well, that's good. Do you think he'll go?"

Jeb wasn't due back from his evaluation until the day after tomorrow. She could call the sheriff in the morning and ask him to rearrange the appointment. The coroner wouldn't mind a change in plans. And one more day couldn't make any difference.

Maybe the children would be back on the playground tomorrow. Maybe she'd see something in one of them to prove—if only to herself—that what Adams was suggesting wasn't true.

He hadn't been able to come up with a credible explanation for how Emma might have come to be separated from her father by a hundred miles. Nor could she. None of it made sense. Which was all the more reason that the delay of one day in going up to Randolph County wouldn't make any difference.

"I think he will."

"I want you to promise me you won't do this alone. That you won't go to that grave by yourself. Swear to me, Suz. You take your friend with you or you take the sheriff, but you don't do that alone."

Susan could hear the agitation in her sister's voice. And that was something Charlotte didn't need right now. Besides, she was right. The journey to that grave was one Susan knew she couldn't afford to make alone, no matter the outcome.

"I won't, Char. I swear to you I won't go up there alone."

# CHAPTER THIRTEEN

AT FIRST SUSAN TRIED to make the ringing phone part of her dream. Eventually its persistence pulled her from the depths of sleep she had achieved after hours of tossing and turning.

The hands of her small travel clock indicated it was almost 2:00 a.m. Her first sleep-drugged thought was that Dave must be calling to tell her she had a nephew. The second, more rational one sent her scrambling across the mattress to grab the phone. Surely her brother-in-law wouldn't call at this time of the morning unless something had gone wrong.

She flipped open its case as she brought the phone to her ear. "What's wrong?"

"I hear you want to find out about your daughter?"

Certainly not Dave. This was not even a man's voice.

"Who *is* this?" She was still brain-fogged from being awakened too quickly after too little sleep. Despite the question, her heart rate had slowed from that first panic-driven gallop.

"Someone who can tell you where she is. *If* you're interested."

"Are you saying that you know something about Emma?"

"Meet me at the school playground. You *do* know where that is, don't you?"

"When?"

"Now or never."

"It's the middle of the night."

"And the only time this is gonna be safe. Like I said, now or never."

Before Susan had time to frame another question, the connection was broken, leaving her holding a dead phone, the caller's words echoing in her head. *And the only time this is gonna be safe…*

That sounded as if the woman feared for her own safety, yet the question about the playground had been mocking. Someone who had seen her repeated visits? Mrs. Perkins? Or one of the parents, trying to scare her away with a prank call?

If so, there should have been some threat involved. A warning to stay away from the children. There hadn't been. There had been enticement instead. *Someone who can tell you where she is…*

Hoax, Susan thought, determinedly tamping down her immediate flare of excitement. There was always someone out there who thought it was amusing to play with people's emotions.

She had heard of this kind of thing before. One man had spent years calling the mother of a missing girl, claiming to be in contact with her daughter. Then finally, after years of taunting, claimed to be her murderer. Susan couldn't remember if he had been, but she certainly had been able to empathize with the victim of that cruel prank and all she'd gone through.

That's all this is, she told herself, punching up the

number of the previous caller on her cell. It wasn't one she recognized, but she hit redial anyhow. The phone rang and rang, but no one picked it up.

Wide awake now, she sat up, turning on the bedside lamp so she could copy down the number. She would give it to Adams in the morning. Maybe he wouldn't pursue it, but she intended to make as much trouble as possible for whoever had called her.

*Someone who can tell you where she is. If you're interested...*

As she wrote down the number on one of the receipts she'd crammed into the drawer of the bedside table, the words repeated over and over in her brain. Despite her belief that the person who'd said them knew nothing about Emma's whereabouts, she couldn't get them out of her head.

She had handed out her business card with her cell phone number on it to everyone she had talked to in this town. She tried to remember the timbre of the caller's voice to see if it reminded her of any of those people.

Gladys Caffrey, maybe? If so, she could hardly be blamed for the innate cruelty of this call.

Despite the similarity of the accents, however, the sarcasm didn't fit. Besides, with that sadly deranged mind would Gladys be capable of putting the phone number on the card together with the significance of Susan's visit that day? Would she even remember what they'd talked about?

Unconsciously she shook her head, discarding the notion. Whoever had called tonight had been in total command of her faculties, as evidenced by the gibe about the schoolyard.

An angry parent as she'd thought before? Or even one of the children? Except how would any of *them* have access to her cell phone number? Which left...

The people she'd talked to. And those were all people who might have had some legitimate reason to come in contact with Richard. And with Emma.

Or maybe this was someone one of them might have passed her card along to. Someone who...

*Someone who can tell you where she is. If you're interested.*

This was why she was here. To talk to anyone who might have information about her daughter. If there was the remotest possibility this hadn't been a prank, she had no choice but to do what the caller suggested.

Go out in the middle of the night? To a deserted schoolyard? She would have to be incredibly stupid to even think about doing that. *Incredibly stupid or a mother who had no other hope of finding her child.*

Rationally, she knew that following those instructions was not only foolish but dangerous. Emotionally, she knew that she had no choice. There was always a chance the person who had called her tonight really did have information. Not keeping that appointment was a risk she couldn't take.

SHE PULLED HER CAR into one of the empty spaces in the same row where she'd parked before. Her headlights shone across the hard-packed dirt of the playground.

It appeared deserted, but the buildings in the school complex, as well as the playground equipment itself, cast long shadows over part of the yard. There were plenty of places for someone to hide, if that was their intent.

She put her fingers over the door handle and opened it. The glare of the interior light was almost a shock in the darkness, making her feel exposed and vulnerable. She climbed out quickly and closed the door. The sound it made seemed to echo in the stillness.

If they hadn't known I'm here before, she thought, they do now.

She had stepped away from the car before she remembered her phone. They'd chosen to communicate with her that way once. What was to say that they wouldn't do that again?

She reopened the door, retrieving the cell, again conscious of the illumination of the overhead light as she fumbled it out of her purse.

She slipped the phone into the pocket of her jacket and closed the door, this time with an effort to make as little noise as possible. She locked the car with the key rather than the remote and then turned, once more looking out over the deserted playground.

A light wind sent dust whirling across it, which disappeared into the shadows on the far side. Her eyes followed the movement, searching that blacker darkness with a sense of foreboding.

Steeling herself, she began to move along the chain-link fence toward the gate on the far side. As she neared it, she became aware for the first time of the halogen light on the road that ran beside the school. Although the building sat between the powerful street lamp and the playground, it provided enough light that she could see how to operate the latch.

Surprised to find the gate wasn't locked, something the caller had obviously known, she let herself in, pulling it closed behind her. Then she waited, listening to the absolute silence around her.

After a long moment, she realized that the woman who'd called hadn't suggested a particular part of the schoolyard for their meeting. If she were waiting in the shadows of the building, it was possible Susan couldn't see her from here.

She started forward, moving through the area mostly used by the younger children, the part that held the play equipment. She circled the raised seat of one of the teeter-totters, which she'd almost missed in the darkness.

Ahead were the swing sets, the kind with metal chains and brightly colored plastic seats. As she neared them, she noticed that one swayed slightly. Despite the earlier dust devil, there didn't seem to be enough wind now to have set it into motion.

The hair on the back of her neck began to lift. Although she'd heard of the phenomenon all her life, she couldn't ever remember experiencing that eerie prickling.

Her instinct was to back away from the swing set, keeping her eyes on the shadowed area next to it as she did. Except she hadn't come here to run away. She had come because it was possible that the woman who'd called *did* have knowledge of Emma. After all, someone in this town had to.

"Hello?" Her voice was too soft, seeming to fade away into the shadows.

She waited, listening for an answer. Listening for anything. And hearing nothing.

"Is anyone here?"

Off in the darkest area of the playground, where all light was blocked by the bulk of the school building itself, there was a faint clink, as if someone had touched glass to glass.

"Is someone there?" Susan called again, walking past the swings and toward the sound.

Again, there was no answer, but she thought she heard a rustle of movement. An animal, maybe? A stray dog who'd been sleeping in the shelter of one of the doorways?

Like a fool, she hadn't even thought to bring a flashlight. There might be one in the glove compartment of the Toyota, but she wasn't sure enough of that to make a return trip to the car. Not if there really was someone here. Someone with information about Emma.

As she moved farther into the shadows cast by the building, she literally couldn't see two feet in front of her. She finally put out her hand, sweeping the darkness before her to keep from running into something. By necessity, she had slowed her pace, feeling her way forward.

From off to her left came that same nearly identifiable clinking noise she'd heard before. Something tapping on one of the windowpanes? A bush or a tree limb? Was that what had lured her into this darkness?

*Lured...*

Suddenly the same primitive instinct for survival that had caused the hair on her neck to lift kicked in again. That's exactly what was happening here, she realized. She had been lured to this place by someone who had no intention of making herself known.

And no matter how much she needed to know about

Emma, she would be an idiot to go any farther. If there *was* someone here, it was obvious by now that they hadn't come to share information. She had given them plenty of opportunity.

She took a step backward, her eyes searching the shadows. And then another. And another. Then, without making a conscious decision to do so, she turned, running from the darkness and toward the more illuminated area of the schoolyard.

The swing she'd noticed before was moving slowly back and forth. This time it clearly could not have been set into motion by the wind. It looked as if someone had pushed it, beginning the pendulum movement that, even as she watched, had begun to wind down.

Someone had been out here while she'd been stumbling through the shadows beside the building. Where they were now, however...

She turned to look behind her, not because of any premonition of danger, but in an attempt to locate the person who had set the swing into motion. As she did, in her peripheral vision she picked up movement.

She tried to make sense of what she saw, a dark shape that rushed toward her out of the shadows. It took a second to identify the object in its hands as a baseball bat and another, nearly fatal one, to realize it was being swung at her head like a scythe.

# CHAPTER FOURTEEN

INSTINCTIVELY SUSAN hunched her shoulders, turning to protect her head from the blow. As she did, she became aware of the swing set behind her. She ducked under the crossbar of the side frame, managing to put it between her and her attacker.

The response had been intuitive rather than planned, but it worked. Instead of coming down on her skull, the bat connected with one of the uprights, metal singing against metal.

Susan had already begun to push through the swings when she realized there would be another attack before she could get out of the reach of the bat. Again she acted on instinct.

She grabbed both chains of the nearest swing, using them to bring the plastic seat up and over her shoulder. As her attacker ran around the frame and toward her, bat raised, Susan swung the seat forward as hard as she could, using it like a medieval mace.

Although it was too light to be truly destructive, she was lucky enough that the bench part of her makeshift weapon struck her assailant on the hands or on the face. The bat fell, and before her attacker's cry of rage or pain had faded, Susan was sprinting toward the gate.

She didn't dare look back, but she didn't need to. She could clearly hear the sounds of pursuit. And whoever was behind her was better prepared for that than she was.

She had dressed in the clothing she'd worn into town today, which included a pair of low-heeled leather moccasins—footwear not designed for speed. She could only hope the few seconds' advantage she had gained with her counterattack would allow her to reach the gate before her attacker could catch her.

As she ran, she tried to think of anything else she could use as a weapon. Especially something that could overcome the advantage the length of the bat gave her assailant.

She glanced up to gauge how far from the gate she was and failed to notice the other end of the teeter-totter she'd skirted on the way in. It rested on a patch of ground shadowed by the oaks that shaded the teachers' parking places. Running at full tilt, she caught her toe on the edge of its plastic seat. It was enough to send her stumbling forward, trying futilely to regain her balance.

She landed hard on her knees and the heels of her hands, expecting a blow from the bat on her back or her head at any second. When it didn't come, she scrambled up, knowing that her fall had obliterated any advantage she'd gained with the swing.

She flew toward the gate. Familiar now with the latch, she had it open in a matter of seconds. As she started down the outside of the chain link, she glanced over her shoulder to locate her pursuer. The quick look she'd intended to take turned into a much longer one, although she didn't stop running.

Once more the playground appeared deserted. She hadn't been aware when the sounds of pursuit had stopped, but even though she slowed to be sure, she could see no sign of the person who had wielded the bat.

Deciding that it might be more dangerous *not* knowing where he was, she sped up again, fumbling in her pocket for her keys as she ran. This time there was no need to worry about noise. She punched the remote as she rounded the back of the Toyota. The resulting beep seemed out of place in the midst of her terror.

She reached for the door handle, again taking the opportunity to survey her surroundings. Her fingers slipped off, either because of the trembling of her hands or because she hadn't been concentrating on it. Forcing herself to focus, she gripped the handle again, successfully opening the door, and slid into the driver's seat.

She pushed the autolock, enormously relieved when she heard the latches engage. In the confined space of the car, she became aware of her breathing. Air ratcheted in and out of her lungs as if she'd run a race.

She had. A life-and-death race. And her competition was still nowhere to be seen, she realized, eyes lifting to scan the schoolyard through the front windshield.

Obviously he knew this area far better than she did. That was why the playground had been chosen as their meeting place, of course, and the sooner she was away from it...

She made a stab at the ignition switch with her key.

By now her hands were shaking so badly she had to make another attempt, this time steadying the key with her other hand. The engine started immediately, producing another surge of relief.

*Too many horror movies.*

From force of habit she glanced in the rearview mirror in preparation for backing the car. There, exactly like one of those relentless entities that haunted the characters in the films she'd just mocked, was the shape that she'd seen emerging from the shadows of the building. This time it was running toward the car, the recovered bat raised again.

Susan floored the accelerator, sending the car backward at a speed that caused the tires to scream against the asphalt. Although she'd been anticipating it, there was no bump to indicate she'd struck her attacker.

As soon as the front of the sedan was pointed in the general direction of the exit, she slammed on the brakes in order to shift into drive. As she did, the windshield on the passenger side shattered.

She gasped in shock, her gaze flying to that side of the car. The starring from the blow was extensive enough that she could see nothing through that part of the glass.

She knew her attacker would be standing right beside the car. As much as she needed to get a look at whoever it was, she needed to get out of the situation even more. If the windshield were hit again she might not be able to see through it well enough to drive away.

She slipped the gearshift into drive and pushed the accelerator to the floor again. The car seemed to leap forward.

She crossed the parking lot and made the turn out onto the street on two wheels. Despite the speed at which she was driving, her eyes flicked back and forth between the undamaged portion of the windshield and the rearview mirror. At any moment she expected the powerful beams of the truck that had driven her off the road to show up behind her.

Just as in the schoolyard, however, her assailant seemed to have inexplicably given up the chase. Taking no chances, even after she had turned off the two-lane that would lead to the Bedford house, she continued to watch the road behind her.

When she pulled into Lorena's long drive, she was surprised to see lights on in the front of the house. Obviously she'd been wrong in thinking she could slip out and start the car without waking her hostess. And she knew Lorena well enough by now to understand that she would have to explain where she'd gone at this time of night and why.

Actually, it would be good to tell someone what had happened. Right now it felt as if she were in the throes of a nightmare. As if she should wake up to the ringing of her cell phone and find everything that had occurred between then and now had been fantasy.

Except it hadn't. That attack on the playground had been real. And this time no one, including the sheriff, could tell her it had been some random act of violence. That assault had been directed at her personally. And it had been premeditated.

As she pulled up in front of the rose garden, she turned to look back at the two-lane. No lights. No traffic. No one was following her. And the front door of Lorena's beckoned.

She killed the engine and grabbed her purse off the seat beside her. Then she was out and running for the steps, pausing only long enough to direct the remote toward the car and press the button. The horn beeped in response to her command.

As she hurried up the steps, the screen door opened with its distinctive creak. She looked up, expecting to see Lorena. Instead, just as they had the night she'd arrived, Jeb's broad shoulders filled the opening.

Her reaction now was far different from what it had been then. She rushed toward him, hearing his muttered, "What the hell?" as she threw herself into his arms.

Incredibly they closed around her, holding her tightly. It was only then, in the safety of Jeb's arms, the tears began.

Hearing her shuddering intake of breath, he put his hands on her shoulders, holding her away from him so that he could look down at her face. With light streaming out from the hall behind him, it would be mercilessly revealed.

She had no idea what he saw, other than the tears she was struggling to control. It was enough, however, that he put his arm around her and pulled her inside, closing the door behind them. He turned the dead bolt and fastened the chain before he asked the question she already dreaded.

"Where the *hell* have you been? Do you have any idea what time it is?"

She didn't. She only knew it had been after two

when she'd left. And that it seemed like forever since she'd felt safe.

"Somebody called me. On my cell. She claimed she had information about Emma, and that if I wanted to hear it, I had to meet her tonight."

Jeb's lips had parted as he listened to that disjointed explanation. At first he said nothing. Then he began to shake his head as if he couldn't believe what he was hearing.

Something in her eyes must have warned him that she was at the end of her endurance. As she stared up at him, hoping that he, at least, would understand, his expression changed from derision to concern. Seeing that set off the tears again.

"Tell me what happened."

His voice this time was free of censure. Apparently he had realized that whatever had occurred was serious enough to send her not only into near hysteria, but also into his arms. And perhaps that she had run there without the slightest hesitation.

"She told me to come to the playground—"

"The *playground?*"

"At the elementary school."

"I don't understand. Why the playground?"

It was time for the truth, no matter how embarrassing. "I thought it was because I'd gone there to watch the children."

Jeb's eyes widened in response to the confession.

"I just watched them. I know how that sounds, but I thought if I could see her—"

"I understand. What happened tonight?"

"I thought at first there was no one there. That the

call had been a prank. That maybe someone had seen me looking through the fence at the school and decided…"

It didn't matter what she thought, she realized. She had no idea who'd been waiting for her. Or why. She took a breath, determined to finish the story as coherently as she could.

"Even after I went *inside* the playground, I thought there was nobody there. And then suddenly…" She paused, shivering at the memory. Putting the ordeal into words not only made it more real, but more immediate. As if it were happening right now. "Someone came out of the shadows with a bat."

"A *bat?* Like…a baseball bat?"

She nodded, wondering only with his question how she had been so sure that's what the weapon was. "When he held it up, I could see the shape against the light from the street lamp."

"When *he* held it up? I thought this was a woman."

"I don't know why I said that. It was a woman who called me, but I never really got a good look… It *could* have been a woman, I guess. It could have been *anybody.*"

"Tall? Short? Thin or heavyset?"

She tried to think, reliving those few seconds when she'd watched that dark shape materialize out of the shadows.

"I don't know. It all happened too quickly." As clichéd as the phrase was, she understood it now.

"Just tell me your impressions."

"I don't know. Not too tall, I think. At least…not much taller than I am."

She was five foot eight, which was tall for a woman, but less than average for a man. Based strictly on height, her attacker could have been either.

"Thin?"

"I didn't *see* him. Or her. Not well enough to give that kind of description. And at the time I was more interested in dodging the bat."

"Wooden or aluminum?" Jeb persisted, ignoring her sarcasm.

*"What?"*

"The bat. Was it wooden or aluminum?"

"What possible difference could that make?"

"It might help us narrow down who would have access to it. Few high-school teams use wooden bats anymore."

"If you're trying to suggest this was those kids from the next county—"

"I'm not. I hadn't even thought about the possibility. Not until you mentioned them."

Which made her wish she hadn't. Of course, Adams wouldn't need any prompting to claim the same thing.

"This *wasn't* some random prank. She called me. She lured me out there—"

"I'm not *saying* it was random. You reported the joyriders, if that's what they were. Adams said he was going to talk to the sheriff in Blount County. If the kids got hassled, maybe this was their way of getting back at you."

"Except whoever this was had my cell phone number."

"Which you've given to half the people in this town."

Jeb was right. She'd thought of that when weighing

her decision to respond to the call. The cards she'd passed out had provided everything anyone would need to set this up.

"But how could they know who called Adams?" she persisted. "*If* they just picked whoever was out on the highway that night."

"I don't know. Maybe he told the sheriff who it was that filed the complaint, and *he* told them. I don't know the sheriff in Blount County, but in my opinion, Wayne's never been the brightest of our elected officials."

Jeb took a step back in order to prop his hip on the hall table. It was an obvious attempt to ease the strain on his leg, and for the first time Susan remembered where he'd been and how much was riding on the outcome of the tests he'd taken.

"What happened at the evaluation?" Even before he told her, she had read the answer in the flash of pain in his eyes.

"There hasn't been enough improvement to justify another extension. It'll take them a couple of weeks to make that official, but I could read between the lines."

"So…does that mean they'll kick you out?"

His lips tilted at the terminology, but the smile was slightly twisted. "Or relegate me to a desk."

She knew he wouldn't want that. He had already told her what being with his unit meant to him.

"Is that why you decided to come home tonight?"

"I didn't see any point in staying. I'd had more than enough of their bullshit, so I changed my reservation. I would have been home sooner, but the flight from Atlanta was delayed."

"I'm sorry."

She knew all about shattered dreams and having your world turned upside down by something beyond your control. That was exactly what had happened to Jeb, and she didn't blame him for being bitter about it.

"About the flight delay?"

His smile this time was almost normal. Self-deprecating. Charming, she realized. It transformed the habitual sternness of his features, showing her what he must have been like when he had lived in Linton as a boy.

"About the evaluation," she said, managing her own smile.

"The irony is they wanted to cut the damn thing off. I thought I was so frigging brilliant talking those bastards into leaving it alone."

"They wanted to amputate your leg?" Her voice was tinged with a natural horror at the thought.

"That's exactly how *I* reacted when they told me. Now they've got guys with prosthetics passing PT with flying colors while I'm still hobbling around. Hindsight's twenty-twenty, I guess."

"What do they tell you at Southeastern? I thought they were supposed to be miracle workers."

"They are. Supposed to be, I mean. They just can't seem to produce the one I need."

She let the silence build a moment before she worked up courage enough to ask, "So what are you going to do?"

"I don't know. I'm *not* sitting behind a desk. I'd go nuts. What about you? What do *you* intend to do?"

"About Emma?"

"About what happened tonight."

She knew the answer she should give, but she'd gotten tired of dealing with the sheriff. He would probably suggest she'd imagined the entire incident.

"I *don't* want to talk to Adams again."

"I don't think you have any choice. He *is* law enforcement in this county."

"Everything I try to tell him, he's got some answer for. He says now that the autopsy report didn't come back with a finding of murder. That the medical examiner is saying the skull fracture could have happened during the wreck."

"That's not what Doc told us."

"Well, it's what Adams says the report says. And he also told me he knows what happened to Emma."

Her stomach tightened as she remembered the scenario the sheriff had outlined. Then she rejected it, just as she had today. Not only did she know Richard would never have harmed Emma, she knew in her heart that her daughter was still alive.

"What did he tell you?"

Jeb's question was careful, both in tone and in phrasing. He might even believe there was some merit in the sheriff's idea, she realized. And the only way to find out...

"Four years ago a hunter found the body of an unidentified baby in Randolph County. She appeared to be approximately the same age as Emma when she disappeared."

Jeb said nothing, but she could see the flare of sympathy in his eyes. She rushed on in an attempt to explain why she knew Adams was wrong.

"I spent the afternoon reading the local newspaper reports of that find. One of them gave the measurements of her skeleton. According to the coroner, the height of that baby was an inch less than Emma's at her last checkup. And that was two months before she disappeared."

"How far from Linton?"

"About a hundred miles north."

When Jeb didn't comment immediately, she knew he was thinking about the possibility that it could have been Emma. She added the thing that had made her know there was nothing to the sheriff's newest theory.

"Adams suggested she'd gotten to be an inconvenience for Richard, so he killed her and left her in a makeshift grave for some wild animal to dig up."

"Susan…"

"That's what happened to the baby they found." Tears threatened, but she refused to give in to them. "Whatever else Richard was capable of—and yes, it's painfully obvious I didn't know him as well as I thought I did—I *know* he wasn't capable of doing that to Emma. He adored her. And she adored him. He would never in a million years—"

"I believe you," Jeb broke in. "And it should be very simple to prove that isn't Emma's. They can identify her the same way they identify bodies in the military after an even longer period of time," Jeb said. "All they need is a DNA sample from you. I'm surprised Wayne didn't suggest that."

# CHAPTER FIFTEEN

"THE MORE INFORMATION you're able to give me, the better chance I have of tracking down whoever did this."

This time Adams hadn't downplayed the seriousness of the attack. Nor had he mentioned the teens from the neighboring county. Like Jeb, however, he had immediately homed in on the lack of detail in her description of her assailant.

"I told you. It was dark. It all happened in a matter of seconds. I couldn't see the person well enough to tell you anything about their appearance."

"How about another vehicle? Any parked near the school?"

Had there been? If so, she hadn't been aware of them. But then, she'd been anxious when she arrived and terrified when she left.

"I didn't notice any. That isn't to say there *wasn't* a car nearby, just that at the time, I wasn't looking for one."

Even Jeb, as supportive as he'd been, thought she'd made a mistake going there alone. But since she'd been determined to meet with the caller she should at least have been conscious of everything in her surroundings.

The sheriff's questions were making her feel even more stupid than Jeb's had.

"You should have called me as soon as you got away. We could have had a cruiser on the scene in a matter of minutes."

Although she'd made a point of taking her cell phone, she hadn't even thought about dialing 911. Not even after she'd gotten away from the school. She'd been terrified, but still, the logical thing would have been to call and report the attack. Instead, she'd driven back to Lorena's.

She wouldn't have done that in Atlanta. Of course, a police car would have been on every corner there. And they didn't seem to doubt everything you told them.

Even after she'd reached the Bedford house, she had debated waiting until morning to report the incident. Jeb had insisted she talk to Adams tonight, and the dispatcher had put her through at once. Buck Jemison, who'd been on duty, had taken down the information, and Adams had called her right back.

"I didn't even think about 911," she confessed. "I just wanted to get away from there. I'm sorry."

"I'll send someone over to the school to take a look. You can't ever tell what's gonna show up at a crime scene, especially if it's dark. People drop things or leave something behind that can lead back to them without their realizing it."

"Believe me, it was dark enough that could have happened. The person was hiding in the shadows of the building. The side by the playground. You might tell the officers to start there."

"And I'd like for you to come down to the department first thing in the morning to file a report. We like people to do that while things are still fresh in their minds."

She was unlikely to forget anything that had happened, but there was no reason not to agree to his request. Not only was it reasonable, Adams actually sounded concerned.

"I'll be glad to. I also wondered if you'd set up the interview with the coroner in Randolph County."

"Two o'clock tomorrow afternoon. *This* afternoon," Adams corrected. "He's expecting you."

"Thank you. We'll come by your office on the way."

"We?"

She glanced at Jeb, who was still propped against the table in the hall. His head was down, so that he appeared to be studying his hands while she talked.

He hadn't even looked up at her use of the plural pronoun. Nor did he seem to notice the pause as she wondered how he would feel about her committing him to appointments tomorrow.

Although she'd told Charlotte she had a friend who would go with her to talk to the Randolph County coroner, she hadn't had a chance to ask Jeb whether he would or not.

"Mrs. Chandler? You said 'we.' Who would that be?"

"Jeb Bedford and I."

Jeb looked up when she said his name, meeting her eyes across the hall. She raised her eyebrows in question. His lips flattened momentarily, but he nodded, the movement abrupt.

"I see," Adams said.

"About ten?"

"That's fine. There's just one more thing before you go, Ms. Chandler."

"Yes?"

"You think there might be any significance to the fact they asked you to come to the playground tonight?"

It was the question she'd dreaded hearing from him earlier today. And coming on top of what had happened tonight…

"What do you mean?"

"I've received a couple of complaints about you hanging around the school. I wasn't going to say anything 'cause I figured I knew why you were there, but…people get real nervous when strangers watch their children."

"I'm trying to find my daughter, Sheriff Adams. And despite what you told me this afternoon, I believe she's alive. And here in Linton."

"Yes, ma'am. I know you do, but…I'm just wondering if that's the case, if what you're doing is the smartest thing. Under the circumstances, I mean."

"I don't understand."

"If she *is* here, Ms. Chandler, then it seems to me that asking all these questions and watching the children… If you really believe she's here, then it occurred to me that might be the very thing that would scare off whoever had her."

"Scare them off?"

"Yes, ma'am. Scare them so they would pick up and leave. Take her somewhere else so you wouldn't ever find her. It just seems to me you might be going about this the wrong way."

"I'm going about it the only way I know how, Sheriff Adams. I'm trying to find my daughter. And I'll do whatever I think is necessary to accomplish that."

"I was just offering a word to the wise. I wouldn't want any of those parents to file a formal complaint. I thought I'd give you an opportunity to think about what I said before that happened. I'll see you folks tomorrow."

He broke the connection before she had a chance to say anything more. Susan closed her phone, realizing as she did how exhausted she was, both physically and emotionally. Since Adams's original phone call, she'd been on a roller-coaster ride between hope and despair. Tonight, sheer, unadulterated terror had been added to the mix. Who could know what tomorrow's journey would bring?

"I promised my sister I wouldn't go to Randolph County alone," she said to Jeb, whose eyes were still on her face.

"Is that what you were telling Adams?"

"I understand if you feel you can't—"

"I didn't say that."

"Then…?"

"You definitely need *somebody* with you. Maybe from now on. Twenty-four hours a day. But I'm not the person for the job."

"I don't understand."

She didn't. Neither his comment that she needed someone with her, or if that were so, why he wouldn't be the right person. Maybe throwing herself into his arms tonight had made him wary of further involvement. After all, despite her abject plea for his help the other night, he hadn't formally agreed.

"Someone tried to kill you tonight," Jeb said. "This may have been their second attempt, except we were slow to realize what the incident out on the highway was all about."

"You think whoever ran me off the road intended to *kill* me?"

Jeb hesitated before he shook his head. "Even in light of what happened tonight, I can't see how they could have hoped for that result. That was an attempt to run you out of town. Maybe they thought if they frightened you enough, you'd just pack up and go home and stop asking questions."

"That's essentially what the sheriff suggested I do. And if Emma's body had been in the car with Richard's, that's exactly what I *would* have done. I didn't know then that there was the remotest possibility his death could have been anything other than the result of an accident."

"According to the sheriff, you still don't."

"Except someone obviously doesn't want me asking questions about it."

"I didn't think you'd *been* asking them about your husband's death." The blue eyes were opaque. Unreadable.

"I haven't," she said, suddenly realizing where he was going with this. "I've been asking about Emma."

"*And* visiting the playground."

Again, she considered what he was implying, reaching the conclusion he already had. "They're afraid I'll find out what happened to Emma."

"It seems that way."

"But…if she's dead, they shouldn't care *how* many

questions I ask. Or how long I search." Her excitement at that realization was reflected in her voice. "After all, the punishment's the same for one murder or two."

"Probably not. Not anymore. And for someone who killed a baby…" He shook his head. "Trust me, Mississippi juries wouldn't take kindly to that, and they haven't abolished the death penalty down here. But…I don't think it's your questions that caused tonight's reaction. You've been asking questions since you got into town."

"Then…?" He waited, again allowing her to arrive at the conclusion herself. "You think this was because I went to the playground. I thought that's probably why they asked me to meet them there."

He nodded. "Some kind of psychological 'gotcha' maybe. You go looking for your daughter there, so that's where they came to answer you."

"By killing me?" The phrase—the very idea— seemed foreign to who and what she was, despite the reality of tonight's attack.

"If you're dead, you can't keep asking questions about Emma. And they're betting that if *you're* dead, no one else will."

Once she might have argued that point, but she'd learned seven years ago that the wheels of bureaucracy, like those of justice, grind exceedingly slow. And not very fine at all. Wayne Adams didn't believe Emma was alive. He wouldn't look for her. He'd be relieved not to have to.

And judging by the efforts of the various governmental agencies she'd encountered through the years, especially those responsible for recovering children taken by their own parents, they wouldn't pursue this new information either. They would delete her husband's file from the databases, but that didn't mean they'd be any more vigorous in searching for his daughter.

"Promise me that won't happen," she said.

Jeb's head tilted as if questioning the request. "That you won't die? I've already told you I'm the wrong person to try to protect you."

"I didn't mean that. Promise me that if whoever this is succeeds, someone will keep looking for Emma. Promise me, Jeb."

"Look, if Emma is alive—"

"Then whoever tried to fracture my skull with a bat tonight is connected to her in some way. And more than likely connected to the murder of her father. I want your word that if anything happens to me, you won't abandon my baby to that person."

She was well aware of what she was asking of him. And that she had no right to make this request of a virtual stranger.

"I'm not asking you to do it yourself," she went on. "I have some money saved. Now that we have somewhere to start, you could hire an investigator to do what I've tried to do here. To find someone who might remember Emma. Who might have seen her."

"You don't need me to do that. Call the private investigator who worked for you before. Tell *him* to keep looking. Or hire someone else. And if you've really got the money to do that, then get the hell out of here before they try some other way to keep you from finding her."

"You know I can't do that. And you also know that no matter who I hire, if I'm not around, they'll take the money, but they won't keep looking for Emma. All I'm asking is that if something happens to me, you won't do what everyone else will and turn a blind eye to what happened here."

"Why me? You must have friends or family who would make that promise."

It seemed disloyal to David and Charlotte, but with a new baby, she really wasn't sure how much time Dave would devote to the search. Even Charlotte, with all her dreams finally coming true, would listen to the explanations of people like Adams and believe them because that was far easier than the other. And because she hadn't been down that empty path before.

"Why you? Because you're the only person I know who's bullheaded enough to stick with this no matter what."

He laughed, the sound mocking. "You're basing that on our long acquaintance, I suppose. You don't know anything about me, Susan. Certainly not enough to make that kind of judgment."

"I know that no matter how much they discouraged you, you kept trying to rejoin your unit."

His mouth closed, lips flat. His expression was set and hard, but he didn't argue with her assessment.

"All I want is to know she's safe." She tried to remove the passion that had crept into her voice. "And that someone will see to it she stays that way if something happens to me."

"Nothing in life comes with a guarantee," Jeb said. "You of all people should know that."

Just as he did. Despite that, he hadn't given up. Neither would she. Not as long as she had breath in her body.

"There's no one else I can ask to do this."

"Nothing's going to happen to you."

The words were dismissive. Not contemptuous, perhaps, but seeming to belittle the scenario he himself had painted for her only a few minutes ago.

"You *are* willing to guarantee *that?*"

His lips tightened again. "I'll go with you tomorrow. After that... Why don't we wait and see."

What he meant was why don't we wait and see if the baby they'd buried in Randolph County was her daughter. Still, he'd agreed to accompany her to the meeting with the coroner. It was more than she had any right to expect.

She should never have asked him about the other. It was just that tonight she had finally recognized the truth. She *had* no one else. And if anything happened to her, neither did Emma.


"ARE YOU SURE you want to do this?" Jeb asked as the Avalanche bumped along the dirt road behind the rural church they'd been directed to.

The hour they'd spent with the Randolph County coroner had been almost anticlimactic. He had confirmed the measurements Susan had found in one of the articles, but he didn't seem impressed with the information that they were different from those taken at Emma's last checkup. After all, he'd told them, they were dealing with incomplete *skeletal* remains. The slight variation in length could be attributed to the loss of cartilage and connective tissue.

He had taken a cheek swab from Susan, promising to get the state lab to run a match with the samples they had stored from Baby Doe. He wouldn't even try to estimate how long that might take, given the current lack of funding. Almost as an afterthought, he'd suggested that they might want to drive out to the baby's grave, which is where they were headed now.

"It isn't Emma," Susan said, turning to look at him.

"Then why come out here?"

She didn't answer for a moment. When she did, her voice was low. "Because whoever she was, she belonged to someone."

There hadn't been a florist in the small county seat, but she'd asked him to stop on the way out of town to pick up an arrangement of flowers at one of the supermarkets. Jeb hadn't recognized any of the blooms, but thankfully they didn't look like a funeral. At least none he'd ever attended. The flowers were in all the colors of autumn—oranges, golds and reds.

As soon as he pulled the truck up behind the church, Susan opened the passenger door. He stayed in the cab as she walked across the browning grass, carrying the simple bouquet.

Scattered across the cemetery were perhaps a hundred monuments, most of them timeworn, covered with lichen and darkened with age. The coroner had given them directions to the baby's grave, but they wouldn't have needed them. The gleam of its white marble and the statue of the cherub on top would have quickly distinguished it from the others.

Taking a deep breath, he climbed down from the cab, feeling the strain of the last couple of days as he put weight on the damaged leg. It was always worse after the military sawbones got through with their prodding and poking. And the outcome was always the same.

By the time he had rounded the front of the truck, Susan had bent to lay the flowers she'd brought against the base of the marker. Then she stepped back, looking down on the grave.

As he limped nearer, he read the incised letters on the stone, their clarity undimmed by time like those on the other markers.

Baby Doe
Rest in Peace, Sweet Angel

Below that, in much smaller script, was a Bible verse.

"Whatsoever you do unto the least of these,
you do also unto Me."

He stood beside her a moment, looking down on the tiny plot, still slightly rounded above the flatness of the surrounding ground.

"Nice stone." He couldn't think of anything else to say, and her continued stillness made him uneasy.

Susan had said repeatedly this wasn't Emma, but there was no way she could be certain of that until the DNA results came back. The possibility that she was standing beside her daughter's grave had to be in her mind right now. Despite the fact that he didn't want it there, it was certainly in his.

"One of the articles said the people of the community collected money for it. They thought she shouldn't be buried without some kind of monument."

He nodded, his eyes again tracing the words on the marble. There were no dates, not even the day she'd been buried. Under the circumstances, there was no way they could have known when this baby had been born or when she'd died.

"How could anyone do that?"

He turned at the question, but Susan wasn't looking at him. Her eyes were still directed at the contours of the small grave.

"Kill a baby?"

"And leave it…that way."

She stooped down beside the stone, reaching out, so that Jeb thought she was going to rearrange the flowers. Instead, she put her palm flat against the ground over the center of the grave plot. She let it rest there a few seconds, and then she straightened, getting to her feet in one smooth motion.

"We can go." This time she did look at him. Her face was colorless, but her eyes were defiantly dry.

He nodded, but he didn't move.

"If this were Emma, don't you think I'd know?" she asked. "Don't you think I'd feel some connection?"

There was nothing he could say to that. He didn't believe she could put her hand on some dirt and tell whether or not her daughter was buried under it, but if it comforted her to think she could, what was the harm?

He looked down one last time on the marker with its Bible verse and conventional platitude. He'd watched a lot of men die through the years, and none of those deaths had been peaceful.

But at least they had chosen to be where they were. And they had had a fighting chance. Something this baby had never had. Maybe not in her entire short life.

Aware of the sudden burn at the back of his eyes, he lifted them, blinking against the unexpected tears. As he did, he was conscious that Susan had moved closer.

He looked down, seeing in her eyes the same sheen of moisture he fought in his own. Without stopping to think about what he was doing, or how she might interpret it, he moved his arm away from his body, inviting her to step into his embrace.

She closed the distance between them to lean against his side, slipping her arm around his waist. He hugged her, knowing that the emotion he felt was only a fraction of what she must be feeling.

Maybe this wasn't Emma, but until they discovered what had happened to her, they couldn't be sure that she wasn't somewhere in a grave just like this. Or, even worse, somewhere without even this simple stone or those comforting words.

*Rest in Peace.* Susan wouldn't, and now, neither would he. Not until they knew.

"I promise," he said, putting his lips against the fragrance of her hair.

The faint, now-familiar sweetness filled his senses. He closed his eyes, fighting the sharp tightening in his groin. An unexpected sexual response that had no place in what was happening here.

"What?"

"I won't stop looking for Emma. Nothing's going to happen to you, but...I wanted you to know that isn't something you have to worry about."

She nodded, her head moving against his shoulder. For a long time neither of them said anything else. They stood together over that small grave, their arms around one another as if they both had some link to the child whose body rested inside its tiny, donated casket.

Except the link wasn't to this child, Jeb thought, but to another. Another little girl who had also had no choice about what had happened to her.

## CHAPTER SIXTEEN

"AND GET WHOEVER you used before, the private investigator in Atlanta, to track down the whereabouts of Travis Caffrey," Jeb suggested over supper that night. "If by some chance Gladys really does remember Richard and Emma, we need to follow up and see if there's any connection between that and Travis leaving town. We probably need to know the date he left in any case."

"His name is Nolan Harbinson," Susan said, "and he's already working on it. I'll call him tomorrow and see if he's found anything."

Jeb had warned her that most of what he would propose tonight was simply brainstorming. Everything he'd mentioned so far, in her opinion at least, was something that needed to be looked into. And if they waited for Adams to do any of it—

"I'll get back with Doc and see if he'll take a look at the autopsy report. He'll give us his honest opinion about that skull fracture, whether Adams likes it or not."

"Do you think that's why the medical examiner changed his report. Because the sheriff brought pressure on him to be *less* definite about the cause of that injury?"

"I think he probably told Doc what he really thought. He may have told Adams what he wanted to hear."

"Do you think Dr. Callaway might be a source of information about the children in town? I know he didn't practice here, but some of the parents probably took their kids to him."

Jeb nodded, lifting another spoonful of Lorena's squash casserole toward his mouth as he answered. "Maybe. If they were his patients, though, I don't know how much he can tell us. There are bound to be confidentiality issues involved."

"Maybe you could just ask him if he knows any little girls in town who are adopted. Girls about the right age, I mean. When we talked to him before, he said something about knowing there were adopted children."

"Doc would know about *that*, all right," Lorena said.

Although she was sitting at the table with them, the old woman had not set a place for herself. Instead of eating, she had kept Jeb's plate full and listened as they talked. This was the first time she'd joined the conversation.

"What do you mean?" Jeb asked.

"His daddy used to do that. 'Course, back then there was more call for that kind of thing than there is now."

"More call for what, Lorena?" Susan prodded.

"Finding homes for unwanted babies."

Neither of them said anything for a moment, trying to digest the information that had just been dumped in their laps.

"Are you saying Doc ran some kind of adoption service?"

"Mostly his daddy, but I know for a fact about one child Doc helped find a home for. When you practice medicine in a town like Linton, you get to know everybody's secrets. And if you're trusted to keep them, then folks come to you when they got a need for something that has to be kept quiet."

"Like a baby born out of wedlock," Susan said.

It was a term that wasn't used anymore, but the world Lorena was talking about, the world in which Doc Callaway's father had practiced medicine, had been an old-fashioned place. Fifty years ago an illegitimate birth in a community in the heart of the Bible Belt would have raised eyebrows. The girl who had made that kind of mistake would have found herself the center of a firestorm of gossip and probably a social outcast as well. If her secret had become known.

"People didn't believe in abortions back then," Lorena went on. "Not here, anyway. 'Course they would have said they didn't believe in premarital sex either, but things happened, no matter what the preachers said on Sunday mornings. Doc Callaway—old Doc, I mean—delivered ninety-five percent of the babies in Linton. And he treated the women who wanted children and couldn't have 'em. Why *wouldn't* he do some matching up? Just more of a good doctor taking care of his patients."

Would his son see that "matching up" in the same light? Susan wondered. After all, they had thought all along that the present-day Dr. Callaway was one of the people Richard might have detoured off the interstate to see.

"But you said that *this* Doc Callaway did some of that, too?" she asked carefully.

"In one case I know about."

"Recently?" Jeb asked.

"That depends on whose perspective we're looking at it from, doesn't it?" the old lady said with a grin. "That particular baby just graduated from high school. I doubt more than half a dozen people in this town know about his adoption or that Doc had anything to do with it. 'Course, there's not as much need now to be discreet about those kinds of things as there was in his daddy's day."

"How did you know about this one?"

"Somebody at church was involved. Somebody who trusted me, as well as Doc."

"Did you recommend they go to him?"

"I might have. If I'd been asked. But none of that's any of your concern, young man. Whatever happened with that has got nothing to do with Susan's baby. Not all those years ago."

Lorena was right, of course, but the story was interesting. And something to keep in mind. If someone had approached Doc Callaway with the right story and asked him to place a baby, given the example of his father, would he have complied?

She met Jeb's eyes across the table. He tilted his head slightly, raising his eyebrows. He was obviously thinking the same thing. With his close relationship to Callaway, maybe he could find some way to ask the old man about that when he talked to him about the autopsy report.

"Anything else?" Susan asked him.

"One thing I thought about last night. We've been assuming all along that Richard turned off the interstate and ended up in Linton because something happened that diverted him from his intended destination. What if that wasn't the case?"

"I don't understand."

"What if Linton was his destination all along?"

The idea was so foreign to everything they had ever talked about that it took her a second or two to put it into context.

"You think he came here deliberately?"

"I think it's a possibility we have to consider."

"But...that makes no sense. Why would he come *here?*"

"Maybe for the same reason he left Atlanta."

And that was something she still didn't know. Harbinson hadn't turned up anything to indicate Richard was having an affair. Nor had he found evidence he was engaged in illegal activities. No gambling. No substance abuse. Nothing but a seemingly ordinary family man who had one day decided to disappear, taking the family bank account and his baby daughter with him.

"You're suggesting that Richard's coming to Linton was connected to whatever made him leave home?"

"I think we have to consider that a possibility."

"But why?"

"Maybe if we find out why he left, we'll know that, too."

It was the same vicious circle she'd been caught in seven years ago. If she'd known why Richard left, then maybe she would have known where he'd taken Emma. Now Susan believed she knew where Emma was—here in Linton—but Jeb was suggesting that they needed to understand why Richard had taken her with him before they could unravel the puzzle and locate her.

"Believe me, I tried to figure out what happened that weekend. So did Harbinson. He kept coming back to it every time we talked."

"Because it's the key to everything. If we knew why Richard took Emma and disappeared—"

"Emma *and* the money," Susan said bitterly. "Don't forget the money. It's not as if he were planning on coming back."

"That's not to say he wasn't planning on getting in touch."

"With me?"

"We can assume he wasn't meeting another woman. No man is going to take a toddler along if he's walking away from his marriage. You'll never make me believe Richard would, no matter how devoted a father he was. And according to your P.I., he wasn't in debt. He wasn't dealing or taking drugs. He hadn't lost his job." Jeb stopped, his mouth remaining open after the last item in his list, his eyes seeming to lose focus.

"What is it?"

"That picture you brought."

"The one of Richard?"

"You told Doc it had been made to announce a promotion."

"That's right."

"How soon before he disappeared?"

"The promotion? Five or six months. Maybe less."

"More money involved?"

"Some. Potentially a lot more. That's what he said."

"And new clients."

That hadn't been phrased as a question, but she answered it anyway. "Several. Some of the biggest accounts the firm had."

"Do you know who they were?"

She shook her head, trying to remember. "I know he must have talked about them. At least when they first gave him the list, but... We were both so busy right then. My maternity leave was up, and I'd gone back to the graphics department full-time. I was trying to break into illustrating children's books, juggling that and taking care of Emma *and* my job. Getting her to and from day care. Getting us all fed without buying takeout every night. We'd talked about finding some help, but I didn't even have time to interview anyone."

"Is there any way you could find out?"

"About the client list? I could ask Richard's boss."

"He's still there?"

"I don't know. Some of the company management stayed in touch for a while, but they were like everyone else. When everything came out, they didn't know what to say."

"How about a co-worker? Someone he might have talked to."

"About...his new clients?" she asked, bewildered by his insistence.

"Someone who would have known the names," Jeb said patiently. "Someone who might remember. Maybe whoever took over his client list. You have any idea who that was?"

She shook her head again, trying to come up with the name of someone at the company that Richard had been close to. "He hadn't really been there that long. We were surprised by the quick promotion, but you don't question something like that. You just assume they like you or your work and are grateful."

"And what was his work exactly?"

"Powell is a regional accounting firm that audits in the Southeast. It wasn't one of the Big Five, of course, but Richard liked the smaller size. He said that meant they knew who you were. The promotion seemed proof he was right."

"The Big Five," Jeb repeated. "Who are now the Big Four, by the way. I wonder if that could possibly…"

"Jeb?"

"Too many clients cooking the books while the accountants looked the other way."

She had heard the term, of course. Who hadn't? But again her bewilderment with where he was headed with this must have been reflected in her face.

"Creative bookkeeping to keep anyone from finding out how badly a company is doing," he explained. "Probably a lot more companies were involved in that then than anyone was aware of."

There had been a ton of publicity about the practice, but she couldn't remember that she and Richard had ever talked about it. Or maybe that had all happened after he'd disappeared.

"You think Richard could have discovered something like that with one of his accounts?"

"You didn't recognize the names of any of his clients in the news during the next few years, did you?"

She hadn't, but then the years after Richard and Emma's disappearance had been a blur. Still, if he'd found something illegal, she believed he would have mentioned it.

*Unless he'd discovered it that weekend. The weekend she'd been out of town. The weekend he'd disappeared.*

"I know the police talked to almost everyone at Powell. And they talked at length to Richard's boss. Surely if there had been anything out of the ordinary he would have told them."

They'd been looking for evidence of a crime Richard might have committed. Embezzlement. Fraud. Insider trading. Anything. And nothing had shown up. Still, that interview would have been the ideal time for Sam Tribble to tell the investigators about anything suspicious with Richard's clients.

"If he'd known about it, he might have. But the climate was different back then, remember. Accounting firms weren't playing watchdog like the public believed they were. After all, if you found too many problems with an account, you'd probably be replaced with someone more willing to look the other way."

Richard had said he had a lot of work to do that weekend. Somewhere in the bulging briefcase he'd brought home had he found something so incriminating that he'd immediately known something criminal was going on?

"But if Richard discovered something suspicious, he would have called Sam. Surely Sam would have told the police that."

"Or maybe Richard asked for clarification from the client first," Jeb suggested.

"And then what? Are you saying they threatened

him? Some of those were Fortune 500 companies. Some of the top businesses in the Southeast."

She *did* remember Richard throwing those phrases around. He had been so excited about the prestige of the firms he was working with. Of course, that was something he would never have divulged to anyone but her. He would have thought expressing that kind of excitement was bush league.

"*Something* happened that weekend to make him leave Atlanta," Jeb said. "And what he did before he left sounds like someone who knew he was going on the run. Cash can't be traced. Not like a credit card. If you don't want someone to know where you're going, you grab all the cash you can get your hands on. Especially if you don't know how long you're going to be gone."

The police had told her the same thing. Richard didn't want to leave a trail when he bought gas or food. They had thought that was because he didn't want her to know where he'd gone, but what if Jeb was right? What if he'd been running from someone else that weekend?

"And Emma? Why in the world would he take Emma?"

"What else could he have done with her?"

Charlotte and Dave had been out of town. So had she, of course. Richard's family lived in San Francisco. And since it was a weekend, the day care was closed.

The police had been skeptical when she couldn't think of a neighbor or friend he might have left Emma with, but it was true. They hadn't been in the new house long. And with their schedules, there had been little time for socializing.

Of course, when the bank teller had come forward with her story, the authorities had discarded that angle and had begun to consider the case as a parental abduction. After a while, even she had accepted their version of things.

"If someone *had* threatened Richard—or his family," Jeb added, "who would he have trusted to take care of Emma? Other than himself?"

It was not so far from the theory Harbinson had advanced. That Richard was running from something. Only he'd believed that it must be from someone he owed money to. Or from something criminal he'd been involved with. And when none of those things had proven to be true...

"You're saying that one of his *clients* threatened him? And that he was frightened enough that he took Emma and left without even leaving a note or making a phone call?"

"Maybe he called the wrong person."

"Why didn't he call me?"

"Maybe because he was afraid that if he did, they'd find out where you were."

"That's ridiculous. Things like that don't really happen—"

"Things like that happen all the time."

"Not to someone like Richard. He was an *accountant,* for God's sake. And his clients were all legitimate businesses."

"With balance sheets in the billions of dollars. That's a very high-stakes game. If you've been cheating at that game, and someone finds out..." He raised his eyebrows, just as when he had questioned Lorena's information about Doc.

Susan didn't know what to say. She didn't even know what to think. Jeb's analysis was something no one else had suggested.

And yet, more than any other scenario she had imagined through the years, it finally made sense of what had happened. So much so she couldn't believe the idea had never been considered.

"We need to see Richard's client list," Jeb said. "But we need to be careful who we ask for it. There's no guarantee someone at the accounting firm *didn't* know what was going on. Maybe they assumed Richard, being new, wouldn't discover whatever he did. Maybe the guy he'd inherited the accounts from had already reported his own suspicions. You don't know what happened to him, do you?"

She didn't, she realized. She'd never thought about the person whose clients Richard had been given. Or about the person who had been given his.

"If not Richard's boss, then...I don't know who to ask for the list."

"Maybe there's somebody at the firm who could tell us who had those accounts before and after your husband."

She nodded, trying to think. "Richard's secretary, maybe."

"That's as good a place to start as any. We'll think up some story to tell her to explain why you're asking."

"Not tonight," Lorena said. "You've done enough tonight. I swear you both look like death eatin' a cracker. You get on to bed now. This'll all be here in the morning to puzzle over some more. It's been a hard day," the old woman said, putting her fingers over

Susan's wrist. "Going to see that baby's grave. You let her get some rest now, you hear me, Jubal."

Susan met Jeb's eyes across the table. They had been focused on her face as his great-aunt concluded her lecture, her fingers still resting comfortingly on Susan's arm.

"Lorena's right. As usual," Jeb said. "There's nothing more we can do tonight."

Susan nodded, looking down on the list he'd given her. Despite her exhaustion, she felt more hopeful than she had in years. So much of what Jeb said made sense. Finally, after all this time, there were new avenues to pursue. New possibilities.

"Thank you."

His eyes widened slightly. "For what?"

"For going with me today. But most of all, for this." She lifted the spiral notebook she'd been writing in. "It's been a long time since anyone has tried to come up with a reason for all of this that makes sense."

"There had to have been one. If only half of what you've said about Richard is true."

"It makes me feel…" She shook her head. "I should have been the one person who didn't believe what they were saying about him. I should have believed in him. I was the one who knew him best."

"They may have been right. We don't know that any of what I just suggested happened. Right now, it's like everything else. A theory. And it will be until we have some proof."

She knew that. But for the first time, something made sense of what Richard had done to their lives that weekend. And no matter how this all turned out in the end, she knew this would make it easier to live with.

## CHAPTER SEVENTEEN

WHEN THE PHONE RANG this time, she came awake instantly, mouth open, breathing rapid and shallow. She glanced at the clock, just as she had last night.

It was only a few minutes after nine. Although her exhaustion had driven her to bed soon after supper, she had thought, given the events of last night and today, that she would probably toss and turn for hours. Instead, she had apparently dropped off to sleep almost immediately.

Her cell shrilled again, bringing her completely awake this time. She reached up and turned on the bedside lamp before she flipped open the case.

This couldn't be the same person who had called last night. The timing was wrong for one thing. And only an idiot would believe she'd fall for that same ruse again. *Fool me once...*

"Hello." Even in her own ears her voice sounded strange. Tentative. Fearful.

"Sorry to call so late, Suz," her brother-in-law said. "I had to wait until Charlotte went up to bed."

It would be after ten in Atlanta, so that made sense. Why Dave would be calling instead of her sister, however...

"What's wrong?" she asked, the question still fearful.

"Nothing's wrong. Everything's fine. It's so fine, in fact, that they've decided the baby's far enough along to induce."

The doctors had talked about doing that from the first. For someone with Charlotte's history, they hoped to get as close to the due date as they could, of course, but they also wanted her labor to be in a safe and totally controlled environment.

Apparently they had now decided she and the baby had made it to that point. She could hear the joy in Dave's voice.

"That's wonderful. Tomorrow?" Susan asked, pulling the second pillow behind her and pushing up so that she was leaning back against the headboard.

"The day after. That's why I'm calling."

"I don't understand."

"Charlotte really wants you here. She won't tell you that. She knows what's going on down there, but... You're the only family she's got, Suz. And you two have always been so close. I just think she'll do better if you're with her. You've been her security blanket, especially since your folks died."

Susan closed her eyes, trying to weigh her sister's needs against her own. This wasn't fair. Dave had said that they knew what was going on down here. Not the attack, of course. She hadn't dared tell Charlotte about that. Nor had she told her sister that she was waiting for the results of a DNA test that would prove whether or not her baby was dead.

*Her baby.* One she had loved and cherished as much as Dave and Charlotte would cherish theirs. A baby who had been taken from her before she had had a chance to really know her. Just as she was developing a personality. Becoming a real person. It wasn't fair of them to ask her to give up the search for Emma when it seemed that finally, with Jeb's help, she might be getting somewhere.

*And how will you feel if you don't go and something happens to Charlotte or the baby?* That was a guilt she knew she couldn't live with.

Besides, despite all the plans she and Jeb had made, there was nothing she could do to speed up the results from the state lab. And until she had those in hand, she suspected Sheriff Adams would continue to drag his feet on everything else.

He had practically forbidden her to visit the schoolyard again or to talk to the children. Even now his warning about the possible consequences if she continued to push that avenue echoed in her head.

"Suz? You still there?"

"I'm here. I'm just..." Unconsciously she shook her head, although her brother-in-law wouldn't be able to see the gesture. "Things are starting to come together down here."

"You've got a lead on Emma?"

He sounded excited. Pleased. All the things that she should be over his good news. And she was. It was just that right now...

Right now she had nothing to do but put some of the things Jeb suggested into action. Get back in touch with Harbinson about the Caffreys' son. Try to find out about Richard's client list. None of which had to be done from Linton.

"A couple of things look as if they might lead somewhere."

"Well, then forget I asked. We'll be fine."

She let the silence after Dave's comment build until it became unbearable. No matter what, she couldn't refuse to be there for Charlotte, who had always tried to be there for her.

"It's not like anything is going to break in the next day or two," she said finally.

"Does that mean you'll come?"

If she had doubted it before, his obvious relief assured her that Dave hadn't exaggerated how much Charlotte wanted her. And now that the decision had been made, there was no doubt in her mind it was the right one.

A few days. That's all they were asking. She owed both of them more than that for the support they'd given her through the years. Even through the difficult days she'd been down here, Charlotte had been the one person she could pour out her heart to with the assurance that her sister would understand even if she didn't agree.

"I'll leave in the morning. I should get in sometime tomorrow afternoon. How about if I come straight to your place and spend the night there? If that's okay," she hedged, wondering if she would be intruding on a time they'd rather spend alone and together.

"That's great. I can't tell you how thrilled Charlotte will be to see you. Only, don't tell her I called."

"Then how am I supposed to know about the induction?" Susan asked with a laugh.

"She's planning to tell you in the morning. Just hang

around down there until she calls. I'll make sure it's early so you can get on the road. I don't want you driving after dark."

For an instant the image of those headlights coming toward her car was in her mind's eye. She destroyed the memory, knowing that wasn't something that would happen again because she wouldn't allow herself to be in that position.

If Charlotte hadn't phoned by the time she needed to leave, she could get on the road and take the call while she was driving. Her sister wouldn't have any idea of the time it took to make the trip.

"No, I won't be," she said aloud. "I'll leave in plenty of time. Anything you need me to pick up?"

"Hell, we been getting ready for this for the last five years." Dave's voice was jovial. Relieved. "Char's had her hospital bag packed for months now. All we need is you."

"I'll be there," Susan promised.

"Call me from the road. I've always worried about my girls, but after what happened to Richard… It just makes you more paranoid, you know."

"I know. I'll keep in touch. Don't worry about me. You just take care of Charlotte and our baby."

*Our baby.* She had said that often through these long months because she had known how much the two of them were looking forward to sharing their child with her. Just as she was looking forward to being a part of her nephew's life. And as for *her* baby…

*A few more days, Emma,* she vowed, closing her phone. After all this time, surely a few more days couldn't matter.

"IT MIGHT EVEN be an advantage to ask those questions in person," Jeb said.

He hadn't questioned her decision when she'd told him at breakfast this morning about the upcoming trip. He hadn't offered to go with her either. And she'd been surprised to discover how disappointed she was that he hadn't.

Of course, he had his biweekly appointment at the rehab center in Pascagoula. Despite his feeling about how the medical review had gone, she knew that he planned to keep it.

And he didn't know Charlotte or Dave. Besides, there was nothing he could do from Atlanta.

*Nothing but offer moral support.*

Again she was a little shocked at how much she wanted that. She'd been alone for seven years. She'd survived the loss of Richard and Emma without Jeb Bedford at her side. She wasn't likely to face anything on this trip to compare with that.

"It's not as if I had much choice," she said, still feeling as if she were leaving at a critical juncture.

"I know. I'll talk to Doc. You check with Richard's secretary at Powell and with your P.I."

She nodded, fingering her keys. Jeb had already put her suitcase in the trunk. There was nothing left to do but get into the car and head toward the interstate. For some reason she couldn't seem to make herself do it.

"Call me."

She looked up at the command. His face was set, the line of his mouth straight and hard.

He held her eyes a moment before he reached up,

touching her cheek with the tips of his fingers. They were warm and callused against the coolness of her skin.

"I will," she promised.

"And be careful."

Her eyes must have widened at that caution. He shook his head slightly.

"Nothing's going to happen. Not like before. I meant be careful on the road."

"I will."

There was so much more she wanted him to say. And so much more she wanted to say to him. Instead, she seemed to be parroting the same inane phrases. As if they were strangers again. As if he hadn't held her at the cemetery yesterday.

He moved, breaking the spell by limping forward to open the car door. Obediently she slid behind the wheel, looking up at him before she inserted the key into the ignition.

"You have my cell phone number?" she asked.

"Along with everyone in Johnson County."

The taut line of his lips had lifted slightly with the comment. He leaned down to look into the car, one hand on the roof and the other on the top of the still-opened door.

What he'd said reminded her of one of the worries that had kept her awake after Dave hung up last night. She needed Jeb's reassurance that what she'd worried about wouldn't happen.

"Do you think the sheriff could be right?"

"Very seldom," Jeb said, his mouth relaxing even more. "About what in particular?"

"That whoever has Emma might take her and run because I've been asking questions."

"If they did, that would be a dead giveaway, wouldn't it? Even to doubters like Adams. I can't believe anyone could be that stupid."

"Maybe, but… I've spent so long looking for her, Jeb. I couldn't bear to come this close and then lose her again."

"That's not going to happen. The smartest thing whoever took Emma can do is try to ride this out."

"Ride out my attempt to find her?"

"I meant the discovery of Richard's body. They just need to avoid doing anything stupid and hope this will die down again. After all, they haven't had to worry about anything for seven years. They've probably been feeling pretty complacent."

"But if they know I'm not going to let it die—"

"What they'll know very soon is that you've gone back to Atlanta. If you're worried about them taking Emma somewhere, your leaving should go a long way to prevent that from happening."

An aspect of her trip she hadn't thought of, but it made sense. And it definitely made her feel better about the decision she'd made last night.

"They'll think I've given up."

"Combined with the fact that you went up to Randolph County yesterday, this should go a long way toward convincing them of that."

She nodded, wanting very much to believe what he was saying. "If they know all of that."

"This is Linton. Everybody knows everything."

As he said the last, Jeb straightened, removing his

hand from the top of the car. He had already started to close the door, when her next comment stopped him.

"Thank you."

"For what?"

"For believing she's here. For helping mc. For keeping me sane," she added with a smile.

"That works both ways."

"I don't understand."

"It doesn't matter. Be careful."

"Jeb—"

The forward motion of the door halted. He bent as if to look into the car again. This time, however, his head lowered until his face was only inches from hers.

He searched her eyes as, lips parted, she held her breath. Although she had anticipated his intent, that didn't prevent a surge of excitement from coursing through her body as his mouth lowered to cover hers.

The kiss was brief. Over before she had time to react.

He straightened, stepping back and closing the door without meeting her eyes again.

She watched him limp toward the front steps of Lorena's house, still aware of the unexpected warmth and softness of his lips against hers.

And aware, too, that another very good reason had just been added to the ones that would bring her back to Linton as quickly as she could possibly manage.

# CHAPTER EIGHTEEN

"So what the M.E. told *you* and what he said in this autopsy report could both be right. Is that what you're saying?"

It wasn't like Doc to equivocate, but Jeb had the feeling that's exactly what was going on. And he didn't like it.

"I'm saying that sharing an opinion with a colleague and giving an official report that you might have to defend in court are two entirely different things. And not mutually exclusive."

"Could you arrange to get a look at the autopsy photographs and tell me what you think?"

"In what capacity?" Callaway asked.

"I don't know, Doc," Jeb said, letting his growing exasperation show. "How about as a concerned friend?"

"Of the medical examiner? Or of Mrs. Chandler?"

"*Ms.* Chandler," Jeb corrected. "That's her maiden name. After her husband disappeared, she went back to it."

"What kind of stake you got in all this, Jeb?"

"The same one everyone else in this town *should* have. A little girl is missing, and she was last seen here."

"Seen? You didn't tell me that. You mean somebody actually saw her after her father's car went into the river?"

"Before. They saw her with him here in Linton."

"Then the logical explanation is that she *died* with him. As hard as that is to swallow, it's probably what happened."

"You sound like Adams. Except her body wasn't *in* that car, Doc. How do you explain that?"

"I don't. I wouldn't venture to try. Sometimes things don't have neat explanations. Believe me, I've seen things in my years of practice—"

"Like disappearing bodies. Come on, Doc. She wasn't in the damn car when they dragged it out of the river. The doors and windows were all closed. The safety seat is there, but the baby isn't. What does that sound like to you?"

"What does it sound like to you?"

"It sounds like whoever killed her father took her."

"*Took* her."

"Carried her off with him."

The old man laughed. And his next comment was in the same nearly patronizing vein. "Well, then I guess all you're left with is the question of why someone would do that."

"Maybe because it's harder to bludgeon a toddler to death than it is a grown man."

With his background, that part was easy for Jeb to believe. He'd killed his share of men, not all of them in combat, and he knew that he could never, under any circumstances, kill a baby.

"Okay, so what happened to her then?"

Doc sounded as if he were humoring him. Given everything that had happened the last few days, especially the attack on Susan, the old man's attitude set Jeb's teeth on edge. Otherwise, he might have been a little more diplomatic in presenting the second reason he'd come by the Callaway house on the way to his appointment in Pascagoula.

"I thought *you* might know something about that."

"Me? Now, why in the world would you think *I'd* know something about that baby?"

"Lorena says that you and your daddy had a lot to do with placing babies in good homes."

"Well, as far as I know, my daddy didn't place any whose fathers had been murdered."

Jeb took note of the word, although he didn't comment on it. Either what the M.E. had told Doc about Richard Kaiser's death had been more definitive than the old man had just indicated, or Callaway had, to some extent at least, bought into the scenario Jeb had outlined for him.

"But he did *place* babies in good homes?"

"What my father did was a service to his patients. And only when they approached him. If you're trying to imply—"

"I'm not implying anything about your father, Doc. All I'm saying is that if someone in this town had a baby who needed a home, they might have come to you."

"Well, they didn't," the old man said. "Whatever happened to Ms. Chandler's baby, I didn't have anything to do with it."

"No one approached you seven years ago to—"

"How many times I got to tell you, boy? I didn't have anything to do with that baby."

"How about someone here in town? You know the women. Was there one of them, maybe someone who'd tried to conceive for a long time, who all of a sudden had a baby girl seven years ago?"

"You know what?" Doc said, his normal good nature destroyed by Jeb's persistence. "It ain't none of your damn business if some poor woman in this town had a baby seven years ago. You gonna go around and take a survey of which of them had a hard time conceiving? I swear you've gone off the deep end with this, Jeb. I can understand Ms. Chandler's obsession. It's her baby. But you? What's made you buy into this like you are?"

It was a fair question, but one Jeb wasn't prepared to answer. Not to someone else. Maybe not even to himself.

"Because I think she's right," he said instead.

"You think somebody in this town killed Mrs. Chandler's husband and took her baby and has then been living right here under our noses with it all this time."

"Why not? Nobody knew about Kaiser *or* his daughter until now. Nobody had any reason to be suspicious."

As he said it, he realized how true it was. Until the SUV had been found, no one had had any reason to question the origins of any of the children in town.

"You gonna take DNA samples of every little girl here?"

He wanted to say yes. He wanted to ask why not. Something about the look in the old man's eyes prevented him.

"If her daughter's alive, Susan Chandler has every right to try to find her."

"*If* she's alive. That's the crux of this, Jeb. You got no real reason to believe she is. Neither has anyone else. You just admitted that your witness saw that baby with her father. And you got no one who saw her after his death."

"Susan's convinced she's here."

"Yeah, I imagine she would be. She lost everything she ever had, boy. Her husband. Her faith in him. *And* her little girl. Wouldn't you be trying to get some of that back? Hell, any of us would be. Only, that doesn't mean that baby's alive. And you, of all people, ought to know that."

Jeb didn't attempt to argue with him. Not only was the reasoning flawless, the respect he'd always had for Doc made him listen—even when he didn't want to hear what he was saying.

"If you got feelings for the woman—and I suspect you have—then do her a kindness. Tell her she's wasting her time. Don't let her heart get broken all over again. 'Cause this time, she just might not get over it."

"I THOUGHT YOU MIGHT have read about the discovery of the body," Jeb said.

Duncan McKey, the renowned surgeon and founder of Southeastern Rehabilitation Services, had sent word for Jeb to come up to his office as soon as his session was over. This was where they usually discussed any changes in his program and evaluated his progress. Or more appropriately, Jeb thought with a trace of bitterness, his current lack of it.

Since McKey had been well aware of the Army reevaluation, he would want to hear the results. And Jeb truly believed the surgeon would be almost as disappointed as he had been.

McKey's continued encouragement had given him reason to hope, but maybe that was a hope that had been misplaced. He knew that was something the doctor would address.

He was sitting now across the big mahogany desk while McKey leafed through the reports from his last two therapy sessions. Talking about Richard's death gave him something to take his mind off the upcoming assessment, which he feared would probably mirror the one he'd received from the medical board.

"Between the professional reading I need to stay current and the staff reports," McKey said without looking up, "I don't read the papers like I should. If it wasn't in the headlines or on the sports page, I probably missed it."

"The guy was an accountant with some firm in Atlanta. One weekend he took his baby and withdrew all the money he and his wife had saved and disappeared. No debts. No criminal involvement anyone can discover. Seven years later, they find his car—with his body inside—in the Escatawpa. He's got a fractured skull, and there's no money and no baby."

The skilled fingers stilled over the pages of the report. McKey's eyes, widened slightly, lifted to his.

"Obviously somebody found out he was carryin' that cash. So what was he doing in Linton?"

"Maybe if we knew that…" Jeb shrugged.

"*We?* You working with the locals on this? Knowing that crew in Johnson County, mind you, I'm not sayin' that's a bad thing."

"Not really working with *them.* I got interested because Kaiser's ex-wife is staying at my great-aunt's. The place used to be a bed-and-breakfast, and someone recommended it to her. Lorena's never said no to anybody in need in her life."

"The wife come down to identify the body?"

"Mostly to find out what happened, especially to the baby."

"So if this guy's walkin' out on his marriage, why bring the kid with him?" McKey's question expressed the central question that puzzled everyone who heard the story.

"Nobody knows. Fourteen-month-old toddler. A little girl. And she definitely wasn't in the car when it was pulled from the river. The windows were up, the doors closed, and the infant seat was still inside."

McKey's lips pursed before he shook his head. "Probably left her with somebody. Planned to come back to get her, and then, before he could…"

"Except that's not what happened. The mother *and* the FBI have been looking for her for seven years."

"Then, as much as I hate to say it, Jeb, I doubt anybody's gonna find her now."

"Somebody reported seeing the baby in Linton. And since the husband never left…"

"They're thinking the baby didn't either. And I take it they're also thinking she's still alive."

"Actually, no one seems to be thinking that but the mother. And me, I guess. At least…I'm thinking it's possible."

"Seems like somebody over there would have to know about her then. Town like that, you can't take a piss without half the population hearing it."

"Maybe if we knew what Kaiser was doing in Linton in the first place. He leaves home without so much as a note left behind, taking all the money in his bank accounts and his kid, and he ends up in the Escatawpa."

"Sounds like something Grisham would write."

The comment was so close to what Jeb had been thinking that he couldn't believe it. If ever there had been an opening…

"I've been trying to come up with some scenario that might have put an accountant on the run."

"You're suggesting that his being an accountant had something to do with what happened." McKey had seen where he was going immediately, but then a man didn't get where this one was without being bright.

"I'm wondering if he could have found something about one of his clients they didn't want revealed."

"Like that they were doctoring the books, maybe?"

"There seems to have been a lot of that going around back then. Most of it didn't come to light until after Kaiser's death, but…maybe he was unlucky enough to be one of the first to discover what was happening in corporate America."

"When that stuff all came to light," McKey said, "the most common defense seemed to be 'everybody's doing it.'"

"That's what I'm wondering. If they were. I figure you'd be more in tune with the corporate climate at that time than I am. As I remember it, I was far more concerned about what was going on in Bosnia right about then."

"Hell, I might as well have *been* in Bosnia. Corporate climate doesn't mean much to me, Jeb. Back then

Court handled that kind of stuff, and I left it to him. I still don't get involved in that side of the business. I leave that to the financial types."

"Even so—"

"I hire extremely good men and let them do their jobs. They tell me when and where to build the clinics. I staff them with the best people I can find, and I run them. And I tell the financial folks to stay the hell out of my side of things. If I wanted some bean counter telling me how to practice medicine, I'd have stuck with the HMOs."

"And they let you get away with that?" Jeb asked, amused at the picture McKey had painted.

"Ray DeCourtney and I had an agreement when we started all this. I made them stick with it after his death. You know, even after all these years, I miss that wonderful, crazy bastard every day of my life."

DeCourtney had been killed in a private-plane crash shortly before the company he and McKey had started turned golden. He hadn't lived to see the fruits of his labor.

"You want somebody to speculate on how many folks were doctoring their books back then," McKey went on, "you're gonna have to talk to somebody else."

"It was just a thought," Jeb said.

He watched as the surgeon closed the file in front of him. McKey's lips pursed again as he looked up from it.

Jeb's former anxiety, which had dissipated somewhat with the distraction of talking about the case, immediately began to churn in the pit of his stomach. He could tell himself that the evaluation board didn't know their ass from a hole in the ground, but McKey did. And he would shoot straight about his chances of appealing their decision when it came down.

"So what did the Army guys tell you?"

"Nothing official. Not yet, but…I don't think they were impressed with what I'd accomplished since the last time."

"There *are* other things you can do, you know," McKey said.

Jeb couldn't read his tone, but it hadn't been particularly sympathetic, which gave him hope. "Other exercises?"

"Other professions. Or other specialties, as far as that goes, if you want to get your twenty in."

"Riding a desk."

"There *are* worse things."

"Not to me. And if you're going to tell me I should be grateful—"

"You know me better than that. You came to us with an injury. We're in the rehab business. I'm not gonna tell you to be grateful for anything. You can be as pissed off as you want at the slowness of your progress. I damn well would be."

"So you're sayin' I should just give up."

"I'm saying there are natural limits on the prospects for improvement with injuries like yours. It's been what? Almost a year? I'm not sayin' you aren't going to get more flexibility back. I *am* sayin' that the chances of anyone doing that decrease as the months pass."

Jeb could argue, as he had at the beginning, that he would be the exception to all those normal expectations. He'd learned a lot of lessons since those days, however, the most important of them that determination alone wasn't always enough to accomplish a goal. Sometimes it took luck. Or divine intervention. He'd found out the hard way that he couldn't depend on either.

"You want to keep tryin'," McKey went on, "you've got the money. And we've got plenty of open appointments. But I can't promise that either of us is going to get the results we want, no matter how much we invest. I'd be dishonest if I told you anything different."

"I appreciate that."

Despite his words, Jeb felt numb with the severity of this second blow. McKey had always been his ally. The two of them against those bastards on the medical review board.

Through the course of these long, difficult months, he had also come to view the doctor as a friend. He had wanted no less from McKey than the absolute truth. He had just been hoping that truth wouldn't be quite so brutal.

"You chose a dangerous profession," the surgeon went on, "and the odds caught up with you. I've never known anybody who's worked harder to come back than you. No matter what, you got nothing to regret about the effort you've devoted to this."

"So what you're saying is that I should give up?"

"What I'm sayin' is that if the medical board comes back with a refusal to either extend your leave or let you rejoin your unit, you should probably consider accepting it."

"I won't have much choice." The bitterness and self-pity he'd fought for so long washed over him in a wave.

"And if you did have a choice?"

"I'd ask them to give me a few more months."

"Even knowing it might not make a difference?"

"I'm not ready to quit. Not yet."

His eyes lifted to the poem he'd read a dozen times through the months while he'd waited for McKey to study his progress reports. The lines had always seemed to echo and fortify his own determination. "Under the bludgeonings of chance, my head is bloody, but unbowed."

"Then I think I still have enough pull to accomplish that."

McKey's words snapped his attention back to the man behind the desk. His lips weren't smiling, but the brown eyes seemed to be.

"To get me more time?"

"I can't guarantee it, but...I haven't worked like a damn dog all these years without some rewards. One of them is a pretty good reputation in this field, if I do say so myself. If I tell them I believe you can make significant progress in say...the next six months, I think they'll go along with it."

It was the reprieve Jeb hadn't dared to hope for. And given McKey's own assessment, one he wasn't sure he deserved.

"So...what if another six months doesn't make a difference? I don't want you going out on a limb for me and putting your reputation on the line. Not if you think—"

"I appreciate the concern, but in all honesty, Jeb, I don't think my standing is that precarious," McKey said with a grin. "If it is, I should probably pack up and retire to the islands."

"I don't know what to say." He didn't. What McKey

was offering to do for him was beyond any expectation of friendship. "Nothing except thank you, of course."

Jeb rose to put out his hand. Although he was by no means a small man, his fingers were dwarfed by McKey's, which closed around his, squeezing encouragingly.

"We've *both* got a lot of time and effort invested here. I'm not ready to call it a day either. Let me get you that extension, and then we'll concentrate on proving those bastards wrong. Which is, by the way, one of my favorite things in the entire world. Proving to somebody that what they're sayin' can't be done really can be."

Jeb nodded, his throat tight with emotion. He owed so much to this man who'd been with him every step of the way.

"I won't let you down."

"I know you won't. If I hadn't believed that, I wouldn't have made the offer. I'm going to get together with Ross and see what kind of changes we need to make in your program. We've got a lot to do and, even with that extension, a very short amount of time to do it. You go on home now and get ready to work harder than you've ever worked in your life."

"You can count on that."

"Believe me, I already am," McKey said with a laugh.

## CHAPTER NINETEEN

AFTER FOUR DAYS in Atlanta, she had been more than ready to return to Linton. Charlotte and the baby were home and both doing well. Her sister had finally decided the temporary nanny was competent, easing Susan's guilt over deserting her so soon.

She would probably have left tomorrow morning in any case, but the courtesy call from the Mississippi state lab, telling her the DNA testing was complete, had given her more than enough reason to start back today. Frustratingly, they had refused to release the results to her on the grounds that, as a state laboratory, they couldn't provide those to private individuals, but only to the official who had originally requested the test.

She had assumed that would be the coroner of Randolph County, but when she reached his office, he explained that he'd put Wayne Adams's name on the form, since the sheriff had initiated the contact. So far, Adams hadn't returned her call.

Although she was now only a few miles from the Linton-Pascagoula exit, she opened her cell and hit redial. Whoever answered at the sheriff's department wasn't the same person she'd talked to before.

"Sheriff Adams, please."

"He's gone home for the day. Can I help you?"

"I'm trying to locate a fax that was sent to your office this afternoon. It was from the state forensics lab, and although it contained information that was intended for me, it was sent in care of Sheriff Adams."

"And you say it came this afternoon?" Paper rustled in the background.

"That's right." Several hours ago, she thought, glancing at her watch.

"Well, it's not here, ma'am," the deputy said. Apparently he'd been checking the fax machine itself. "Of course, the sheriff may have it in his office."

"Could you look, please?"

She waited while he put her on hold. After less than a minute, he returned.

"Ma'am? Sorry, but the sheriff's office is locked."

"And no one there has a key? Is that what you're saying?"

"I'm saying that the sheriff's office is locked. I don't have authorization to open it and give you whatever information is in that fax. Even if I managed to locate it."

"You *do* understand that it contains material that was intended for me."

"Yes, ma'am, you told me. But since it was sent to the sheriff, seems like it would be up to him to pass it on to you."

Everybody has rules and regulations, she had told herself. And she supposed everyone also had a chain of command. The deputy, who sounded very young, probably didn't have the authority to do what she was asking of him.

Knowing that didn't keep her from wanting him to.

It did, however, allow her to control her anger at the bureaucratic runaround she seemed to be getting this afternoon.

"That's the lab's procedure," she said. "They always send it to the investigative agency."

"Yes, ma'am. Well, this is our procedure. Sorry, but you're gonna have to talk to the sheriff."

"Could I have his number, please?" She used her shoulder to hold the cell against her ear as she rummaged in her purse for a pen and something to write on, left hand on the wheel.

"You mean his home phone number? Sorry, ma'am, I'm not allowed to give out that information."

"Then how can I call him?" Her frustration came through in the tone of that question. By this time, she didn't care.

"If you give me a number where you can be reached, I can call him and ask him to return your call."

"I did that. Hours ago. And I haven't heard from him."

"Well, then, there's not much else I can do. The sheriff's office hours are from nine to five. He'll be in tomorrow morning. You can ask him about that fax then."

For a few seconds she considered trying to explain exactly what the fax contained. Judging by the enjoyment the deputy seemed to be taking in turning down her requests, she decided that would be another exercise in futility.

"Thank you," she said instead.

She closed her phone with a snap, tossing it onto the seat beside her. She took a deep breath, fighting to control her fury. After a moment she picked the cell up again, punching in the number of the Bedford house.

As she listened to the slow rings, she repeated mentally, like a litany, *"Pick up. Pick up. Pick up."* Given the way her day had gone, she was almost surprised when Lorena answered.

"Hello."

"Lorena, it's Susan. Is Jeb there?"

"Susan? How are you, dear?"

"I'm fine, thank you. I really need to talk to Jeb right now. Is he there?"

"He's gone into Pascagoula. It's not his usual appointment, but they called him yesterday and asked him to come in. Something about trying a new therapy."

Jeb had told her about McKey's offer when she talked to him two nights ago. She had called to tell him that the address Ed Caffrey had provided for his son had proved to be a dead end. And, she admitted, to hear his voice again. Of course, he hadn't mentioned the extra session since he hadn't known about it then.

"What time do you expect him back?"

"Same as usual, I imagine. Six or thereabouts. Is something wrong, dear?"

Susan glanced down at her watch. It was almost five-forty.

"Not really. I just wanted to ask him—"

The sudden thought put an end to that half-formed sentence. If there was anyone in Linton who could give her directions to the sheriff's house, it was the woman she was talking to.

"Ask him what, dear? You need to speak up. I can barely hear you. You must be on your cell phone."

"Yes, I am. Sorry. Could you tell me where Sheriff Adams lives?"

"Wayne? You want to know how to get to his *house?*"

"He's already left the office for the day, and I really need to talk to him. Do you know his address?"

"Not his address, but I can get you there. You got a pencil and paper?"

Susan balanced the phone between her ear and her shoulder, again searching her bag. When she had her pen in hand, the back of a receipt spread out on the seat beside her, she spoke into the phone again. "Okay, Lorena. I'm ready when you are."

THE NAME WAYNE ADAMS was neatly lettered on the side of the mailbox. The end of the *Johnson County Star,* rolled and enclosed in a plastic bag, extended slightly from the delivery box beside it. And there was no cruiser parked in the driveway.

The house was the same white clapboard as dozens of others she'd passed on the narrow road Lorena had directed her to. The tiny front porch contained only a solitary white pine rocker that looked as if it had never been occupied. Petunias, left over from the summer and clinging to life, drooped sadly over the sides of a couple of hanging baskets.

She turned into the dirt drive, bending her head to examine the house through the windshield as she approached. She couldn't see lights inside, despite the fact that the front door was open.

As she pulled the Toyota up a few feet from the porch, she realized that what she was seeing was a glass storm door. Beyond it, the unlit entry hall was dimly visible. Maybe Adams would hear her car and come out, so she wouldn't have to go knock on his door.

She took a breath, feeling her anxiety build. She hadn't expected to hear from the test this soon, so she hadn't had time to prepare herself. *That wasn't Emma. I would have known. I would have felt something.*

Banishing the unwanted fear that she could be wrong, she turned her head, looking at the front door again. Nothing had changed. Either her first impression—that the sheriff wasn't here—had been right, or he hadn't heard her car.

She wondered if he had brought the fax home with him. Maybe even now he was inside, looking for the business card she'd given him. Or maybe he was dialing Lorena's number.

Or maybe he'd already done that, she realized. She picked up her cell and hit redial, once more waiting through the seemingly endless rings.

"Hello?"

"Lorena, it's Susan again. Did someone call for me this afternoon?"

"Jeb, you mean?"

"No, someone else. Anyone else."

"I don't think so. If they did, I didn't hear the phone. 'Course, I was pruning the roses most of the afternoon. We won't get many more days like this."

"And there were no messages on the machine when you came inside?"

"I didn't think to look. Let me see." The slow seconds ticked by as the old woman checked the machine. "No, dear, no messages."

"Okay. Thanks. That's all I wanted to know."

"Will you be home in time for dinner? I can keep it warm on the back of the stove if you won't."

"Why don't you do that. I shouldn't be too late."

"All right. I will. You take care now. And be careful driving home."

The caution made Susan remember the night of the rainstorm when she'd been forced off the road. She glanced again at her watch. Almost six. And almost dark.

She raised her eyes, focusing on the front of the house. Her fingers closed around the handle of the door. She hesitated only a second or two before she opened it, stepping out into the deepening twilight.

She walked over to the low steps and then up onto the narrow porch. Through the glass of the storm door she could see into the hall.

She hadn't even thought, until this minute, to wonder if the sheriff was married. Something about the entryway, empty of ornamentation or furniture except for a tall gun cabinet, seemed to indicate this was strictly a man's domain.

She reached out to push the bell and heard a distant buzz. She waited, but there was no response.

Just as when she'd been trying to get someone to the door at Lorena's the evening she'd arrived in Linton, she put her forehead against her cupped hand and peered into the dark interior. Despite the sound of the bell, nothing had changed. No lights had come on in the back of the house.

She glanced out at the narrow two-lane, devoid of traffic. Daylight was fading as the sun sank below the pines on the western side of the house. With the approaching darkness, a hint of apprehension, much like the kind she'd felt before she'd entered the playground that night, shivered through her body.

In a few minutes, it would be fully dark. And again she would be alone. And vulnerable.

She hated the thought of waiting overnight to find out what the lab had discovered. And the deputy had assured her the sheriff had gone home.

*Or out to supper. To a movie. Almost anywhere.*

She ignored those caveats, punching the bell again and then tapping on the glass door. It reverberated in the frame. Surely in a house the size of this one, those noises would have been heard by anyone inside.

Admitting defeat, she crossed the porch and walked back to her car. She got in and turned the key in the ignition. As she guided the Toyota around the other side of the circular driveway, she looked down the side of the house.

Sticking out from the back corner was the rear end of a county patrol car, distinctive because of the emergency number stenciled on the trunk. She pressed down hard on the brakes, stopping the Camry again.

She got out of the car, leaving her keys, and walked along the grass-centered tracks that led toward the back of the house. The vehicle she'd seen was definitely a cruiser. And just as obviously it belonged to the sheriff.

Either Adams was avoiding her or he wasn't inside. She surveyed the backyard. An old-fashioned detached garage sat directly behind the house. In the gathering darkness, a crack of light shone between the center of its double wooden doors.

Without giving herself time to think, she walked toward it, her footsteps crunching along the mix of crushed stones and dirt in the driveway. As she neared the garage, she could hear the faint strains of country music spilling out into the night.

She reached up to knock on one of the doors, but for some reason her hand hesitated in the act. She listened, and then put her ear against the rough planks from which it had been fashioned. There was no sound, other than the soft, soulful rendition of a Hank Williams classic.

"Sheriff Adams?"

She waited in the fading light, night literally closing in around her as she listened to the words of the song, their drawn-out, mournful message adding to her sense of desolation. *"I'm so lonesome I could die."*

She raised her hand again, but her knuckles made little noise against the heavy door. It moved, however, rocking back and forth slightly under her puny knocks.

The padlock that was normally used to secure the two doors had been inserted, open, into the hasp on one of them. *Not locked.*

If the sheriff was inside listening to country music, then he could damn well take time to go with her down to the office and get her fax. *Her* fax, damn it.

She grasped the hasp and pulled. The wooden door creaked, protesting, but it moved, creating a narrow opening.

She listened again, but still heard nothing but the music. She slipped through the space, pausing as soon as she was inside the garage, its air redolent of old grease and gasoline.

"Sheriff Adams?" As she waited for an answer, her eyes surveyed her surroundings.

The light that had shone through the crack came from a single bulb on an insulated cord that had been looped over one of the rafters. It illuminated the side of the building in which she was standing, but the other half was cast into shadow by a tall, antique pickup that took up most of the center portion of the interior.

Its front bumper rested almost flat on the dirt floor, the cab and bed slanting upward. Oil had seeped from underneath the engine to pool in a dark puddle just inside the double doors.

The wall illuminated by the lightbulb was lined with counters, disappearing into the dimness at the back. They were cluttered with tools, paint cans, and what appeared to be used auto parts. Above them, almost every inch of the unfinished wall was covered with pinup calendars, most yellow with age. There were more tools, haphazardly hung from ten-penny nails. The music came from a battered transistor radio, which sat on one of the workbenches, propped upright against an exposed stud.

"Sheriff Adams?" Her voice seemed to echo in the enclosed space. Again there was no answer.

She released the breath she'd been holding as she waited. Apparently, despite the cruiser outside and the radio, Adams really wasn't at home.

Maybe he'd come back to get his personal car or change clothes and had then gone out to eat. There didn't seem to be much point in wasting any more time—

A sudden creak from the side of the garage shrouded in shadows interrupted that decision. It hadn't sounded like the noise the door made when she'd pushed it open. Just as it had that night on the playground, the hair on the back of her neck began to lift.

Not daring to breathe, she waited for the noise to be repeated. After a small eternity, it was. Or at least something very close to what she'd heard before came from the area on the other side of the truck.

Her eyes made another quick survey of the counters, searching for a flashlight. She didn't find one.

Keeping her back to the door, she took a single step to her left, trying to see over the high hood of the ancient vehicle. Then she took another, careful to avoid the dark puddle that seeped from under the bumper.

Just as she reached the headlight on the far side of the truck, the noise she'd heard was repeated. This time she recognized it. Metal creaking against metal. It sounded as if the truck were settling, which made no sense unless—

She leaned to her left, straining to make out the shape on the floor, almost hidden by the shadows. For a heartbeat, none of what she was seeing made sense, and then, in a sickening burst of comprehension, it all did. The man's long, uniform-clad legs extending from beneath the wheel well. The long metal handle of the jack that was supposed to hold up the front end of the truck so its engine could be worked on.

That was supposed to hold it up... And was not.

Retching, she backed away, bumping into the door behind her. It moved, creaking loudly. Her shoe slipped in the dark pool of what she had thought was oil and now, in a rush of horror, recognized was blood.

With that, blind panic took control. She turned, pushing against the door she'd just come through. She burst out of it, running at full tilt by the time she had taken a step or two.

That was all she managed before she slammed into something hard and very solid. Not something, she realized in nearly mindless terror, but someone. Someone whose hands closed over her upper arms, holding her powerless, despite her struggles to break free.

## CHAPTER TWENTY

"WHAT THE HELL are you doing?"

*Jeb's voice. And Jeb's hands.* As soon as she had made the identification, her panic eased enough to allow her to gasp out the words that were unthinkable.

"I think it's the sheriff. Under the truck." She half turned, looking back over her shoulder at the garage. "The jack must have slipped. There's blood coming out from under the front. A lot of it. I though it was oil at first, but…" She ran out of breath and story at the same time.

"Slow down. You think Adams is under a *truck?*"

She nodded. "I think it fell on him."

Jeb had been holding her slightly away from him so that he could look down at her face. Now his eyes lifted to focus on the open garage doors behind her.

"Stay here," he ordered.

Despite the fact that had obviously been a command, she wasn't about to be left alone out here. Better the horror she knew…

She turned as he brushed past her, following him to the garage. He pulled open the heavy door and entered, leaving it ajar. She slipped through behind him.

Jeb had already reached the other side of the truck.

He stooped as she entered, disappearing from sight for maybe thirty seconds. When he stood again, his face was grim.

"You have your cell?"

"In the car."

"Come on."

He walked around the front of the pickup, avoiding the pool of blood, to push open the other door. Instead of heading down the drive, however, he limped toward the back of the frame house. She followed, forcing herself not to take a final look into the darkness of the garage.

As Jeb obviously expected it to be, the screen door at the back of the house wasn't locked. He entered, flipping all the switches inside the doorway, flooding both the yard and the utility room they'd entered with light.

"What are you going to do?"

Instead of answering, he continued through the kitchen and then toward the front of the small house. He turned left in the dining room. She trailed him through each room, finding him finally in what appeared to be a second bedroom that had at some time been converted into a home office. As she entered, Jeb picked the phone up off a battered desk, which had been set in front of the room's double windows.

He punched in three numbers and then stood waiting for the dispatcher to answer. While he did, her eyes moved around the room, taking in the cheaply framed certificates, plaques and photographs. They all seemed to have been hung just as they had been received through the years, without any consideration of aesthetics.

"There's been an accident," Jeb said, bringing her eyes back to him. "I don't have the address, but the victim is Sheriff Adams. It looks as if he was working under a truck he's restoring. Somehow the jack slipped and pinned him."

He listened, and then, his eyes meeting hers, he said, "I don't think there's any question that he's dead."

She had known that intellectually. To hear it stated so bluntly, despite the near dispassion of Jeb's tone, made it more real than it had been before. She crossed her arms over her chest, but the cold she felt was an inward chill.

"Jeb Bedford. Ms. Chandler and I had come to talk to the sheriff and found the body." He listened again, nodding an agreement the dispatcher couldn't see. "We'll be here."

He hung up, his eyes holding hers. "They're going to send the paramedics. And someone from the department, of course."

"You don't think there's any chance…"

He shook his head, knowing immediately what she was asking. His certainty only confirmed her first impression. No one could lose that much blood and still be alive.

"I need to call Lorena. We're probably going to be here a while."

She nodded and only then remembered why she had come. "The lab faxed him the results from the DNA comparison they made."

Jeb frowned. "The state lab? Why would they do that?"

"Because he's the one who initiated the inquiry. It

didn't make any sense to me either, but I talked to the coroner in Randolph County *and* the lab. They both said that's how they had to do it."

"That's why you're here?"

"They said he'd come home for the day. I thought maybe he'd brought the fax with him. That he was planning to call me from here or something. Or that he'd go back to the office with me."

"You want to look for it?"

"Here?" She considered the cluttered desk.

"Why not?"

Jeb was right. No one would ever know. After all, the report should, by rights, have come to her. It was her DNA they had tested.

She walked over to the desk. As she did, Jeb moved to his left, giving her room to slip behind it. For a moment she was reluctant to touch the papers scattered over its surface. It seemed an invasion of privacy.

Except Adams was dead, and if she didn't look for the report now, there was no way to know how long it might be before someone in the department would take time to go through his things and locate it for her. Judging by the attitude of the deputy this afternoon, there was no way to know whether the department would release it to her at all under the circumstances.

She started with the pile of papers neatly stacked on the right side of the desk. She picked them up, her eyes scanning each page quickly and then putting it back down as soon as she'd determined it wasn't what she was looking for.

Most of them seemed to be articles that had been printed off the Internet or photocopied from some other source. New techniques concerning police work. How-to articles. There were even a couple of human-interest stories that involved police departments. Nothing that even remotely resembled a lab report.

When she finished with the first group, she began gathering up those that were spread over the blotter. In the distance she heard the wail of a siren. She turned her head, looking at Jeb for confirmation that she should continue. He nodded.

As she returned to her task, her gaze moved across a small, framed photograph sitting on the left side of the desk. It was the picture of a child, a little girl, her broad smile revealing a missing front tooth.

Her sweeping glance passed on and then, recognition kicking in, snapped back to the photo. Although the hairstyle and clothing were different, she knew that small, heart-shaped face.

And now, perhaps because of the deep blue of the dress she wore, the eyes that stared as directly into the camera as they had into hers that day on the playground appeared to be blue, too, rather than gray. Fingers trembling, Susan reached out and picked up the frame, questions ricocheting through her brain.

"What is it?"

"I know her," she said softly.

Jeb leaned forward so he could see what she was staring at. "From here, you mean?"

She nodded. "I met her at the school. Her name's Alexandra. And she's in the third grade."

"Third grade. That means—"

"That she's eight years old. She told me that."

*The exact same age as Emma.*

"What's her picture doing on Adams's desk?" Jeb asked.

"I don't know, but… Even when he was warning me away from the playground, he never mentioned her. He never indicated he knew any of those children. Don't you think that's strange?" she asked, looking up at him. "Especially since he must have realized Emma would have been in the same grade as—"

"Mr. Bedford?"

The masculine voice came from the back of the house. Susan quickly set the picture back down on the desk, attempting to straighten the papers she'd been looking through.

"In here," Jeb called, squeezing around behind her. As he did, his hand closed over her shoulder, the gesture obviously intended to offer strength or comfort.

Before Jeb could reach the doorway, a deputy poked his head into the opening. He was deeply tanned and sported a dark, neatly trimmed mustache that was obviously intended to make him look older. It wasn't effective, unless he really *was* sixteen.

"You the one who made the call about the sheriff?"

Since he'd called Jeb by name, it was obvious he knew the answer. Despite the ridiculousness of the question, Jeb nodded.

"You found the body?" the kid asked.

"Ms. Chandler did."

The deputy's eyes focused on her face. "*You're* Ms. Chandler? I talked to you a little while ago. Something about a fax you were trying to locate."

She nodded, but didn't offer any other information.

"Ms. Chandler came out here to see the sheriff about her fax and discovered the body."

"That right, ma'am?"

"That's right."

"And the sheriff was...like that when you arrived."

She wasn't sure about the legal implications of that question. Whatever he meant, she didn't particularly like the sound of his phrasing.

"He was pinned under the truck. There was blood pooled in front of it, but at the time I didn't know what it was. I thought it was oil. Then I heard something creak and walked around to the other side. That's when I saw his body."

"What kind of creak?"

"It sounded like metal moving against metal."

The deputy's brows rose as if that information were somehow surprising or important.

"The jack may have slipped farther, or the truck may have been settling," Jeb supplied.

"That's possible, I guess. You didn't see the truck fall?"

"It was already at that angle when I opened the door."

"Angle?"

"You haven't seen it?" Jeb asked.

"I saw the lights and figured you folks must be inside. The paramedics were already out there when I arrived."

"The front bumper of the pickup is almost touching the ground. There are no tires, so when it fell..." Jeb shrugged.

There was an uncomfortable silence.

"Okay," the deputy said. "Well, you folks are still gonna need to come down to the department and fill out a report."

Susan looked at Jeb, hoping he'd object. He was nodding instead.

"I need to make a call first, if that's all right. My great-aunt is waiting supper for us at home. She'll be worried if we don't show up pretty soon."

"I'll wait on you all outside. Ma'am."

The deputy nodded to her, touching the brim of his hat as he did. Then he took a step back toward the doorway.

"Did he have any children?"

Her question stopped him in midstride. "Ma'am?"

"Sheriff Adams. I was just wondering if he had a family."

"Sheriff wasn't married. Folks in the department always said he was married to the job. He's gonna be missed in this town."

It was obvious he had already slipped into deification mode. Whatever shortcomings Adams had would be lost, at least temporarily, in the tragedy of his death.

"Then…" Susan picked up the photograph from the desk and held it out to him. "I was wondering who this is."

The deputy crossed the room, taking the frame from her. "That's Alex," he said, smiling. "She's his niece. Sheriff's sister and her husband have been divorced for years. Since before she moved back here, actually. Sheriff's always been like a daddy to that little girl. She's gonna miss him, too."

"You said they moved back here? So…she had moved away for a time?"

"Diane? As I remember it, her husband wasn't from around these parts. Maybe they lived where his family come from. I don't know all the details, but Diane moved back when Alex was just a baby. Must be five or six years ago now. I think the sheriff was the only family she had, so naturally she come on home when her marriage fell apart. Most folks do. Nothing like family in hard times," he said, handing her the photograph, his face arranged in an appropriate expression of grief.

"That reminds me," he added. "Somebody's gonna have to call Diane and give her the news. I don't envy 'em that job. She's gonna take it hard, especially the way it happened."

"I assume whoever makes that call would be Sheriff Adams's second in command," Jeb said.

The deputy nodded. "Buck Jemison. I'll need to get in touch with him."

"When you do, mention that Ms. Chandler has a very important fax that was sent to the sheriff's department. It's information she needs immediate access to. I'm assuming that since the sheriff is dead, Jemison is the one who can authorize its release."

For a moment the deputy looked as if he wanted to argue the point. Something about Jeb's tone or that unthinking air of command made him think better of it.

"I'll tell him. You go on and make your phone call, and I'll see you outside."

He nodded dismissal again with the same brief gesture toward the brim of his hat. This time his exit was successful.

Susan waited until she heard the screen door at the back of the house slam shut behind him. She turned to

Jeb, her heart pounding with the information they'd just been given.

"The sheriff's sister brought a baby to Linton six years ago. A little girl Adams failed to mention to me, despite his talk about my watching the children at the elementary school. Do you realize what that means?"

"Don't," Jeb advised.

"Don't what? You have to see—"

"I admit it looks strange he didn't mention his niece, but maybe he didn't see a connection. It could have happened just as the deputy said. A nasty divorce. She moves back home, bringing her daughter with her."

"Adams did everything in his power to discourage me from looking for Emma. Since the day I got into town. You *know* that."

"I know that if you get your hopes up, and this proves to be nothing—"

"Then what?" she interrupted. "I'm back right where I was before—having no idea what happened to Emma. If I'm *right*…" Her heart ached with the thought of what that could mean. "She might be my little girl," she said. "And I've seen her. I've even talked to her. She's safe, and she's right here—" Her voice broke with the enormity of that.

"Susan."

"I know. But…it *is* possible. At least admit that much. It *is* possible. Don't pretend I'm crazy. God, I had enough of that from *him*."

"You're not crazy. And it is possible. But until we know more, that's *all* it is. I just want you to be careful what you're thinking."

Jeb was right. She had come too far and searched too

long to get her hopes up before she knew the whole story. What he had said was just common sense.

However, the place in her heart that had once guarded the precious memories of a baby who'd reached her arms up to be held had already begun to thaw from the long freeze she had imposed on it. Alexandra was the right age. She was in the right place. And she had connections to someone who had thrown obstacles and objections into Susan's path every step of the way.

Despite Jeb's warning, the warmth of hope began to spread outward from that cold, long-dead center.

# CHAPTER TWENTY-ONE

"LORENA WILL KNOW," Susan said.

Jeb took his eyes off the road to glance over at her. Only her profile, backlit by moonlight, was visible in the dark interior of the car. "Know what?"

She'd been quiet since the deputy, whose name they'd learned was Byron Ahern, had told them about the sheriff's niece. In spite of his warning to slow down, Jeb knew she was already thinking of that little girl as her Emma.

"Diane's name. She may even know her address."

"Diane Paul. I asked one of the officers."

There was no way Susan was going to let this go. He was surprised she hadn't asked him to take her to the home of Adams's sister as soon as they left the sheriff's department.

They'd told their stories again, in separate rooms this time. Although Jeb had dragged his feet about leaving, waiting for Buck Jemison to show up, he hadn't. When he finally asked Ahern, he'd been told Jemison was unavailable because he was heading up the investigation of Adams's death.

When Jeb had expressed surprise at the term, he'd been told they considered the inquiry into any accidental death an investigation. What they would do in this case might be more thorough, given the victim's relationship to the department, but in circumstances like this an investigation was routine.

"Did you ask him where she lived?"

"I thought that might seem a little inappropriate," he said, "given what just happened to her brother. I didn't want to create any suspicion in anyone's mind."

"I don't care if they're suspicious. You *know* there's something strange about the fact that Adams didn't mention his niece. That has to mean *something*. We can't just let it go."

"I keep thinking about his warning that if you push whoever this is, they'll take Emma and disappear," Jeb said. "I'm wondering if he said that because it's already the plan."

"He said that to discourage me from looking for her."

"That doesn't preclude the possibility that his sister really *is* planning to run. If we show up at her house tonight, without any authority to take Emma…"

"How do we get that 'authority'?"

"First of all, we have to have some evidence that the little girl Diane Paul brought to Linton isn't her daughter. And I mean something more substantial than the fact that Adams never mentioned his niece to you."

He wondered if Susan had been thinking about just taking the little girl. He couldn't blame her, but without proof, he couldn't let her do that. This would have to be done legally because otherwise, if she were wrong, she'd be opening herself up to a charge of kidnapping.

"Do you think Adams had something to do with Richard's death? I don't see how he could have taken Emma if he didn't."

"There are other scenarios that might explain it."

"Like what?"

"Maybe Wayne found the body. *And* the baby."

"And if he reported finding the body," Susan said, quickly following his thinking, "he would have to report finding the baby, too. And he didn't want to do that."

A lifelong resident, Adams knew this area as well as anyone. He would certainly have been aware of the currents at the entrance to the bridge, as well as its reputation. Maybe he hadn't had a hand in Richard's death, but he might well have had a hand in seeing that his car ended up in the river there.

"All of that's speculation," he warned. "And with Adams dead, there's no way to prove any of it."

"A DNA test wouldn't be speculation."

"Do you think Diane will allow you to take a sample from her daughter?"

"Don't you think that under the circumstances a court would order her to?"

"Maybe." *If they could get this to court before Diane and Alex disappeared.* "But we'll need something other than suspicions and guesswork before we get that far."

"Like what?"

"Maybe Alex's birth certificate."

"Her *birth* certificate?"

"Diane would have to have one to get her into school. If Alex is Emma, then the one she provided can't be the original."

"People use copies all the time. Maybe they forged it. Or maybe Adams helped her to get one that *said* Emma was her daughter. He may have handled it here where he had some pull."

"If you're right about Alex," Jeb hedged, "then I'm sure he did. I'm just saying that's one thing we need to have the authorities take a look at."

The plural pronoun echoed in his head, but he didn't bother to retract it. That's how he felt. As if he were part of this. As if he had some stake in seeing Susan reunited with her daughter, a little girl he'd never met.

"I just don't think there's anything we can do tonight."

"Jeb, I can't go back to Lorena's and just go to bed, knowing what I know."

"You don't *know* anything. You *suspect* something based on a lot of circumstantial stuff that wouldn't convince anyone, much less a judge. In any case, I don't think Diane would take her daughter over there tonight. Do you?"

"To Adams's house?"

"I think she'll probably go herself, but I don't think she'd want to take Alex. Not at her age."

"You think she'd leave her at home alone?"

Jeb could hear the sudden excitement in her voice, an excitement he needed to temper with reality. "Would *you?*"

"She'd probably leave her with someone," Susan admitted. "A neighbor or a friend."

"That makes sense. And without approaching Diane directly, something we can't afford to do because she might run, there's no way to know where Alex is right now."

"What if the deputy tells her I asked about the photo?"

"Ahern? I doubt he'll go back out to Wayne's. Someone else is in charge of the investigation."

"*Investigation?* Do they think there was something suspicious about his death?"

"I asked that. Apparently it's routine with any death not attributable to natural causes."

"Well, I would certainly say there was nothing natural about that one."

Jeb glanced at her again. Her arms were wrapped around her body as if she were cold.

"How could that happen?" she asked. "The jack, I mean."

"How could it slip? Age maybe. Or carelessness on Adams's part. It's designed to go under the chassis and hold the weight of the axle, but if you bump it hard, the handle can release. Believe me, this isn't the first time something like that has happened."

"But someone *could* have done it, couldn't they? Someone *could* have lowered the jack so that the truck would fall on him?"

"You think someone deliberately—" He stopped, thinking about what she'd just suggested. "Why would anyone do that?"

"Because if it's possible he found Richard's body, maybe it's also possible he knew who killed him."

"And didn't tell anyone?"

"He couldn't. Not and keep Emma."

"Despite what you and I may think about Adams, he held his job for a lot of years. And in all that time I never heard any intimation he was corrupt. Or even particularly incompetent. Certainly no more so than any other rural sheriff down here."

"I haven't been here two weeks, and *I* thought he was incompetent. He couldn't even tell me if the doors and windows were closed when they pulled Richard's car out of the river. That should have been one of the first things he'd check. Then, when I told him about Emma, he came up with half a dozen things that could have happened to her. When those didn't work, he tried to warn me off by saying that whoever had her might take her and run. So...save the testimonials, please. He may be dead, but unlike Ahern, I'm not ready to assign him sainthood."

Jeb couldn't argue with Susan's assessment of the sheriff's mishandling of things following the discovery of Richard's body. And he *had* opposed almost everything she'd tried to do to get to the bottom of her daughter's disappearance.

"If they ever found out he had the baby," Susan said, going back to her theory, "then they would know he'd found the body. Whoever killed Richard, I mean. After he took Emma, revealing *any* of what had happened was a chance he couldn't take."

"Wayne would know where to push the SUV into the river to keep it out of the reach of the current," Jeb admitted. "He would also know that if it were found at that location, everyone would assume it was just another accident."

"So why didn't he open a window? Then if the car *were* ever found, he wouldn't have had to answer questions about Emma's disappearance."

"Because something might have floated to the surface."

"Like Richard's body," she said bitterly. "And it might have happened *before* the soft tissue disappeared."

"What?"

"He told me that if they'd had soft tissue, they could determine cause of death. So he knew the longer the body stayed in the water—"

"The fewer clues there would be," he finished for her.

Although it was all speculation, it fit. Adams had taken the baby for his sister. Or maybe to satisfy his own desire for a family. He'd weighed his chances of Richard's body being found, deciding they were fewer if he left the windows closed. And he'd been right. If it hadn't been for the derailment...

"You think someone killed him for the money and left his body and Emma wherever Adams found them?"

"That's something we can't know right now." With Adams dead, maybe they never would. "What'd you find out in Atlanta?"

"That Powell is no longer in existence. I couldn't even find a listing in the phone directory. I did get in touch with Richard's secretary. She was going to get back to me with the names of any of his clients she could come up with, but she was working with several of the other accountants at the same time. She couldn't remember any Powell clients having problems when the fraud cases began hitting the headlines. I don't know, Jeb. This is all beginning to look as if whatever happened, happened right here in Linton."

"Then the question of why Richard left home remains."

"Maybe all those people were right. Maybe he *did* have someone waiting for him. Maybe someone in this area."

"Another woman? Do you really believe that?"

"I didn't then. Nobody thinks that about their marriage, but don't they say the wife is always the last to know?"

There was nothing he could say to that. No comfort he could offer. Just because he couldn't imagine any man being unfaithful to her, that didn't mean it hadn't happened.

"What are you doing?" Susan questioned as he drove past the turn to Lorena's.

"I just thought of someone who might be able to give us some information about Diane Paul. Something that might be even more important right now than her address."

THERE WERE LIGHTS ON inside the imposing Victorian mansion, showcasing the rich elegance of the front rooms. The same melodic chimes sounded deep inside the house, but this time it didn't take Callaway but a moment to answer the door.

Jeb hardly gave the old man a chance to get it open before he began. "I need your help, Doc, and don't give me any crap about patient confidentiality."

"What's that supposed to mean?" Callaway's voice was cold.

"It means two people are dead, and a little girl has been missing for seven years. If you've got answers for any of this, I want them. And I want them now."

"If *I've* got answers? I swear, Jeb, I don't know what

you're talking about. I don't even know *who* you're talking about, other than maybe Ms. Chandler's husband and daughter. And what the hell you think I'd know about either of them—"

"I'm talking about Wayne Adams. And a little girl named Alexandra Paul."

"*Wayne?* What's Wayne got to do with this?"

"We just found him crushed under a truck."

"Crushed? Are you saying…he's dead?"

"Very. And I think he may have been murdered, Doc."

"*Murdered?* Why would somebody murder Wayne?"

"Maybe because he knew too much about Richard Kaiser's death. I think he may have found Kaiser's body and the baby. And maybe he also found evidence of who was involved."

"Whoa. Slow down. You think *Wayne* found Ms. Chandler's husband and daughter?"

"I think he hid the body in the river and took the baby."

"Now why in the world—?"

Something changed in the old man's eyes, making Jeb know he'd been on the right track in coming here. Doc had just realized he *did* know something about what had happened that night. Something he hadn't put together before.

Now that he had, Jeb had to convince him to tell them what it was. Even if this wasn't the kind of evidence they could take to a judge, it might be enough to justify the risk of going after Emma themselves.

"Alex Paul," Jeb said again. "What do you know about her?"

"That she was never a patient of mine."

"But you *do* know who she is?"

"I know she's Wayne Adams's niece."

Jeb waited, but Callaway seemed to have nothing to add to that statement.

"How about Diane Paul, née Adams? Was *she* your patient?"

"At one time. Years ago."

"So what can you tell me about her?"

"If you're asking what I can tell you medically, then you know better. How would you like it if the folks who are seeing you started talking to other people about your treatment?"

"If it would right the kinds of wrongs that have taken place in this town, I'd say go ahead. There are all kinds of ethics, Doc, and standards of morality that outweigh the ones you're hiding behind."

There was a flash of fury in the old man's eyes that made Jeb wonder if he'd gone too far. Indignation flushed the thin skin of Callaway's cheeks.

"How dare you talk like that to me."

"If you know anything about Diane Paul that might help us figure out what happened seven years ago, then you damn well owe it to this woman to tell her."

Doc's eyes moved to Susan's face before he said, "You know I can't breach patient confidentiality. Not even if I wanted to. And I don't. Whatever treatment I provided for Diane Adams, I'm bound by law not to reveal it to anyone. I could lose my license to practice. I could also be sued. And rightly so."

"Except you're no longer practicing medicine. And if we're right about Diane, she isn't going to be suing anyone. She's going to be serving time as an accessory to kidnapping."

"*If* you're right," Callaway reiterated stubbornly.

"Damn it, Doc, are you telling me that if someone has committed a criminal act, you can't discuss something in their history that might be relevant? Legal or not, that's insane."

"If there was a court order—"

"We don't have time for a court order. Adams is dead, and we believe Diane may be preparing to leave town. If she does, she'll take her 'daughter' with her. Only we think the little girl she and Wayne raised might not *be* her daughter. And if she isn't, maybe she and Diane are next in line for whoever murdered both Richard Kaiser and Adams."

For a long time the old man said nothing. "I've lived my whole life by a certain code. And now you're telling me I should discard everything I've sworn to uphold—"

"To save a child's life. Funny, I always thought that was part of that code you lived by. This isn't a court of law, Doc," Jeb said, pressing his advantage. "And you aren't on the stand. This is just me, Jeb Bedford, asking somebody I admire almost as much as I did my own father to do the right thing. Help us find out what happened to a baby who disappeared right here in this town. *Your* town."

"Please, Dr. Callaway," Susan said, "if you know something that might be related to Emma—"

The dark eyes shifted to her face again, as if he had forgotten she was here, before they tracked back to Jeb's. "I never thought I'd hear you talk to me that way, boy."

"I never thought I'd have to," Jeb said, his voice equally cold. "All I'm asking you for is the truth."

"And if that *truth* isn't your business?"

"Is it mine?" Susan asked, bringing the old man's gaze back to her face once more. "*Is* Alexandra Paul my daughter?"

For a long time no one spoke. Jeb was afraid Callaway might step inside, closing the door in their faces. And by now it was obvious that he did know something about Diane Paul or her daughter. Whether or not it was the proof they needed—

"I don't know," the doctor said finally. "And that's the God's truth," he added, looking back at Jeb.

"But you *do* know something, don't you, Doc? You know something you *think* might be related to what happened."

There was another silence. Through it, the old man's eyes remained locked on Jeb's face.

"Wayne brought her to see me one night."

For a second Jeb thought he was talking about Emma before he realized who Doc meant. "He brought Diane here?"

"She was maybe fourteen or fifteen at the time. She had a fever. Chills. Looked like death warmed over. He wanted me to prescribe an antibiotic or give her a shot, but I told him I'd have to examine her first. Throat looked good. Ears. Chest sounded okay. There was something about her eyes, though..." Callaway seemed to recall himself from the past. "I told Wayne I wanted to examine her more thoroughly and that I needed him to leave the room. Soon as he was outside, it didn't take more than a couple of questions to bring the whole story pouring out.

"She'd gotten pregnant and was too scared to tell anybody. She and the boy had skipped school one day and gone to New Orleans, where somebody had butchered her. She might as well have taken a knife or a coat hanger to herself. She'd probably have been better off if she *had*."

"And Adams knew?" Jeb asked.

"Not then, but there was no way to keep him from finding out. The infection was so massive by that time I ended up having to put her in the hospital to save her life. I'll give him credit though. He never said a harsh word to her. Not in my presence anyway. And he seemed far more concerned about her welfare than about what she'd done."

"And what about Diane?"

"Antibiotics, of course. Powerful ones. And I called in a specialist, but the damage was pretty severe."

"Severe enough to keep her from conceiving a child?" Jeb prodded, knowing that question was at the heart of Doc's story.

"Nature's a far better healer than most of us with medical degrees. I've seen some miraculous—"

"In your professional opinion, Doc," Jeb broke in, "after that botched abortion, would you have expected Diane Paul to conceive a child?"

"The truth?" the old man said.

"That's all we've asked you for."

"Then no. In my professional opinion, I wouldn't have expected her to conceive, much less carry a fetus to term."

# CHAPTER TWENTY-TWO

"WHAT DOC TOLD US doesn't change the fact that we can't possibly know where Alex is."

"Emma," Susan said stubbornly.

"You can't confront Diane tonight," Jeb went on, ignoring the correction. "If you do, you'll scare her off, and you may never see Emma again. Think," he demanded.

She was trying to. All she could think about, however, were Callaway's words. Confirmation of what she'd suspected since she found that photograph on Wayne Adams's desk.

"What do you think I should do?"

"Call the FBI. Based on what we know right now, I'm pretty sure they'll send an agent down here. Once they do, all of this will be out of the jurisdiction of the Johnson County Sheriff's Department."

"It's out of their jurisdiction now. As a kidnap victim, Emma is, at least."

"And who do you think the deputies are going to believe about that? You or Diane?"

"I can't just leave her with that woman—"

"Yes. Yes, you can." Jeb modulated his tone from that first abrupt affirmation. "That's *exactly* what you can do. Diane isn't going anywhere until after her brother's funeral. Not unless you force her hand. If you do, you'll leave her no option but to run. And to take Emma with her. You may never see her again, Susan. Despite how close you are right now."

"And you could be wrong. She could have Emma with her at Wayne's house right now. If she does—"

"If she does, they'll be surrounded by half the deputies in this county. If you go there, then you'll have warned Diane, and Wayne's followers won't allow you to take Emma away with you. You *know* that."

"I can't risk that she might—"

"Tomorrow," he interrupted again. "After the FBI arrives. You'll have a better chance to protect her then."

"Chance? I can't *take* a chance, Jeb. Not with Emma. Why can't you understand that?"

"I do understand. Believe me. But as far as these people are concerned, you *have* no rights here. Diane does. Including the right to put her daughter into a car and drive away."

"What guarantee do I have she isn't doing that right now?"

"Her brother's funeral for one thing. You heard Ahern. Wayne was the only family she has. No matter what else happens, she isn't going to leave before her brother is buried."

"You can't know that. What if she suspects the same thing we do?"

She had tried to put herself in Diane's place. If she thought her brother's death wasn't an accident, wouldn't she fear for the baby he'd brought her? Or was it possible Diane really didn't know where the little girl she'd named Alexandra had come from?

Maybe that had been the case before Richard's body had been found, but there was no way she didn't know after Susan arrived in Linton and began searching so publicly for Emma. Diane had to have suspected the truth at that point.

"I don't think anyone else is suspicious of Wayne's death," Jeb said. "They all seem to accept it was an accident."

"Diane has to know that he stole the baby he gave her. Even if she didn't know before, Jeb, she has to now. She must be terrified I'm going to take her daughter from her." Susan had only one standard by which to measure Diane's degree of desperation. That was what she might do in the same situation. "I can't wait until tomorrow."

"We'll call the FBI as soon as we get home. We'll lay it all out for them, including what Doc told us. They can have someone from the field office in Jackson down here in the morning. That's when we confront her. Not until we have someone who can overrule Jemison."

"Jeb—"

"It's the only way. And the only chance you've got to keep her from taking Emma and running. I wouldn't tell you that unless I believed it."

The quiet conviction in his voice made her know he did. The problem was that all the people she'd listened to the first time had been just as convincing. Just as sure of what they'd told her. And that time...

"I can't lose her again. I couldn't survive that."

"You aren't going to. I'm not going to let that happen. I swear to you, Susan. Just...trust me."

Despite everything that had gone wrong before, despite the outcome—the endless nightmare of the last seven years—she *did* trust him. But the stakes in the gamble he was asking her to take were too high. All her instincts screamed she should just go find Emma and then defy anyone to take her away again.

She came out of that fog of despair to realize Jeb was guiding the truck alongside Lorena's front steps. He cut off the engine and then turned to look at her, blue eyes reflecting the light from the open front door.

"We call the FBI, and then we wait until they get here. That's all we can do tonight."

She didn't try to reason with him again. He had already heard all her arguments and rejected them.

And she couldn't deny the possibility of what Jeb believed they should fear the most. If Diane learned that they knew the truth about Alexandra, then with Buck Jemison and the rest of the deputies as her willing allies, she would be gone before they had a chance to stop her.

She understood all that. At least intellectually. She just couldn't help thinking that sometime tomorrow she was once more going to walk through the empty rooms of another house, fruitlessly searching for her daughter.

"Susan?"

Unable to sleep, she had finally retreated onto the cool, protective darkness of the veranda. Just as on the night she'd begged Jeb to help her, she was sitting on the top step, arms wrapped around her knees as she stared unseeingly at the roses.

"What are you doing out here?"

This time she turned, looking at Jeb over her shoulder. The light in the hall was off, but he was silhouetted against the dim illumination coming from the back of the house.

"Trying not to think."

She had been. Trying not to think about what it would mean if Jeb was wrong. Or about the indifference in the voice of whomever she'd talked to at the Bureau tonight. Most of all, trying not to think about a little girl who should, please dear God, be sleeping in a bed only a few short miles from the one where Susan had tossed and turned.

Despite the fact that Jeb hadn't answered her comment, she wasn't surprised to hear his uneven footsteps cross the wooden floor behind her. She was surprised when he eased down on the step beside her, seeming to contemplate the same moonlit garden that stretched before them.

After a moment he put his arm around her shoulders, attempting to draw her to his side. Unthinkingly she resisted, her body stiff with an anger she hadn't realized she harbored until he'd touched her.

Her resistance didn't deter him. He increased the pressure, pulling her cold body against his solid strength. Holding her close enough that she could feel the steady beat of his heart against her ribs.

She couldn't remember the last time she had been this near to a man. Near enough to feel his heartbeat. Near enough to feel the warmth of his skin against hers.

Once, a long time ago, leaning against a man's chest and being comforted had been as familiar as the scent of baby lotion and formula. Then, in a heartbeat, both had been taken from her.

She had acknowledged the impact of the loss of one, but until tonight—until now—in her long bitterness over Richard's desertion, she had never admitted how much she had missed being held. Or how badly she needed to be tonight.

She closed her eyes against the sting of tears. As she did, locked in that self-imposed darkness, she became aware of a dozen other sensations. The clean, masculine scent of soap. The hair-roughened texture of Jeb's forearm resting against her bare shoulder. The firmness of the muscles under her cheek. And underlying all of them, the steadiness of his heartbeat.

Trust me, he'd said. And she had. Maybe, as he'd warned her, she hadn't really had a choice, but once more she had put her fate—and Emma's—in the hands of another person, something she had sworn she would never do again.

"Do you want to talk about it?" he asked.

"Not really."

"Do you want to talk about her?"

If she did, then she would have to think about the self-possessed little girl who she now believed was her daughter. And she already knew where those thoughts would lead. In the same endless circle of fear and hope that had driven her out here more than an hour ago.

"How can I? I don't even know her."

"You will."

She let the assurance lie between them, too tired of the uncertainties to argue the point. After a moment Jeb turned his head, his lips moving against her hair.

She'd done the same thing a thousand times as she'd held Emma. It was a gesture of caring. Concern. Love.

Except Jeb didn't love her. And no matter how welcome the solidness of his body against hers, she needed to remember that.

This was friendship. Fellow feeling for someone who was suffering. Nothing more.

And of course, she didn't want it to be more. Not now. Not until...

The realization was sudden. And unsettling.

If she recovered Emma tomorrow, there would be no reason to stay in Linton. No reason to spend another minute in the company of the man at her side. No reason...

Except that she wanted to. Even if she had Emma, this, too, was something she now knew she needed. Something she had needed almost as much as being able to press her lips against the softness of her daughter's hair.

She moved slightly, an obvious withdrawal. Jeb responded immediately. He leaned back, removing his arm from around her shoulders.

She turned her head, looking into his eyes, her awareness of him colored by the newness of the emotion she'd just discovered. She had been physically attracted to him from the first. That instinctive response had now changed into something much different. Something based, not on physicality, but on respect. Friendship. Admiration. Trust.

*Trust me...*

What she felt must somehow have been reflected in her face. His eyes narrowed, some thought shifting behind them, before he lowered his head, tilted so that his mouth aligned with hers.

There was a heartbeat of hesitation before his lips closed possessively over hers. This was nothing like the abrupt kiss the morning she'd left for Atlanta. This was a slow, unhurried caress. His tongue explored, melding with hers before it slipped away to trace the outline of her lips.

In spite of the stress of the last few hours, she responded, trying to deepen the kiss by placing her hand at the back of his head. Opened, her fingers spread through the softness of his hair.

With that encouragement, his arms tightened, crushing her to him so that her breasts were flattened against the hard wall of his chest. For a fleeting second guilt intruded, reminding her of the worries that had driven her into the darkness. Unable to act on them, she had not wanted to think.

And that was exactly the gift Jeb now offered, she realized. Freedom from those circling thoughts and fears. A span of time during which she wouldn't be aware with every breath she drew of how near—and yet how far—from Emma she was.

*Make me forget...*

She didn't speak the words, but as if in response to them, Jeb leaned back again, creating a narrow space between their bodies. His hand cupped under her breast, the sudden pressure of those strong, dark fingers verging on pain. She gasped, and immediately the pressure eased, to be replaced by the back-and-forth glide of his thumb across her nipple.

His mouth found hers, more demanding than before, as his fingers continued to tease the tightening nub. Sexual heat shimmered like summer lightning along nerve endings that were almost atrophied from disuse.

*Too long. Too long.*

His lips deserted hers, causing a small wordless protest. They found the hardened nipple his thumb had created, suckling it. All thought of protest was lost as moisture surged through her lower body, releasing in a sweet, hot flood of desire.

Her fingers convulsed, tightening unconsciously in the darkness of his hair. In response, Jeb raised his head far enough to allow his hand to sweep the wide lace strap of her nightgown down and over her shoulder. The night air brushed the dampness left on her skin, cool against its heat.

Almost before that sensation had registered, his mouth closed over her bare flesh. With his lips, teeth and tongue he teased her already sensitized breast, evoking a gasp of pleasure and surprise.

Again he leaned back, his desertion creating another wordless protest. Her fingers, still locked in his hair, urged his head down again, but he ignored their entreaty.

"Come on," he said instead.

She opened her eyes, shocked that he would chance an interruption. She couldn't. If she stopped to think about what she was doing… "What's wrong?"

"Not here." His hand closed over her fingers, which rested against the fabric of his shirt.

Bewildered, she shook her head. She was again aware of the night air, chill against her skin. Aware of how little she had on. Conscious, when she didn't want to be, of what she knew was about to happen between them.

"Why?"

"The beds are inside."

*Beds.* The reminder of how this was going to end was almost a shock. It was one thing to allow herself to be caught up in the heat of the moment and quite another to deliberately seek a sexual encounter with a man she barely knew.

"Maybe this isn't such a good idea." All the reasons why it wasn't came crashing in on her, destroying both need and desire with the cold, hard reality of the situation.

"Like hell it isn't," Jeb said. "If you think you're doing Emma some kind of favor by being alone tonight, you're wrong."

"It just seems…"

"I know how it seems. But I also know that waiting out these hours shouldn't be an act of martyrdom."

"Is that what you think? That I'm trying to be a martyr."

"I think you're scared to death that I may be wrong."

He was right. She just hadn't realized he understood her fears.

"The thing you don't know," he went on, the words seeming to be dragged from him against his will, "is that I'm just as terrified as you are."

"Then—"

"Admitting I'm afraid doesn't change a thing. Waiting is still the best thing you can do. Just…don't do it alone."

"Is not wanting to be alone a good enough reason for something that should be… I don't know *what* it should be. It just seems that when two people make love it should be about more than that."

She hesitated, hoping he would say the right thing. That he would find the words that would free her from the constraint she felt. Words that would let her know she wasn't taking anything away from Emma tonight by wanting to be held. Not even by wanting Jeb to make love to her.

And she did. Despite the fact that his lips and hands were no longer seducing her. Despite the fact that this would no longer be a situation that had simply happened, but one she had made a conscious decision to allow.

She still wanted him. His strength. His warmth. His heartbeat against hers.

And he was right. Denying herself those comforts wouldn't change whatever was going to happen.

"I thought you knew," he said.

"Knew what?" Her heart rate accelerated, anticipating.

"How much more there is than that."

She examined the words, realizing that more than anything else he might have said, these really *were* the right ones.

"I'm out of practice at reading between the lines."

There had been a few men in her life since Richard's death, but those relationships had been brief and for the most part meaningless. She had always accepted the blame for that, but this time...

"I'm afraid I'm not very good at this," Jeb said. "The way my life has been—" He stopped, seeming to think about what he wanted to say. "To be honest, I don't know how much my current situation has to do with it, but you're the first woman I can ever remember thinking about in terms other than sexual. And temporary."

She wasn't sure for a second whether to be flattered or appalled. Given that confession, however, she couldn't doubt he was trying to tell her the truth. Even if that didn't rebound to his credit.

"I'm not proud of that," he went on, speaking hesitantly for almost the first time since she'd met him, "but…my job didn't lend itself to permanency. And it always came first."

Now that had been taken from him. Just as her life had once been taken from her. And neither of them could be sure they would ever recover what they'd lost.

All they could be sure of… All they could be sure of was what they had together tonight. Although it might not be what they sought, it was, in itself, something of value, no matter their reasons for embracing it.

Something of value. Something to cling to. Something they both needed right now.

Without a word, and knowing that he couldn't possibly understand what had changed her mind, she held her hand out to him. After a moment, he pushed up from the step where they were sitting, looking down into her face. Then he reached out and took her fingers into his.

She was aware again of their strength. Aware of the slightly callused abrasiveness of their skin. So aware…

She allowed him to pull her to her feet. For a few seconds they stood silently at the top of the steps before his arm once more came around her waist, drawing her to his side.

Arm in arm they walked to the door before he stepped aside, allowing her to precede him through it. Without any hesitation she crossed the hall to the foot of the stairs. Once there she turned back to find him watching her.

Again she held out her hand, smiling at him until he took the first limping step toward her and all that lay ahead.

# CHAPTER TWENTY-THREE

THERE HAD BEEN another awkward moment when they reached the landing on the second floor. Lorena's room was at the head of the stairs, next door to the suite Susan had been given. She'd hesitated, realizing what that proximity might mean. Jeb's hand at the small of her back reminded her there was another option.

She followed his lead to the suite at the far end of the hall. She had known those were his rooms, but she'd never been in them, of course.

He turned the handle, opening the door for her. The lamp on the bedside table had been left on, its low light revealing the disordered sheets of the bed he'd left to come looking for her. An open hardback lay facedown on the table. Beside it stood a small brown prescription bottle.

Painkillers or sleeping pills? She had time to wonder before the door to the hall closed behind her. She turned to find Jeb standing before it, his eyes luminous in the dimness.

"I should probably warn you," she said.

"Warn me? About what?"

"I'm a little out of practice at this."

"I've always heard it's like riding a bicycle."

"Somehow it doesn't feel like that right now."

It didn't. Despite what Jeb had said downstairs, despite her acknowledgment that this was something she, too, devotedly desired, everything felt strange. Almost disjointed. As if she were watching it unfold between two other people.

"There's nothing to be afraid of," Jeb said.

"I'm not. I'm just…" There was no single word for what she was feeling. No simple explanation for why something that had seemed so right downstairs seemed suddenly so wrong. "It's just been a very long time."

His lips moved, a small upward tilt at their corners. "Funny. I was thinking the same thing."

*I was thinking the same thing.* Since he could have no idea about the deprivations of her sex life, there seemed to be only one interpretation of that. But the idea that someone as intensely masculine as Jeb…

*They told me you were half-dead,* Dr. Callaway had said. For the first time she thought about what injuries that severe might mean to any man, especially one whose entire adult life had, of necessity, been lived at a peak of physical perfection.

Although there was now no outward sign of infirmity—other than the limp she hardly noticed anymore—she could imagine the psychological toll his injuries must have taken. Whether the lack of sexual activity he'd just confessed was a result of that or of the injuries themselves, she couldn't begin to guess.

The only thing she was sure of was that after a long abstinence, she was the one he had chosen to make love to, a choice that carried with it an unwitting burden. One she wondered if he was even aware of.

"In that case I hope you're right about the bicycle."

She smiled at him, seeking both to reassure him and, at the same time, to acknowledge the absurdity of her own worries. She had never met anyone who exuded more sexual magnetism.

Jeb Bedford didn't need—or want—her concern. All he wanted was the same thing she did right now. The mindless oblivion of this very human connection.

"Would you feel better with the lights off?"

He'd already started toward the lamp, making that logical assumption from her behavior. But she knew the images that waited in the darkness. She'd wrestled with them before she'd given up and fled to the comforting moonlight of the veranda.

"No, I wouldn't."

Surprised, he turned to look at her.

"The dark is full of things I don't want to think about."

He didn't ask because he knew what she feared. And that trying *not* to think about that was why she was in his room.

"Then maybe I should warn *you*."

He said nothing else, letting her puzzle out the meaning of that cryptic phrase. As she did, his eyes didn't leave her face. And seeing what was in them, she knew she was again being tested.

She had just acknowledged how terrible Jeb's wounds must have been psychologically. In only a few minutes she would be forced to confront the physical reality of them. And she had no idea what she should prepare herself for. Scars, of course, but beyond that, she was as much in the dark—

Would being in the dark be better? Safer, at least, because then there would be no chance she might betray shock or dismay. Except she wasn't a child. Or a fool.

Although the fire she'd been through was in no way similar to that Jeb had suffered, it had taught her the things in life—and in people—that mattered. Appearance wasn't one of them.

"Consider me warned," she said, smiling at him again.

Tension built in the resulting stillness, but she didn't allow her smile to falter. It wasn't important what his body looked like. She'd felt its strength. And whatever else she saw tonight, she had already seen the goodness of his soul.

Finally Jeb took a step toward her, holding out his hand. As she had on the porch, she put her fingers into his, allowing him to draw her toward the bed and the tangled sheets to which she knew would still cling the warm, clean scent of his body.

HIS FINGERS TRACED the halo of lamplight that limned the peak of her breast. Under their sensitive tips, the clear translucence of her skin was cool. Incredibly smooth.

She lay watching him, her eyes almost slate in the dimness. Her face was calm and composed. A little mysterious, even now that he knew every inch, every perfect centimeter of her body.

He had wanted to make love to her from the moment she'd handed him her car keys that first evening. He had drawn her to him tonight with such anticipation it had almost destroyed the dread that had kept him celibate through these long, painful months.

He had told himself then that he didn't have time for romantic involvement. Not of any kind. Every minute had to be devoted to the goal that had driven him since he'd awakened in the field hospital in Iraq, his body broken and helpless.

He had told himself that, and all along, on some level at least, he'd known it for a lie. He'd been afraid. Afraid of what he would see in a woman's eyes when she looked at him.

Before he'd been wounded, he would have said that, although he was guilty of a lot of sins, vanity wasn't one of them. Despite the dread with which he'd approached tonight, he still believed that. He'd had his share of women through the years, but he'd never believed his looks had a lot to do with that.

Still, having to expose his body to Susan was the hardest thing he'd ever done in his life. Far harder than the rigorous training Delta had demanded. Harder even than the long, painful hours of therapy he'd endured during the past ten months.

And because of that, he had approached it the same way he always approached something he dreaded. Or feared. Even before he had eased the lace straps off Susan's shoulders and allowed the sheer nightgown she wore to puddle at her feet, he'd methodically stripped off his own clothes. First the T-shirt, locking his fist in the material at the back of his shoulders and pulling it off over his head.

Her eyes had fallen, just as he'd known they would. And he had known exactly what she would see. He had deliberately looked at the scars that marred his chest and stomach in the mirror as he stepped out of the shower every day until they no longer had the power to repel him.

And as she'd studied them, he had refused to look down. He waited instead, anticipating what might be in her eyes when she looked up again.

When she did, there was nothing there of what he'd dreaded. No shock. No horror. No pity.

Untroubled, her gaze had held his, waiting for whatever came next. Almost defiantly he'd begun unfastening the metal buttons on the fly of his jeans. He'd worked quickly, hurrying over the task in order to hide the slight tremor that made his fingers clumsy and uncertain.

When they were finally done, he glanced up again, only to find the same calm certainty in the depths of her eyes. Still he hesitated, wondering what he'd do if this time...

Then, instead of trying to imagine either of their reactions, he pushed his thumbs inside the waistband of the worn jeans, forcing them over his hips and allowing them to fall down the length of his legs. He stepped out of them, standing before her just as he'd gone to bed hours ago, completely nude.

For an eternity she held his eyes. Afraid, after what he had already revealed, that she wouldn't be able to control her reaction this time?

"It doesn't matter," she said softly.

*Prove* it.

That challenge had been issued only in his head, but her lips tightened, as if in response. Her gaze fell, examining the damage in the cruel, revealing light of the lamp. When her eyes came up, they were again clear, seemingly undismayed.

*Now what?* He wasn't sure if he'd read that question in them or in his own mind. The only thing he *was* sure of...

He took a step, avoiding the jeans at his feet, and then another. As he approached, her chin had tilted slightly until she was looking up into his eyes.

Just as he'd stripped the waistband of his jeans over his hips, he put his thumbs under the straps of her nightgown and slipped them off her shoulders. Although she'd made no protest as the garment fell, he had expected that familiar protective gesture, her arms crossing over her breasts.

They didn't. Instead, she stood still, exactly as he had only seconds before, while his gaze examined the slender perfection of her body.

He had known she'd look like this. Her breasts small and high, despite the fact she had borne a child. There was no evidence of that pregnancy in the flat stomach or the narrow hips. Almost as if the baby she'd lost had never existed.

Except she had. She still did. Sleeping tonight within a few miles of where they now lay together.

"What are you thinking?"

Her question brought him quickly back to the present. His fingers hesitated before they renewed the journey upward, moving over the same smooth skin they had just caressed.

"How different this was from what I expected."

Her lips curved. "I told you I was out of practice."

"Not that," he said, answering her smile. "Besides, I'm not sure, given my delicate state of health, that I could deal with anything more 'practiced.'"

Release had been quick for both of them. He'd felt a ridiculous sense of relief that he hadn't exploded inside her until he'd felt the first telltale tremor of her body. It had, however, been a very close thing.

"I think what you told Doc was the truth."

"What I told Doc?" He couldn't think of anything he'd said to the old man that made sense in this context.

"That reports of your demise have been greatly exaggerated. I didn't notice anything delicate about your...responses."

"And here I was flattering myself on their subtlety."

"Subtlety wasn't on the agenda. Not for either of us," she added, her smile fading.

"Don't," he advised softly.

"Don't what?"

"Don't think about it." *Don't think about Emma.*

She took a breath, deep enough that the tip of her breast made contact with his fingers. "I thought that was your job."

To keep her from thinking. She was right. That's what this had all been about. At least at the beginning. Now...

"Do I detect a note of criticism?"

The teasing lightness of seconds ago fell flat. The life had gone out of her eyes and the curve from her lips.

The reality this interlude was designed to deny was always on the periphery, the anxiety it produced tearing at any peace she found in his arms. He understood that, but in the sweet satiation of their lovemaking, he'd forgotten those thoughts must be kept at bay. That was his job. And she couldn't know how much he relished it.

He leaned forward, putting his lips against her forehead. Her eyes followed the movement, but when he pulled back, looking down on her face, they were closed. Beneath the fan of lashes, the light from the bedside lamp illuminated a sheen of moisture.

He leaned forward again, putting his lips against the delicate skin. He kissed away the salt-sweet taste of her tears, first from one eye and then the other.

And when he leaned back this time, she opened them, again looking up into his. Her lips parted as she lifted her head.

He met her halfway, mouths aligned at the perfect angle. Their tongues engaged, mirroring the movements of the ageless duet that would follow. Thrusts and retreat.

The small niggling question that this might be happening too soon dissipated as her body moved over his, pushing him down against the mattress. Their mouths never broke contact throughout the transition.

Her hardened nipples brushed sensuously against the hair on his chest, awakening an aching need that immediately tightened his groin. It took a second or two for him to realize that the slightly guttural sound he heard had come from his own mouth.

Her hand slipped between their bodies, flattening as it slid downward. She hadn't touched him before. Not like this. As her palm encountered the first ridge of scar tissue he wondered—briefly—if that could have been why.

Although no longer painful in the normal course of

bathing or dressing, he was always aware of the traumatized nerve endings in the damaged skin and underlying muscle. The sensation of her hand moving across it was strangely erotic, pleasure balancing on the delicate edge of pain.

Something of what he was feeling must have been communicated to her, either through the sudden tension in his body or by another unconscious sound. Her hand hesitated, lifting until it was no longer in contact with his stomach.

For the first time since she'd leaned forward to meet his kiss, she raised her head enough to whisper, "What's wrong?"

He put his fingers over hers, pushing them down again until the hard ridge of scar lay under their joined hands. His breath was coming in small, audible gasps.

"Jeb?"

"Nothing." The word was breathless. Torn from his lips.

He guided her hand downward, anticipation stirring in his lower body so that he knew she must be able to feel the quick heat and strength of his erection. After a moment her fingers closed around it, again taking his breath.

His mouth found hers, trying to tell her how he felt. Trying to thank her for touching him. For all the ways she had touched him.

She moved again, her left knee sliding to the other side of his hip as her body settled over his. Her hand guided him into the sweet hot wetness created by their previous lovemaking.

He closed his eyes, feeling the silken muscles enclose him as she slowly, so slowly lowered her body. His hands found her waist. Her palms flattened against his lower chest as she leaned forward. Even the slight shift of position was enough to send him too near the edge. Too near the point of no return.

He tried to think of anything other than what she was doing. Snow-topped mountains in Afghanistan. Icy streams tumbling down rock slopes in Colorado. Cold showers.

And then she moved, her body lifting away from his so deliberately its ascension could be measured in millimeters. Each one intended to drive him mad.

His hands tightened around her waist, trying to keep her still. She ignored the entreaty, rising until he thought she'd gone too far. Hoping for that reprieve, even while praying she hadn't.

And then, before he had time to realize his prayer had been granted, she began to lower her body over his again, the wet heat of it slipping downward over his aching hardness like a glove. Enclosing him. Accepting every inch.

*Accepting him.*

The thought was enough to destroy what little control he had left. The cataclysm began before he had time to visualize any of the images that had kept his climax at bay.

Not that they would have had any effect this time. The reality of what she was doing was too powerful. Too real.

*Too late.*

His back arched, thrusting his hips upward as hers descended the last few centimeters. His fingers clenched, holding her body over his as convulsion after convulsion racked his frame. All thought of taking her with him was lost. He was conscious of nothing but the driving force of his own desire. For endless minutes it left him mindless, unable to do anything but ride out the storm of sensation.

When it had passed, leaving him breathless and again sated, he opened his eyes to find her lost in her own ecstasy. Her head was back, her eyes closed as her body shook in orgasm.

Unable to do anything else, he watched her, reveling in her release, as he had in his own. Finally her eyes opened. They were slightly glazed, almost disoriented, but when she realized he was watching her, she smiled at him.

Hands at the small of her back, he urged her forward. She lay down on top of him, her cheek against the damp, heaving muscles of his chest.

His arms tightened around her, trying to say without the words he couldn't formulate how sorry he was to have left her behind, even momentarily. The fingers of her left hand found his cheek, resting there a moment before they moved over his mouth. Although his breath was still coming between them in audible gasps, his lips pursed, kissing the tips.

He wished he could see her face, but he was too exhausted to move. And almost afraid of what he might find in her eyes.

"Sorry."

"For what?" she asked, moving her fingers again so that they lay on his opposite shoulder.

"For not waiting."

She laughed, the sound a breath.

"Waiting also *wasn't* on the agenda. I didn't expect you to. I didn't want you to."

There was nothing he could say to that, so he wisely said nothing. He held her instead, gradually feeling her heartbeat slow as did his own. Their bodies were still joined, but the connection now had nothing to do with need. At least not the kind that had driven their frenzied climaxes.

This was a mutual need for closeness. For human comfort perhaps. For love.

She stirred against him, settling her leg into a more comfortable position over his thighs. The weight of it was pleasant, her skin silken in contrast to the hair-roughened texture of his. Feminine. Right.

*As if it belonged there.*

The thought was so foreign to those that normally occupied his mind in the few minutes after good sex that he examined it again, trying to be objective. He couldn't be. He wanted her here. Not because they would make love again, but because he wanted *her* here. Because he enjoyed holding her. Comforting her. Keeping the darkness at bay.

All the darkness, both his and hers. He had never before realized this was as much a part of lovemaking as what had just happened between them physically. And never before realized how much he needed this, too.

Eyes wide in the dimness, he lay holding Susan in his arms as her breathing slowed, becoming deep and regular, her breath softly fluttering over the moisture on his skin.

As she slept against his chest, he knew he'd given

her what she wanted—freedom from thought. And what she'd given him…

What she had given him was another kind of freedom. For the first time in his adult life he was thinking more about someone else's needs and desires than his own. Thinking about someone in terms of permanency and commitment, something that would have been inconceivable to him only a few weeks ago. And thinking about what he'd found tonight rather than of what he had lost ten months ago.

# CHAPTER TWENTY-FOUR

DESPITE THOSE TERRIBLE weeks after Richard and Emma disappeared, today had ranked as the longest in Susan's memory. Unlike last night, there had been nothing Jeb could do to distract her while they waited.

As the afternoon hours had ground away, Jeb had still been determined they couldn't afford to confront Diane. Not without some authority to back up their demand that she hand over Emma. And the FBI agent from Jackson, whose name the Bureau had given her last night, had yet to return Susan's repeated calls.

Just when she thought she couldn't stand the searing anxiety a second longer, Jeb had relented, agreeing to at least drive her by Diane's house, which she'd found listed in the local phone directory. As impeccably maintained as Callaway's Victorian, the modern brick two-story sat at the end of a cul-de-sac in what was, certainly by Linton standards, an upscale neighborhood. The contrast between it and her brother's shabby bungalow was striking.

In response to Susan's pleas, Jeb had agreed to knock on the door as long as she agreed to stay in the truck. His prepared excuse, to pretend to have come to offer Lorena's condolences, wasn't needed. No one answered the door.

When he'd returned to the truck, his eyes had reflected the same fear she felt. Seeing it, she didn't have the heart to rant at him or even to say that she'd told him this would happen. He had done what he'd believed was right, and if he'd been wrong…

She refused to consider that possibility. After all, as he'd told her all day, Adams's funeral was set for tomorrow afternoon. Diane would stay long enough for that.

"The funeral home," she suggested. At least the trip back toward town would give them something to do. Something other than worry about Emma.

"You think she might be there?"

"Making the arrangements, maybe? After all, she's got to be somewhere."

It was what she'd been saying about Emma since she'd been in Linton. And she'd been right. Maybe she would be again.

The funeral director had been politely surprised by their visit, but he'd readily provided information about the sheriff's viewing and the service. He'd also confided that, under the circumstances, it would be "closed casket," of course.

When they returned to the truck this time, Jeb had sat with his hands gripping the top of the steering wheel for several long, silent minutes. A muscle flexed in his jaw as he stared unseeingly at the building they'd just left. When he turned toward her, the fear she'd seen in his eyes earlier had been replaced by determination.

"I don't believe Diane's left, but…if she has, I swear to you I'll find her. I won't rest until I do."

It was the promise Susan had tried to extract before. And she couldn't doubt its sincerity now.

"There's one more place we haven't looked," she said. "I don't know if she's there, but…I think it's somewhere she'd feel safe."

"Safe?"

"If Diane knows where and how Wayne got Emma—and we both agreed last night that by now she must at least suspect—then she has to be wondering if his death had anything to do with what happened here seven years ago."

"You think she's afraid that if someone *did* kill Wayne—"

"That she might be next. And I think the only people she would trust to make sure that didn't happen…"

Even before she had completed the thought, Jeb had started the truck, backing out of the funeral home's tree-shaded lot and heading downtown.

WHEN THEY ARRIVED at the sheriff's department, they discovered Buck Jemison had wasted no time in taking over, apparently relishing his new position. Using the pretext of the missing fax, they were quickly ushered into his office, which still had Wayne Adams's name on the door.

"Sorry, folks, but the fax doesn't seem to have turned up yet. We're still looking, though. I'm gonna send one of the boys out to Wayne's house to see if he took it home with him."

"They finished up the investigation out there?" Jeb asked.

There had been no visible activity going on when they'd driven by. The closed garage had been marked off limits to curiosity seekers with a strip of yellow caution tape.

"Pretty much. Hell of a thing to happen, but that jack was about as worn out as that '38 Chevy Wayne was so proud of. But I guess that ain't such a bad way to go, doing something you love as much as he loved working on that old truck."

"I'm sure that's a comfort to his family," Jeb managed with a straight face. "Wayne had a sister, didn't he? It seems like I remember that."

"Diane," Jemison said readily. "*And* a niece. She would have been since your time. They're pretty broken up about his death. 'Course, Wayne took care of them. We've been talking around here about pitching in to keep things up out at Diane's place."

"She didn't live with Wayne, then?" Jeb's question sounded perfectly natural, despite their recent visit.

"Diane's got a house out in Ravenswood. Subdivision probably wasn't even here the last time you were in town."

"Do you think they'll stay in Linton?" Susan asked. "Now that he's gone, I mean?"

"Why, where else would they go, Ms. Chandler?"

Jemison's mud-colored eyes expressed more interest in her question than anything else that had been said, making her wonder if Diane's departure *had* already been planned. Although if so, why she would tell Jemison—

"I'm going on home now, Buck."

They turned to find a woman standing in the doorway of what had yesterday been Adams's office. Although Jemison didn't offer an introduction, Susan knew immediately who she was.

Tall and angular as her brother, and almost as deeply

tanned, Diane Paul was dressed in a dark sweatshirt and a pair of white jeans. Her light brown hair was cut short and highlighted in chunky streaks. The only signs of her recent grief were the red-rimmed eyes, eerily reminiscent of Wayne's.

"You need me to take you?" Jemison asked.

"Byron's going to do it. Just call me later."

Buck nodded. "You try to get some rest now, you hear? Tomorrow's going to be another long, hard day."

Diane nodded, but by then her eyes had fastened on Susan. Her head tilted as if she were trying to figure out who she was.

"You're the one who found Wayne."

"Yes, I am. I'm Susan Chandler."

"Buck said you went out to Wayne's because they might have found your baby up in Randolph County."

"They found *a* baby." Susan wanted to add "but she wasn't mine." Only Jeb's eyes, harder than she'd ever seen them, prevented her.

"I don't know what I'd do if something like that happened to my daughter," Diane said. "I can't even bear to think about it. Especially not after what happened to Wayne."

Although the words were appropriate enough in the situation, there was something about them that seemed almost challenging. While Susan was trying to figure out how she could possibly answer them, Diane turned back to Jemison.

"I'll see you later, Buck."

"Don't forget what we talked about," he said.

"No, I won't. I'll call you later."

Diane looked at Jeb assessingly before she smiled

at him. "You're Jeb Bedford, aren't you? I heard you were home. Welcome back."

Susan couldn't decide if Diane was making a play for Jeb or for Jemison. Or maybe this was the only way she knew how to relate to men. That slightly flirtatious-schoolgirl approach.

"Ms. Paul," Jeb said.

The smile widened, but when Jeb didn't return it, Diane turned back to Susan. "Good luck finding your baby."

"She's a little girl now."

"She would be, wouldn't she? I guess I didn't think. Well, good luck finding her."

"Thank you."

"See you later, Buck," Diane said again.

This time she made good her departure. No one said anything for a few seconds after she'd disappeared down the hall.

"Funeral's at two tomorrow," Jemison informed them. "Hopewell Baptist. I guess Miz Lorena will be there."

"My aunt seldom misses a funeral," Jeb said. "I think it's some form of self-congratulation."

"Self-congratulation?"

"That it isn't hers."

Jemison laughed. "What is she now? Pushing ninety? She's liable to outlive us all."

Especially if jacks keep falling on people or if they go off bridges and into the river, Susan thought.

"About that. Let us know as soon as that fax turns up, will you? Ms. Chandler is eager to put all this behind her."

"I understand," Jemison said, his eyes meeting hers again. "I'll get a couple of people onto looking for it right away."

"WHAT DID YOU THINK?" she asked as soon as they were back in the truck.

"About what?"

"About Diane."

"I don't think there's any doubt she knows."

"About Emma?"

"I thought she was warning you off."

Susan wasn't sure what she had wanted him to say in response to her question, but it was disturbing to hear that his reading of Diane's attitude so clearly mirrored hers.

"I didn't like that cryptic exchange with Buck. It felt like they had something already set up. Maybe he's going to help her try to get Emma out of town."

"Why don't you call the FBI again?"

Jeb's lack of reassurance was frightening, considering he'd been the one assuring her that Diane wasn't going anywhere. If he no longer believed that...

"Let's drive out to her house again and see if she picked Emma up on her way home."

"What about the FBI?"

"I'll call them on the way."

DESPITE THE NUMBER of times she had now called the Jackson office, she jumped when her cell phone finally rang. She reached out, grabbing it off the console. Despite her eagerness, she hesitated, trying to control her breathing, before she flipped open the case.

"Hello?"

"Ms. Chandler? Susan Chandler?"

"That's right."

"This is Special Agent Rob Hill, Ms. Chandler. How are you, ma'am?"

"Very anxious to know when you'll arrive in Linton," Susan said. "I've been trying to reach you all day. Did they explain the situation to you?"

"Yes, ma'am, they did, and—"

"Then you understand that every minute could be critical. There's no way I can stop this woman from taking my daughter and leaving the area. Her brother was the former sheriff here, and the local department won't step into this. Not if it means taking Emma away from her."

"Emma? That's your daughter."

"That's right. Emma Kaiser. She's been listed as missing for the last seven years."

"This was a parental abduction, right?"

He was probably reading that from the old case file. Susan took a deep breath, trying to control the automatic anger that term provoked.

"That's what we believed at the time, but now that her father's body has been found, we know that isn't true. I believe that the sheriff here may have taken Emma when he found my husband's body."

"That would be Sheriff Adams. He's the one whose body you found last night."

"That's right. He may even have had a hand in Richard's murder. In any case, however it happened, he ended up with Emma, and now his sister—"

"Richard? That would be your husband?"

"Look, I know this is complicated. I told whoever I spoke to last night it was. I'll be glad to go over it all again when you arrive."

"Actually, ma'am, before I called you back, I spoke to the Johnson County sheriff myself."

"The sheriff? But…"

"Sorry. I should have said the *acting* sheriff."

"Buck Jemison."

There was a crackle of paper as Hill apparently checked the name against his notes. "That's right. Henry Jemison."

"So you've already explained the situation to him."

For the first time since she'd picked up the photograph off Adams's desk, the tightness in her chest eased. No matter how much his newly acquired authority had gone to his head, Jemison would have to listen to the FBI. They had jurisdiction in a kidnapping, and Emma had long been on their list of victims.

"Have you *talked* to the sheriff's office this afternoon, Ms. Chandler?"

At something in the disembodied voice, the tension that had begun to ease was suddenly back in force. She couldn't even think to tell him she had just left there.

"What's wrong?" She fought to control the surge of panic she couldn't explain.

When Hill responded, his voice was imbued with compassion. "It seems the sheriff's department received a fax from the state forensics lab yesterday afternoon."

Somehow she knew what Special Agent Rob Hill was going to say before his words came across the line. They were words she had feared for more than seven years. Words she had thought last night she need never fear again.

"I'm terribly sorry, Ms. Chandler, but according to the DNA test the state lab performed, it turns out that the body the officials in Randolph County found and subsequently interred was indeed your daughter."

# CHAPTER TWENTY-FIVE

"HOW DID JEMISON THINK he could get away with that?" Susan asked. She was holding on to the grip above the door as Jeb took the last in a series of hairpin curves far too fast.

"Remember, he only has to get away with it long enough to carry out whatever he and Diane have got planned. If he can keep the FBI at bay until then…" He let the sentence trail in order to concentrate on the winding road that led out to the subdivision they'd visited only a couple of hours ago.

As soon as Jeb had taken the phone away from Susan, who'd obviously been stunned by whatever Hill had told her, it had taken only a quick comparison of the times Jemison had told his conflicting stories to prove that the acting sheriff had lied. It would have been to Buck's advantage to convince Susan that what he had told the FBI was true. Since he hadn't tried to do that, despite the fact that they'd been in his office less than fifteen minutes ago, the logical conclusion was that he hadn't produced the fax because it didn't say what he had claimed.

After Jeb had explained to the FBI agent what he believed was going on in Johnson County, using all the persuasive power and presence of command he had acquired during his years in the Army, Hill had promised to get down there as quickly as he could. They'd all known, however, that it wouldn't be quick enough to prevent what Jeb was now convinced was going to happen. Not tomorrow after the funeral as he'd thought, but tonight.

"Jeb."

He had been slowing to make the entry into the subdivision where Diane lived. Something in Susan's voice caused him to turn to find her looking out the back window of the truck.

He glanced up into the rearview mirror, but the two-lane was deserted as far back as he could see. "What is it?"

"That truck that just pulled out…"

He looked up into the mirror once more, this time spotting the black pickup that had passed them, headed in the opposite direction. It must have come out of the neighborhood street they were about to enter.

Thinking about what might lie ahead, Jeb hadn't paid any attention to it until Susan's comment. He watched until the vehicle disappeared around the curve he'd just negotiated before he looked back at her.

"What about it?"

She shook her head slightly, staring out through the front windshield as he guided the truck through the turn. "I don't know. It just seemed… I think it could be the one that chased me that night."

Whatever he had expected her to say, it wasn't that. His eyes automatically lifted to the mirror again, but there was no longer any sign of the pickup.

"What made you think that?" She'd seen it only at night. And in a situation that hadn't lent itself to noting details.

"I don't know. Something about the headlights. Or the size. It just…" She shook her head again, almost as if she were trying to convince herself she was mistaken.

"The headlights?"

"They were on. Something about them…looked familiar."

Even though the sun hovered just above the horizon, the pickup was new enough that it would have been equipped with automatic lights. That was about all he could tell from the glimpse he'd gotten. That and the color.

The night Susan had been forced off the road, she had described the truck as big and dark. The one that had just pulled out of Diane's neighborhood had been both. Not as large as his vehicle, perhaps, but close. Neither characteristic, however, seemed like grounds for a positive identification.

"There are a hell of a lot of pickups down here."

"I know. It doesn't matter."

He made the second turn, approaching the spot where he'd parked before. Only the side of Diane's house was visible from this point, along with a small section of browning lawn.

Instead of stopping, Jeb pulled into the cul-de-sac, realizing immediately what was different from the last time he'd seen the house. The garage door was up, the space inside empty.

He didn't look at Susan, unsure whether she understood the implications. He didn't have long to wonder.

"Her car's gone," Susan said. "She's gone to get Emma. I know it."

He didn't argue. He gunned the engine instead, sending the truck shooting around the narrow cul-de-sac.

"Oh, God, Jeb, that pickup."

As he approached the entrance, he expected to see the vehicle returning. There was nothing there.

"What about it?"

"It's hers," Susan said. "It's Diane's. *She's* the one who didn't want me asking questions. She's the one who tried to run me off the road."

The conclusions fell into place like the missing pieces of a nearly completed puzzle. Of all the people in Linton, Diane Paul had the most to lose from Susan's questions. Only she and Wayne knew what had happened the night Richard died. And both had done their best to discourage Susan from her attempts to find out. Now one of them was dead, and the other...

Without bothering to articulate any of that, he floored the accelerator, sending the truck out into the neighborhood street with a squeal of tires. Although there were a limited number of roads around Linton, if he didn't catch up with the black pickup and keep in visual contact with it, there was a good chance he might lose her. And if he did...

"Hold on," he warned, roaring toward the turn that would put them out of the residential section and back on the state highway. He took it as fast as he dared, the Avalanche hugging the curve as he pushed the accelerator down again.

"Jeb."

He took his eyes off the road a second to glance toward Susan again. The way she'd said his name hadn't sounded like a protest of his speed.

"What?" he asked, eyes back on the road as he urged the truck along at a speed far faster than he normally drove.

"Maybe she's the one who called me."

It took a second. "To come to the playground that night?"

"It was a woman's voice on the phone. It might have been a woman wielding that bat."

He didn't know a lot about Adams's sister, but a mother desperate to hold on to her child was probably capable of anything. Even if the child she was trying to keep wasn't hers. Maybe more so if that were the case.

Despite the speed at which he was driving, Jeb couldn't see any sign of the black pickup ahead. And they were rapidly approaching the Linton turnoff. Both roads would eventually lead to Pascagoula, the narrow two-lane Richard had taken going through the center of town and the other, the more modern four-lane, although longer, going straight to the city. If the truck he was looking for had already reached that fork…

He topped a slight rise, looking down on it. In the gathering twilight there was no other vehicle in sight. And no way to know which road Diane Paul had chosen.

"What is it?" Susan asked as he slowed.

"I'm not sure which way she went."

"Into town," Susan said. As if there was no doubt.

Without questioning her reasoning, he swung the Avalanche into the turn that would take them through Linton.

"She's going to pick up Emma."

He hoped to hell Susan was right. Because if she wasn't, by the time they backtracked, it would be full dark. There would be no way to recognize that pickup in the traffic on the state road. It would be like looking for a needle in a haystack.

Or, to make an even more frighteningly appropriate analogy, it would be like looking for a little girl who'd been hidden among a dozen others in a place no one ever expected her to be.

"MAYBE SHE WAS STAYING with a friend from school," Susan said, peering into the growing darkness as they drove through the heart of the small community.

Jeb didn't bother to comment, trying to catch sight of the pickup they'd sought through these narrow streets. There was nothing wrong with Susan's speculation, except they had no way to know which friend, which street, or even the direction in which they should be searching.

"Jeb, look."

He turned in time to see taillights disappear at the other end of a side road. Surely Susan wasn't suggesting she could recognize Diane's pickup from it taillights.

"You think that's it?"

"I think it may be," she said, her voice full of excitement. "There isn't that much traffic. Maybe…"

By the time she'd finished the second sentence, he'd begun to turn the truck, swinging it around to make a U-turn in the middle of the narrow street. Although he had to back up and then complete the arc, it was a matter of seconds before he was headed toward the place where Susan had spotted the taillights.

When he reached the end of that street, his instinct was to turn right, which would take them back toward Diane's house. As he turned his head to the left, however, checking for oncoming traffic, he saw a flicker of red wink out in the darkness.

Feeling strongly that if Diane *had* come into town to pick up her daughter, she should now be headed home, he looked to his right again. And into black, unbroken night. Without asking Susan's opinion, he turned left and then gunned the big truck.

"Where do you think she's going?" she asked.

"Obviously not home."

"Maybe that wasn't her."

Maybe not, but their options were running out. The thing Susan had feared, the thing he'd assured her wouldn't happen, seemed to be coming to pass. And unless they got lucky...

For endless minutes they rode in silence, their eyes straining for any sign of the pickup that seemed to have vanished into thin air. As they approached the small downtown section, better illuminated because of its streetlights, he slowed, eyes searching every parking lot and side street.

When he spotted the black truck, it was parked exactly where he should have expected it to be. At the Johnson County Sheriff's Department.

He slowed, trying to see if there was anyone inside. The angle of the light streaming from the windows of the sheriff's office didn't reach out that far, however.

"That's it," he said as he drove by. He turned right

at the corner, planning to circle the block and then park where he could keep an eye on the vehicle.

"What's she doing?"

"Maybe arranging protection."

"From us?"

"Or from whoever killed her brother."

"But if Jemison—"

"All we know is that Jemison didn't tell the truth about the fax. Maybe he did that to protect Diane as much as to keep the FBI out of this."

"You don't believe that," Susan said.

"At this point, I'm not sure of anyone's motives. All I know is that someone in this town knows why Richard was murdered that night. And that Diane Paul is the only link that can lead us back to his killer."

"And to Emma."

*If we're lucky...*

He eased the Avalanche into one of the parallel-parking spots across the street and down the block from the sheriff's department, killing the lights. All they could do now was wait. And hope they were right about Diane's ownership of the pickup they were watching.

It didn't take long for that to be confirmed. Less than ten minutes after they'd begun their vigil, the door to the office opened. Diane, recognizable by the pale jeans she'd been wearing as well as by her height, stepped through it. She was followed by a little girl and then by Buck Jemison, easily identifiable by his size.

"Jeb." Susan's low whisper was filled with excitement.

"I see them."

He assumed that Buck would escort the two out to

the truck. Instead, as Diane opened the passenger-side door for the child, Jemison crawled into the driver's seat, starting the pickup before Diane could get the door closed. He backed out of the lot and, in another surprising move, headed out of town in the opposite direction from Diane's house.

"Now what?" Susan asked.

Jeb pulled the truck out of the space, leaving the headlights off as he followed. "I don't know," he said truthfully.

All he knew was that two of the three people connected to whatever had happened the night Richard Kaiser died were in the vehicle ahead of them. And that wherever they were headed, he didn't intend to lose them.

"THAT'S WHERE Richard's car went off."

Although she'd remained silent while they followed Diane's pickup through the darkness, something about the entrance to the bridge where her husband died had wrenched the sentence from her. It was as if tonight they were repeating the journey he and Emma had made seven years ago. With the same outcome?

She held her breath as Jeb negotiated the treacherous turn with only the moonlight to guide him. The red taillights still beckoned in the distance. Only someone who knew the road with a long and intimate familiarity could do what Jeb was doing.

After perhaps twenty minutes the Avalanche began to slow, causing her to look away from the twin dots so far ahead. Jeb was leaning forward, his hands positioned high on either side of the steering wheel, the tension of trying to follow those taillights through the darkness visible in his posture.

"What is it?"

"They're slowing," he said.

"Out here? For what?"

"I don't know."

She stared through the windshield again, realizing what he obviously had. No longer pinpoints, the telltale oval shape of the lights she'd recognized were once again becoming distinct.

Jeb continued to let the Avalanche lose momentum gradually rather than using the brakes. As they watched, the taillights disappeared off to the right of the two-lane.

Unable to risk using his own headlights, Jeb missed the dirt track Jemison had taken, running by it in the darkness. Just as he had the night Lorena had sent him to find her after Diane ran her off the road, he swung the his truck in a wide arc, using both shoulders of the road to turn it.

"Hurry," she urged, unable to bear the thought of what might be going on at the other end of that dirt track. Instead of turning into it, however, Jeb parked the Avalanche as far off the shoulder on the other side of the two-lane as he could.

"Come on," he said as he opened the driver's-side door. He was out before she could find the handle, waiting for her when she came around the back of the truck.

"I think it's safer if we walk."

"Wouldn't it be quicker to drive?"

"The river parallels this road. They aren't going far."

The implications of that had barely sunk in before his hand in the small of her back urged her forward.

They crossed the deserted two-lane at a run, entering the shadowed track down which the pickup had disappeared.

After only a few steps she discovered its major component was sand rather than dirt, and that the shoes she wore, the same leather moccasins she'd worn that night on the playground, were less than suitable for this. Even with his limp, Jeb had to slow his pace so she could keep up.

She peered through the darkness around them, trying to find the pickup. The thickness of the foliage that surrounded the trail they followed, as well as the over-arching branches, festooned with Spanish moss, blocked the moonlight.

"Shh..." Jeb's hand on her arm reinforced his warning.

The track, large enough for the passage of one vehicle, had begun to widen. Beyond the end lay a clearing, centered by a sprawling structure that hugged the riverbank, visible behind it. The pattern of moonlight on the slow-moving water was broken by patches of marsh grasses and the long stumps of rotting trees.

"What is this?"

Despite the softness of her whispered question, Jeb's fingers tightened over her arm. He shook his head, the motion abrupt. She wasn't sure if it were intended as a warning not to talk or as an acknowledgment that he knew as little about the structure as she did.

Applying pressure to the wrist he held, he pulled her with him, continuing to hug the edge of the woods surrounding the clearing. They moved to the right of the building, which she had now identified as either a fishing camp or summer cabin.

After they'd gone only a few feet, she could see the pickup parked at its back. There was no sign of the occupants. Beyond the truck, a wooden pier stretched over the marsh and out into the river.

The sight of that dark water created a coldness in the pit of her stomach. Although she had never seen it at night, she knew this must be very much like the area around the bridge where Richard's car had been pushed into this same river.

Was that what Jemison planned for Diane? Was that why he'd driven Diane's car here rather than following in the cruiser?

A noise, sounding like a stifled scream, tore her attention from the river. It was followed by a solid thump, like wood striking wood, and then by a muffled curse, clearly masculine.

Jeb reacted more quickly than she did. She grabbed at him as he ran by her, and then she saw what he must already have seen.

Across the opening in the trees where the moon revealed the dark, marshy waters darted a small figure. Before her mind could remember the name her daughter might recognize, Susan became aware of the man who followed her. Jemison's size and longer stride made the outcome of the chase obvious. And inevitable.

She began to run, following Jeb, who was perhaps ten or twelve yards ahead of her now. Again her eyes strained through the darkness, trying to distinguish the little girl against the backdrop of misshapen stumps and tall grasses.

"Alex," she called. "It's all right. We're here."

Although Jeb didn't slow, she knew he would have preferred that she not warn Jemison of their presence. He would have known soon enough, however, and the thought of Emma's terror was enough to drive any other consideration from her mind.

Whether it was the sound of her voice or the promise of the words, the little girl hesitated, turning to look for her.

"Run, Alex. Run," Jeb shouted.

Emma started to obey, but not before she had instinctively glanced behind her, searching for her pursuer. The motion of her daughter's head drew Susan's gaze back to Jemison as well.

The moonlight that glinted off the water behind Emma now also captured the sheen of metal of the upraised cane knife he carried in his right hand.

## CHAPTER TWENTY-SIX

THERE WAS NO TIME to try anything else. And every second of Jeb's professional life had prepared him to make that decision.

Ignoring the agony in his shattered ankle, a pain so intense that not even the adrenaline flooding his system could block it, he sprinted across the last few yards that separated them. He launched himself at Jemison as the deputy brought the cane cutter up over his head.

Jeb hit the deputy low, taking the man's legs out from under him. The momentum of his run drove both of them backward toward the river.

Although he anticipated the blow, the thought of the damage the heavy blade might inflict was not even a consideration. All he cared about was getting the weapon far enough away from Emma that she was no longer within its range.

As soon as he made contact with his enemy, he deliberately forced any concern about the child from his mind. His job was to disarm or disable her assailant. He couldn't do that without focusing entirely on the fight he was engaged in.

Susan would take care of her daughter. All she had to do was to hide her until—

They hit the ground together, the air rushing out of Jemison's lungs in a satisfying whoosh as Jeb's body landed solidly on his chest and stomach. The force of the fall wasn't enough to keep the larger man from attempting to roll—carrying Jeb with him—in order to put himself on top.

That the maneuver had begun so immediately was either the result of the well-honed instincts of a street fighter or professional training. Jeb hadn't wanted to discover either in an opponent. Especially not one who outweighed him by fifty pounds and was still armed.

Even as he denied Jemison's attempt to put him on the ground, Jeb lunged upward over the deputy's body, searching for the wrist of the hand that held the machete-like blade. With his other hand, he reached for Jemison's eyes, trying to get his stiffened fingers into their sockets.

Again his assailant attempted to throw him off, bucking under his weight like a bronc gone mad. In response, Jeb slammed the heel of his hand down as hard as he could on the middle of his face. He felt bone give as Jemison's nose broke under the blow.

The shock of it seemed to infuriate the deputy, giving renewed strength and determination to his efforts. By now the fingers of Jeb's left hand were locked around the wrist of Jemison's right. He banged it repeatedly on the ground, trying to loosen the other man's grip on the cane knife.

At the same time, the fingers of Jeb's right hand were again reaching for Jemison's eyes. The fist that connected with his temple was expected, but the blow was surprisingly powerful, enough to cause his ears to ring and the air to thin and darken around his head for a few seconds.

The roundhouse swing gave Jeb the opening he needed. He managed to poke two fingers into his opponent's eye. With a roar of rage, the deputy wrenched his hand out of Jeb's grip, regaining control of the machete.

As soon as he felt that wrist slip from his grasp, Jeb threw himself to the side and continued the roll, taking him away from Jemison's body.

As soon as he'd put enough distance between them to escape the reach of the blade he scrambled to his feet. Jemison was also attempting to rise and momentarily vulnerable. Wishing he were wearing boots, Jeb kicked out, striking the deputy solidly in the ribs with the toe of his shoe.

Once again he thought he'd felt bone snap, but he couldn't be sure. As soon as his foot connected, he had had to dodge the backswing of the cane knife. Its razor-sharp tip sliced through his jeans and seared a path across his thigh.

*Not life-threatening.* His evaluation of the injury was instantaneous. One he'd been trained to make automatically.

This cut wasn't serious enough to slow him down. Not under normal circumstances. Except he was rapidly discovering these were anything but normal. And given the extent of the wounds he'd suffered in Iraq, he was forced to acknowledge they might never be again.

This, then, was to be the test he'd hoped never to face, not even if he'd been allowed to rejoin his unit. The kind of hand-to-hand, physical combat in which he had once believed he could hold his own against anyone.

*Please, God, let that still be true...*

Jemison was on his feet, the weapon held in front of him. Like wary dogs, they faced one another in the moonlight, their bodies crouched slightly forward. Arms away from their sides. Alert for any movement.

Jemison struck first. The sweep of the hooked blade was close enough that Jeb had to jump back, feeling the force of its passage through the air in front of him. His damaged ankle protested the awkward landing, causing him to stagger slightly.

Jemison didn't miss the opportunity. He swung the cane knife again, the deadly tip missing Jeb's chest by a hairsbreadth, driving him farther back toward the water.

Its length was too great an advantage. The deputy could keep him at a distance, forced to dodge until his damaged leg betrayed him. One slip in the mud of the riverbank, one more awkward landing, and Jeb knew he would go down.

Jemison was too good not to take advantage of that kind of mistake. Too proficient at what he had come here tonight to do.

Jeb tried to think of something he could use to counter the attacks that were becoming increasingly bold as his opponent realized his vulnerabilities. The odds were all in Jemison's favor, and unless he could change them...

The sudden thought seemed too simple. The more he considered it, however, the more sense it made. He'd always been good in the water. He'd grown up around it, and his Delta training had only heightened his confidence.

Underwater, the machete became an ineffective weapon. More important than that, the disadvantage of his damaged leg would be minimized.

Just at that moment Jemison changed tactics, apparently tiring of thrust and parry. He charged with the blade raised over his head rather than swiping with it at Jeb's body. Realizing that he had no other option but the river, Jeb turned and ran for it, trying to catch a glimpse of Emma or Susan in the darkness as he did.

He couldn't see them. That didn't mean they weren't there, of course. And Jemison was still focused on him, which meant they would have a few more minutes to find a hiding place in case this didn't work.

He ran across the wooden planks of the pier, his footsteps more uneven than usual due to pain and fatigue. He tried to judge by sound how far behind him the deputy was. All he had to do was to keep more than the length of the blade between them until he reached the end of the pier.

He had no idea how deep the river was here at this season, but he didn't have the luxury of worrying about it. It was clear from the sound of feet thudding over the boards that Jemison was gaining on him. Since the original separation between them had been a matter of feet rather than yards, any narrowing of that distance put Jeb in immediate danger of having the blade of the cane cutter buried in his skull.

He made it almost to the end of the pier before he decided his luck had run out. With the next step he vaulted off the side, pulling his legs up under him as tightly as he could.

He struck water at once, praying it would be deep enough. As it closed over his head, he began to swim, the powerful, controlled crawl he'd been taught as a child in this same river propelling him toward its center channel.

As he turned his head to make the next stroke, bringing the side of his head out of the water, he strained to hear the splash that would signal Jemison's entry. He heard nothing. At the end of the next stroke, he rotated his body in the water, changing to a backstroke as his gaze frantically searched the empty pier and then the riverbank.

It was possible Jemison had plunged in while Jeb was still underwater. Or maybe he was familiar enough with the river here to feel confident about diving in. If so, then he might be gliding toward him right now through the dark, concealing water.

Still on his back, Jeb slowed enough to raise his head, studying the smooth flow of the current around him. He looked for the telltale signs of cross motion or for a trail of bubbles. Despite the flood of moonlight, he spotted neither.

The bastard had to be somewhere out here. He couldn't believe Jemison would just let him go in order to try to find Emma. Besides, there was no doubt in his mind Susan would have taken advantage of the distraction to get the little girl safely hidden, hopefully making that scenario impossible.

*So where the hell is Jemison?* His eyes scanned the bank again, this time tracking toward the low building.

If Diane was inside, it was obvious by now that she'd been incapacitated. That had probably been the scream they'd heard, either hers or the child's reaction. Maybe Jemison had planned all along to kill Diane first, believing Emma would be an easier target with her mother out of the way.

Except Emma had turned the tables on him. She had gotten away, once more cheating the death that had been planned.

Warned either by some subliminal sound or by his own well-defined instincts, he turned just in time to see Jemison's head and shoulders break the surface behind him. The deputy popped up like a cork, towering above him for a heartbeat.

As soon as he emerged, however, Jemison was forced to suck air into lungs starved for it by his long underwater swim. Taking advantage of his need, Jeb dove, opening his eyes to a world that was far darker than that above.

It took a second or two before he was able to see anything. And then the pale khaki of the uniform he wore betrayed Jemison's location, almost directly in front of him.

With a couple of kicks, Jeb was able to reach the deputy. He wrapped his arms around the other man's hips, jerking him down under the water again. He hoped he'd been quick enough to catch his opponent with his mouth open, still sucking in what he had believed would be lifesaving oxygen.

Whatever the results, it didn't prevent the deputy from mounting a powerful resistance. He struggled against Jeb's hold, kicking at him ineffectually as Jeb held on grimly, dragging Jemison down with him by slowly releasing the air he'd grabbed just before his own dive.

He had once known to the second how long he could stay underwater. Of course, that had been when he was in training. In shape. *Perfect.*

It didn't really matter, he told himself doggedly. Nothing mattered but ensuring that if one of them emerged from the river to search for Susan and Emma, it wouldn't be Jemison.

He was suddenly aware of a bone-numbing blow to the back of his shoulder. It was far stronger than those water-deadened kicks, but it was not until Jemison began to struggle to pull out the knife he'd stabbed him with in order to use it again that Jeb realized what had happened.

First the cane cutter and then a knife. The deputy had obviously come prepared to kill and to kill silently.

Sound traveled along the river, especially at night. Shots would be heard. They might even be reported. And they were no longer in Johnson County.

Jeb locked the fingers of his right hand around Jemison's belt, freeing his left to knock away the arm that had wielded the knife. The wound in his back didn't hurt, but he had no idea how deep it was or how much it was bleeding. And it was the inevitable weakness that would come with blood loss he had to fear.

He had managed to get his left arm over Jemison's right, pinning it against the other man's side. The position gave him less control, and the deputy's struggles had become more frenzied. Apparently he had reached his limits for lack of air.

Only a few more seconds, Jeb told himself. Panic would set in, and that's when the bastard would try to breathe, taking in the tepid, brackish water of the river instead of the blessed oxygen he wanted. Only a few more seconds...

Jemison began to kick again, this time trying to propel himself to the surface. He twisted and turned, fighting to free himself from the weight of Jeb's body, which continued to drag him down.

*A few more seconds...*

Jeb's own lungs burned with a raw, aching need that seemed more powerful even than his will to survive. He knew what would happen if he attempted to take the breath they screamed for. If he gave in to that desperate urge, he would lose.

*And so would Emma and Susan.*

Better that he and Jemison both die in the shadowy depths of the river than that Jemison should be the one to survive. All he had to do to prevent that was to hang on, despite the increasingly frantic thrashing of his opponent.

The desire to give up and shoot upward for the surface had become almost unbearable. He would take only one breath. Just one. Just one.

He could pull Jemison under again, his madness reasoned. And this time he'd last him out. This time—

Suddenly there was a change in the frenetic movements of the man he held. His stomach expanded, moving outward against Jeb's chest. His frame seemed to shudder and then convulse, before finally going limp in his arms.

Still Jeb hung on. They began to sink together, going down farther and farther into the pitch-black darkness.

He could no longer remember why it was important he hold on. He only knew it was. A matter of life and death, but he couldn't remember whose life was involved.

The water no longer seemed cold. It was almost comforting to sink into its warm depths. Safe. Familiar. Soothing.

*Snug as a bug in a rug.* The phrase, so quintessentially Southern, echoed in his mind. And he knew it was Gladys Caffrey's voice that said the words.

She'd been talking to Susan. Talking about Emma the night Richard had brought her into the store. Telling Susan that—

*Susan.* Susan and Emma were waiting up there for him. He'd done what he had set out to do. Jemison was dead. All he had to do now...

With arms so numb they seemed to belong to someone else, he released the body. He watched it fall away from him until he couldn't see the pale uniform anymore. Then he looked up, finding only darkness there as well.

With an effort that seemed beyond his strength, he moved one foot and then the other, feeling his body begin to rise as he kicked. Almost without his conscious direction, his arms began to move too, pushing water away from his body as it rose.

The pressure in his chest was unbearable. Beyond pain. Beyond need. There was no way that he would be able to keep doing this. Not another second. Not another heartbeat.

His lungs were on fire, and still there was no sign of light above him. He must surely be nearing the surface by now, he thought, unless somehow during the struggle with Jemison he'd become disoriented. He'd heard of that happening to divers. Was it possible that instead of swimming upward, he was sinking toward the bottom of the channel...and to his death?

Just as he had begun to despair, he burst into the cool night air, trying to pull it in almost before he'd cleared the surface. Long, whooping gasps filled his lungs with lifesaving oxygen, soothing their agony of deprivation. As it did, the fog that had enclosed his brain began to clear.

Despite the fact that he had felt Jemison's body go slack, had felt it slide into the cold, black heart of the river, he turned in a tight circle, looking across the water in every direction. Expecting the deputy to slip up behind him just as before.

The harshness of his own breathing was the only sound in the stillness surrounding him. There was no sign of Jemison. No movement disturbed the flow of the river but his own tired dog paddle, designed to do nothing more than to keep him afloat.

The danger was over. For all of them.

Only when that sank in did he become aware of the depth of his exhaustion. His eyes searched for the pier and saw that the current had carried him past it and into the center of the river perhaps a hundred feet, a distance that seemed insurmountable.

It was the only way to get back to Susan, he told himself. He had to swim to the end of the pier and then drag his body up the wooden slats that had been nailed to one of the pilings.

He lifted his arm to take the first stroke and was forcibly reminded of the wound in his back. *Only pain.* Something with which he had a long and intimate relationship.

And this would be dealt with the same way he had dealt with all the others. With a dogged determination to ignore it and get on with the task at hand.

One more repetition with the weights, despite damaged muscles that trembled with fatigue. Another hour on the stationary bike, pushing his body until the salt of his own sweat and tears blinded him.

This was no different, he told himself as he began to swim. All he had to do was take one stroke at a time, each carrying him nearer the end of this nightmare.

A nightmare that hadn't been his. At least not in the beginning. And now was.

With the next stroke he lifted his head above the water far enough to locate the pier. It beckoned in the moonlight, perhaps half the distance it had been when he'd started.

He didn't dare look up again. He was afraid that if he did, he would once more feel that seductive pull just to let go and let the river support him. Just to let the waters cushion his aching body.

He was surprised when his fingers brushed the rough, creosote-treated piling. He wrapped one arm around it and rested his cheek against its cool, solid wood, hanging on until his breathing eased.

Then, keeping a hand on the ends of the boards, he moved along the pier to the primitive ladder, grasping one of the narrow two-by-fours that had been nailed to the piling. Beside them hung a weathered sign, made from the same planks as the pier. It was obviously intended to identify the property to anyone arriving by boat.

There was one word painted on it in script. *Invictus*.

The name nagged at him, but he was too tired to remember why. Maybe he'd seen it in the days when he and his friends had skied the river all summer. At least knowing the name of the house would give the locals a place to start searching for Jemison's body.

Giving up the puzzle of the familiar word as too difficult to solve right now, he dragged himself up the ladder, crawling onto the boards of the pier, still warm from the afternoon sun.

He fought the urge to simply sprawl facedown on them. To lie against that warmth, absorbing it through his chilled skin. To rest. Just to lie here for one brief minute before he went to find Susan and Emma. After all, there was no hurry now. And nothing left to fear.

He closed his eyes, almost giving in to the lethargy. He opened them again, knowing there was something he still had to do. Something—

*Susan.*

He tried to push his torso off the planks by straightening his arms and locking his elbows. The wound in the back of his shoulder protested, the skin seeming to tear further with the movement. Reminding him.

Given his exhaustion and growing disorientation, he knew he had lost a lot of blood. And that he was running out of time.

He needed to find Susan. She could fashion some kind of pad to staunch the bleeding until they could get to Pascagoula. Susan could drive.

All he had to do…

He managed to get to his hands and knees, head hanging as he swayed slightly from side to side. With an effort that pushed air from his lungs and through his open mouth in a moan, he got to his knees, one hand against the pier for balance.

The house on the bank was still dark. There was no sign of life anywhere.

*No sign of life.* The words echoed in his head, just as the name on the wooden sign had done.

Except he knew Susan and her daughter were out there somewhere. He had done what he'd set out to accomplish. He'd kept Jemison away from them. Now, all he had to do was to find where they were hiding and get them out of here.

He climbed to his feet, staggering a few yards before he seemed to get feeling back into his legs. One step at a time. That's all he had to do. Just as he'd done everything else for the last year. One slow, painful step at a time.

# CHAPTER TWENTY-SEVEN

SUSAN WASN'T SURE which was worse—knowing nothing about what was going on or knowing just enough to be completely terrified. Or maybe recognizing she couldn't do anything to influence the outcome of what was happening.

She pulled Emma closer, laying her cheek against the top of the little girl's head. Her hair smelled of shampoo and the sweet warmth of children in summer.

She closed her eyes, reminding herself that if she tried to help Jeb, she would reveal their hiding place, giving Emma over to whoever intended to kill her. No matter what was happening out in the river, there was no way she could do that.

She couldn't sacrifice Emma's life, now that she'd finally found her. Not even to save Jeb's. And he would never expect her to, although there was small comfort in that knowledge.

"Susan?"

She held her breath, waiting for the call to be repeated. Wanting to reevaluate the voice to be absolutely certain it had been Jeb's. If he was calling for her to come out of hiding, then that must mean—

"Susan? It's okay. It's over."

Beneath the protection of her arm, Emma shivered, trying to burrow closer to her side. "It's all right," Susan whispered. "That's Jeb. He's…"

There were no words that could express what Jeb had become to her in these few short days. Someone who had bought into her certainty that her daughter was still alive. Someone who had risked his life to help find her. Someone who even now—

"Susan." The voice was closer, its tone impatient.

"Come on." She took Emma's hand to draw her out of the tall grasses at the verge of the river where they'd hidden.

Their shoes made sucking noises as they splashed through the shallow water of the marsh. She hadn't spotted Jeb, but then there were a lot of trees along the bank here. That had been one reason she'd chosen this spot. The shadows their moss-hung branches cast would make it harder for anyone to see them.

"We're here," she called, pitching her voice to carry through the stillness.

Although Emma had been trailing behind obediently, she suddenly resisted the pull of Susan's hand. Surprised, she turned back to find that the child wasn't looking at her. Instead, she was staring toward the low structure Susan had noticed when they'd first reached the clearing.

"What is it?" she asked, glancing from the building back to Emma before she remembered.

The little girl had been brought here by the woman she believed to be her mother. Whatever happened before she and Jeb arrived must have taken place in that house. Given the scream they'd heard, Susan was afraid she knew what that had been. And Emma, of course, had been a witness to it.

"It's okay, baby. I know you're confused, but..."

There was no way she could explain everything that was going on to a terrified eight-year-old. Especially one who had no reason to believe anything she said. This was what Jeb had warned her about. Emma didn't know her. She had no reason to trust her or anyone else. Not after what had happened to the two people at the center of her small world.

Despite the fact that Wayne Adams had stolen her daughter, he and Diane were the only family Emma had ever known. To lose both of them—suddenly and violently—was more than any child should be expected to endure.

"That's Jeb," Susan said, trying to make her voice reassuring. "He's a friend. Everything's all right now, I promise. Nothing bad is going to happen to you."

The child had looked at her as she talked, but almost immediately her eyes darted back to the house. She shook her head as Susan attempted to urge her forward again.

"You don't have to go back inside. We're going to walk along the track back to the highway—"

"Susan?"

"We're here."

Again, she tried to locate Jeb. He turned at the sound of her voice, the motion drawing her eyes. With the darkness of the soaked T-shirt and jeans he wore, it had been almost impossible to spot him until he was facing her.

Limping more heavily than usual, he started toward

them at once. Afraid that Emma would think it was
Jemison, Susan looked back at her to explain.

"That's my friend Jeb. His truck's out on the highway. We'll walk back to it and call the police."

She realized suddenly there was no reason to wait
until they reached the truck. She had stuffed her cell
phone in the pocket of her slacks before they'd locked
the truck.

She reached into her pocket to retrieve it, feeling the
clammy, wet fabric in dismay. As she'd crouched in the
water, shielding Emma as much as she could, she had
never once thought about the damage the river would
do to her phone.

It was too late to worry about it now. They needed
to get away from here and drive into Pascagoula. It
couldn't be far, not given the distance they'd followed
Diane's pickup along that narrow, twisting road.

"You okay?"

She looked up in response to Jeb's question. Every
stitch he wore was wet. Water trickled from his hair and
down his face, colorless in the moonlight. His mouth was
slightly open, his breathing shallow but audible.

"What's wrong?"

He shook his head, holding out his hand to her. Pulling Emma with her, she moved into his arms instead,
which closed around her so tightly it took her breath.

*They were safe.* Thank God, all of them were safe.

After a moment he leaned back, increasing the distance between them. "She all right?" he asked, nodding
toward Emma.

"Considering."

"Then let's get her out of here."

He turned, and for the first time she saw the stain on the back of his shirt. The splotch was frighteningly large, obviously blacker than the water-soaked material around it.

"You're bleeding."

"Yeah. It's okay." Something about the quality of that attempted reassurance wasn't at all reassuring.

"Jeb?"

He wasn't a man who would welcome her solicitousness. She had recognized that the night they met. This, however...

"We need to get into town. To get *her* into town," he said, nodding again toward Emma before he continued his slow progress toward the track that led out of the clearing.

"What about the other one?"

It took a second for the import of Emma's question to register. Susan had already opened her mouth to ask who she meant, when Jeb whirled around.

He glanced questioningly at Susan. When she shook her head in bewilderment, he closed the distance between them as quickly as his limp and obvious exhaustion would allow.

"What *other* one, Alex?" Jeb stooped down so that he was on eye level with the little girl. As he did, an involuntary grunt of effort or pain escaped between his set lips.

"I think she means me." The voice came from the darkness behind him. "I'm really sorry, Jeb, especially since you worked so damn hard to take care of Jemison, but...sometimes that's the way things play out. We don't always get what we want."

WITHOUT ATTEMPTING to get to his feet again, a task that seemed Herculean despite the sudden sickening surge of adrenaline, Jeb pivoted in the speaker's direction. He had to put his hand on the ground as vertigo washed over him.

He blinked, trying to clear his vision enough to find the man among the shadows that stretched across the clearing. When he opened them again, he discovered that the figure was frighteningly close. Close enough that Jeb could identify, despite the darkness and his light-headedness, what the man carried.

Apparently the need to get this over and done now outweighed any desire for silence. The crack of that high-powered rifle would echo a long way down the river. Of course, by the time someone reacted to it, it would be far too late.

Jeb straightened the elbow of the arm he'd been holding himself upright with, using it to push up off the ground. Then he stood, swaying slightly, trying to think of something he could do as the last person on earth he would have expected to be involved in this advanced across the clearing.

No wonder the sign at the end of the pier had seemed so familiar. He must have seen that word a dozen times atop that damn poem in Duncan McKey's office.

> I thank whatever gods may be
> For my unconquerable soul…

You vicious bastard, he thought, watching the surgeon's advance. Always so goddamn concerned. So supportive. And all the time—

"The surprisin' thing is that I really *am* sorry it's got to end this way," McKey said. "I knew once you got your teeth into this, you wouldn't give up. But then, neither can I. Not now. There's too much at stake. My whole life's work. You, better than anyone, should be able to understand that. Besides, love and war have no rules."

The familiar drawl reverberated in his head like an echo. If the bastard was going to shoot him, Jeb thought bitterly, he should have the decency to do it without talking him to death.

*Death.* The harsh reality of the word stopped his attempt at bravado. Although he wasn't unaccustomed to the possibility, this was in no way how he'd ever envisioned his own death. Not the kind of combat in which he had thought he might fall.

But McKey had it right. What he'd said about love and war. This whole thing, from the beginning to the end, had been about both. He just hadn't figured out in time who his enemy was.

*And as for the other...*

He wished he'd told her, he acknowledged, watching McKey come closer, his stride unhurried. He had foolishly believed he'd have plenty of time when everything else had been resolved. After she found Emma. After his reevaluation. And now? With a bitterness as caustic as bile, he knew it was too late.

There had to be *something* he could do, he told himself, fighting the lethargy that spread deeper into his brain with every heartbeat. At the least, he could try to prolong it.

"Why?"

There was no reason for McKey to respond to his question except ego, which was exactly what Jeb was counting on. After all, no one reached the position McKey held without a very healthy dose of self-esteem. Add to that the god complex inherent in the personalities of most doctors...

"Why? Because it turns out the bastard wasn't only cheatin' the stockholders, he was cheatin' me as well."

Not Richard. The only person that description fit was McKey's former partner, Ray DeCourtney.

"So you killed him."

It wasn't a question. DeCourtney's death shortly after Richard's disappearance now seemed too obviously coincidental. Another of the dots Jeb hadn't connected in time.

"Hell, if I hadn't, his greed would have brought it all down. And me with it. If somebody like Kaiser, some shit-ass low-level bean counter, could figure out what Ray had been doin', it stood to reason somebody else would."

"Richard Kaiser called you when he found DeCourtney was cooking the books," Jeb said, finally putting it all together despite the growing buzz in his head.

"Said he needed somebody he could trust to do 'the right thing.'" Amusement colored the deep accent. "Seems his boss wasn't too happy with him accusing a major client of some pretty serious criminal activity."

"And that's when Kaiser made the mistake of trusting you."

"I told him whatever he did, not to tell anybody where he was going. That until I had the proof he said he had in my hands, I was as vulnerable as he was. He bought it hook, line and sinker."

Poor stupid bastard. He had bundled up his baby and headed down here to meet the world-famous surgeon with the spotless reputation. The man who had been building DeCourtney's company into the household name it would become. Following McKey's advice, Richard had been careful not to use his cell or his credit cards or leave a message for his wife. And then he'd walked straight into the trap set for him by a man who was every bit as ruthless as his dead partner.

"And then you killed him."

"If I *hadn't*, Ray would have. He'd already tried once and botched it. That's what sent the stupid son of a bitch running to me. Pretty much par for the course."

"Except you botched it, too."

Jeb had realized with a dawning sense of hope that McKey was exactly what he'd always been. Overconfident. Almost cocky. So sure of his own success and his omnipotence.

Despite the range of the weapon he carried, the doctor had moved in too close. Another foot or two…

"Yeah, well, it's hard to get good help around here," McKey said, again clearly amused. "We live in a world of shiftless white trash, Jeb. You know it, and I know it. We may not talk about it openly—"

"Adams." He and Susan had been wrong. Wayne hadn't *found* Richard's body, he'd been sent to kill him.

"Wayne had done some things for me in the past. Nothing like that, of course, but he was always short of money. Goes with the territory, I guess."

And that piece of information made sense of Diane's big house and truck and everything else. Ironically, that's where the money Adams had gotten for Richard's murder—and maybe even Richard and Susan's savings—had gone. To provide a suitable home for Emma.

And the fact that Wayne hadn't been ruthless enough to murder a baby girl had been the thing that had eventually caused this to unravel. McKey could have afforded to hire the best for his dirty work, a professional who would have had no qualms about doing what he'd been asked to do, but this had apparently been set up on short notice. Probably as soon as Richard had placed that fatal call to him.

McKey had been the one who'd warned him about using his cell again. About the danger of leaving a message for Susan. All the things that had made it so easy for him and Adams to do exactly what they'd done seven years ago. Make Richard Kaiser disappear.

"But then that stupid bastard took the baby for his slut of a sister."

The bastard the surgeon made reference to this time was Adams, Jeb realized. Of course, in McKey's world that's what they all were. Stupid bastards to be manipulated by him. Kaiser, Adams, Buck Jemison and even Jeb.

"If he hadn't," the doctor went on, "none of this would be happening now. We'd all be home, not having to bother with any of this…unpleasantness."

"He was supposed to leave Emma in the SUV with her father."

There was an intake of breath or a shift of position behind him. Susan or the little girl reacting to that revelation?

"Who the hell coulda guessed Kaiser would bring

his *baby* with him? I didn't have any idea he had. Not until I read in the papers that she was missing along with him. I called Wayne as soon as I saw that. Bastard swore to me she'd been in the car when he'd pushed it into the river. I didn't know he'd lied to me until you told me."

That day after his therapy session. His words were what had gotten Wayne killed.

Again McKey hadn't dirtied his own hands. He'd called on another of his henchmen to take care of the problem Wayne represented. Just as when Richard phoned him.

In the process Jemison had gotten what he wanted— Adams's job. But he had also sold his soul to the devil to keep it. When McKey called on him to carry out tonight's murders, Buck couldn't refuse.

"Stupid redneck. All Adams had to do was think for himself. For once in his life, just figure out the smart thing to do. Do what anybody with half a brain would have done in that situation. Instead, he takes the kid home with him."

"It's hard to kill a baby," Jeb said, putting his right hand under the elbow of his injured arm.

He shifted his weight off his bad leg as he did, managing to move half a step forward. There was no reaction from McKey. Again that tiny spark of hope flared inside his chest.

McKey had probably evaluated his physical condition by now, discounting any possibility Jeb might try to attack. What the surgeon didn't understand, however, because he *wasn't* a soldier, was that there *were* some rules of war. And the primary one of them was: Never underestimate your enemy.

He charged, watching McKey's eyes widen as he tried to bring the weapon into the firing position. Time seemed to slow as Jeb closed the few feet that separated them, his entire focus on reaching the tip of the barrel before McKey could pull the trigger.

He was aware of nothing but that. Forgotten were the wound in his shoulder, the loss of blood, the damaged leg. He was totally concentrated on what he had to do to save their lives.

The fingers of his outstretched hand touched the bottom of the barrel, shoving it upward. The report of the shot, which occurred almost simultaneously with the contact, was right in his ear. He could feel the powder burn across his cheek. Apparently the split-second delay between his touch and McKey's squeeze of the trigger, however, had allowed his eyelids to close enough to protect his sight.

Ears ringing, he careened into the doctor, carrying him to the ground. Whatever McKey's credentials as a sportsman, he wasn't a fighter like Jemison had been. Instead of trying to roll and take Jeb over with him, he was attempting to maneuver the gun to get off another shot.

Running on sheer adrenaline, Jeb wrenched the weapon out of his hands. Without a moment's hesitation, he used both hands on the barrel to bring the butt down in the middle of McKey's face.

Panting, he raised the weapon once more, prepared to hit him again if the murdering son of a bitch so much as twitched. He waited, rifle raised, through endless seconds.

He could feel the effects of the adrenaline that had fueled his desperate charge begin to fade. As it did, weakness, like the effects of anesthesia, invaded his limbs.

The rifle seemed too heavy. And the task of climbing off the man he'd just struck with it too difficult to contemplate. The only other option, however, was to fall face forward onto McKey's body. Which was a definite possibility right now.

He closed his mouth, trying to control his ragged breathing. Then he laid the rifle across McKey's throat, intending to use it to push himself up.

Someone touched his shoulder. Still in combat mode, Jeb swung the gun he'd just thought he couldn't hold a second longer around. And found he was pointing it at Susan.

He had no idea how she'd gotten there. He hadn't heard movement behind him. Of course, given the nearness of the rifle shot, he was probably still deaf. She might have been talking to him before she touched him, and he wouldn't have heard her.

"Here."

He lip-read the word as she stretched out her hand. He started to take it and realized he still held the rifle. And then realized that was what she was reaching for.

"Ask her if there's anybody else."

"Emma? Ask Emma?"

He nodded, feeling the scene around him waver with the motion. He needed to get them away from here before he passed out. He released the barrel of the gun, letting it fall onto McKey's chest. He turned his head, watching Susan because he couldn't hear her.

Although he knew the effect would fade shortly, the temporary deafness was one more thing to be dealt with. Right now, he wasn't dealing with any of them too well.

This time Susan knelt beside him before she spoke. He watched her lips, trying to make sure that despite the darkness, he didn't miss anything.

"She says there were just the two of them."

He nodded. "Can you guard him until I get the truck?"

She glanced down at the body he was astride and then quickly back up. "He's *dead,* Jeb. *Nobody* has to guard him."

She took his hand, guiding his fingers to the artery at the side of McKey's neck. He waited a long time, the tips of his fingers pressed against cooling flesh of the man who was the reason he'd come to Linton. His miracle worker. His last chance.

Finally Susan put her hand on his wrist, drawing his attention back to her. He'd almost forgotten she was there.

"He's dead, Jeb. I need your keys."

He shook his head, unsure what she meant.

"The keys to the truck. I'm going to go get it and come back and pick you up. And I'm going to take Emma with me. Just... Just stay here, and we'll be back as soon as we can."

He nodded, pushing himself upright so that he could fish the keys out of the pocket of his jeans. He held them out to her, dropping them onto her palm. He watched her fingers close around them, but he'd already forgotten why she needed them.

She stood up, reaching back to take her daughter's hand. "Are you going to be all right?"

He raised his head, the motion almost beyond his

strength. The moonlight formed a halo around Susan's head. It shimmered, as if the light were reflecting off the surface of the river.

He nodded, although he had no idea if he could remain upright until she got back. He didn't want them to go alone, but he knew he'd finally reached the end of his strength. There was no way in hell he could make it back to the highway.

"Be careful."

"You just be here when we get back," Susan said. "You hear me? You wait right here for us."

He nodded again, almost the only response he seemed capable of. And then he remembered what he'd been thinking before he'd gone after McKey. Something he needed to tell her.

Maybe this wasn't the time nor the place, but he wasn't all that sure he would get another opportunity. And if he didn't, he still wanted her to know.

Maybe that was selfish, but there were too many things he *hadn't* done in his life. This wasn't going to be one of them.

"I love you," he whispered.

She had already taken a step, heading toward the track that would lead back to the highway. She turned, her eyes wide in the moonlight.

"What did you say?"

He caught the words this time, thankful he no longer had to rely on reading her lips. This was far too important.

"You heard me."

She released Emma's hand and came back to where he was kneeling over McKey's body. She bent, putting her hand along his cheek. She left it there, looking down into his eyes for a long time. Then, still without saying anything, she put her lips over his.

They were cold, trembling either with the stress of the situation or with emotion. His mouth opened, welcoming her kiss. After a moment she broke it, putting her forehead against his. He leaned against her strength.

"Promise me," she whispered.

"Promise you what?"

"That you'll be here when I get back."

He swallowed, wondering if he wanted to die with a lie on his lips. But if he didn't tell her what she wanted to hear, she might not go.

"Jeb? You promise me, you hear?"

"I hear."

"Say it."

"I'll be here. I promise."

She nodded, still looking into his eyes. Her lips tightened, before she bent and pressed them against his forehead.

He shut his eyes, thankful for the reprieve from her scrutiny. He opened them again as she straightened.

Without saying anything else, she took Emma's arm and began to run. He watched as long as he could see them, and when he couldn't anymore, he lowered his head and closed his eyes.

This, too, was the same kind of journey he'd become familiar with in the last year. Just like the one that had taken place out in the river tonight. Just like the long, difficult months after he'd gotten home from Iraq.

All he had to do was what he'd done before.

Manage one more breath. One more heartbeat. And one last journey.

"THAT MAN YOUR FRIEND KILLED. He was talking about me, wasn't he?"

Emma's question pulled Susan's mind from its frenzied anxiety about Jeb. She'd been so concerned with getting help for him, she'd forgotten to worry about how her daughter might interpret the things McKey had said before he died.

"I promise I'll explain everything," Susan said, glancing over at the small figure huddled in the passenger seat of Avalanche. "It's just that now we need to watch for the ambulance."

Although she had desperately wanted to go back to the riverbank as soon as she finished the 911 call, the dispatcher had assured her that help would get to Jeb much quicker if she waited at the turnoff and led them directly to him. So she and Emma were sitting in the big truck, its flashers on to signal the location for the paramedics who were on their way.

"He said Uncle Wayne was supposed to leave the baby in the SUV," the little girl went on, her face a pale oval in the dimness of the interior. "But that he didn't. Then he said he took that baby home with him and gave it to his sister."

Emma left out the derogatory descriptive McKey had used for the woman she believed was her mother. Other than that, she seemed to have grasped all the implications.

"That's right," Susan said.

She still didn't want to deal with this right now. The violence the child had witnessed tonight made it seem as if this would be the worst possible time to explain that everything she'd known her entire life had been a lie. And that the people she had loved—and lost—had been as guilty in what had happened as the surgeon himself.

"Then that means..." The little girl hesitated, obviously trying to work out what it *did* mean. And perhaps trying to come to grips with the enormity of what had been revealed tonight.

She had already heard too much, Susan realized. Now Emma needed assurance that, even though the world she'd known had just fallen apart, there was another waiting for her. One that had been waiting for her for seven years.

"It means that you're my baby," Susan said softly. "The one I lost when your father's car went into the river all those years ago. I've been looking for you ever since."

Her voice broke on the last, with the realization that her long search was finally over. Her daughter, the one she had last seen holding up chubby arms begging to be held, was sitting beside her.

"Then...*I'm* the one you came to school to find? *I'm* the Emma you were looking for?"

After she'd found the picture on Wayne Adams's desk, Susan had wondered through what act of Providence it had been Emma who had come to the fence that day. Was it possible that some unconscious memory had drawn Emma to her?

She would never know how much, if anything, a toddler that age might remember, but it didn't seem beyond the realm of possibility that it might be enough to respond to her mother's face. And enough to trust that she would keep her safe, as Emma had tonight.

"I never stopped looking for you," Susan said. "Not since the day you disappeared. I just had no way to know where you were. Not until..."

*Not until your father's body was recovered.* She allowed the sentence to trail. There was no reason to remind Emma of another loss to add to those she'd already suffered.

"And as soon as I can," she went on, "I'm going to take you home with me."

"To live there? With you?"

Susan nodded, her throat aching with the promise of that.

"Forever?" The little girl's eyes were wide in the darkness, her question only a whisper.

"Forever and ever and ever." The tears Susan had denied so long could not be contained. With a stifled sob, she attempted to regain control. She had to. *For Jeb's sake.*

"Don't cry," Emma said, reaching out to put her hand on top of Susan's, which lay on the wide console between them. "It will be all right."

"Yes, it will." Susan attempted a smile, clasping the small, cold fingers in her own.

Then, unable to resist, she leaned toward her daughter, halfway expecting the child to recoil. With the fingers of her left hand, she stroked the baby-fine hair away from Emma's cheek before allowing them to close around her daughter's head to draw her close.

Emma leaned into the embrace, allowing Susan's lips to rest against the softness of her hair, just as they had done so long ago. Conveying the same unmistakable message of love they had then.

Unspeaking, they didn't move again until a distant siren announced the arrival of the paramedics.

## CHAPTER TWENTY-EIGHT

"SHE'S WITH Child Protective Services until the results of the DNA test comes back. I can visit her, but I can't take her out of the state."

"And that's what you plan to do?"

"Since I live in Atlanta," Susan said with a smile, "I don't think I have any choice."

Maybe he wasn't clear about all that had happened the night he'd killed McKey, but Jeb had thought she'd made a choice then. Or maybe she'd just said anything she believed would keep him hanging on until she could get help. If that *had* been the case, it had obviously worked.

He supposed he should be grateful, no matter what her motives were. Right now, he wasn't. Not in the least. He was confused as hell because he'd been lying here for two days thinking some kind of commitment had been made between them.

One thing he was *very* clear about was that he was tired of being in the freaking hospital. He'd had his fill of them a long time ago. No matter where they were or who ran them, there were certain commonalities, none of which he liked. The loss of control and dignity. The fact that doctors treated you as if you weren't quite bright.

He realized with a jolt of regret that McKey had been the only one who'd ever treated him like an equal. Like someone who not only had the right to straight answers, but who should have an active role in his own course of treatment.

"So when are they going to release you?"

Susan's question seemed like an attempt to move the conversation away from the personal. Especially away from the possibility that he might ask her *not* to go back to Atlanta.

Maybe with the effects of the blood loss, he had gotten it all wrong. The fact that they'd made love, something that to him had signified a major change in their relationship, didn't mean she owed him anything. Not even an explanation.

Susan didn't seem like a woman who made that kind of decision lightly, but there had been extenuating circumstances. He had known that going in. None of which explained why he felt as if he'd been kicked in the stomach.

Maybe it was being back in a hospital bed. Or the knowledge that McKey wouldn't be pulling any strings on his behalf now. Or maybe, he admitted, it was the fact that for the first time in his adult life, he wanted some kind of permanence in a relationship. And the woman he wanted it with was talking about taking her daughter back to Atlanta as soon as the authorities would allow it.

"Jeb?"

*Suck it up, Bedford. You've never allowed yourself to wallow in self-pity before. For God's sake, don't start now. Not while she's around. And apparently that won't be too long.*

"I don't know," he said aloud.

"They haven't told you?"

"All I know is it can't be soon enough. I thought nowadays they kicked you out as soon as they slapped the stitches in."

Her relieved smile erased the furrow that had formed between her brows. "Yeah, well, considering you were almost dead by the time they got you here…"

He knew she'd used his phone to call 911 when she reached the Avalanche. He hadn't been conscious when the paramedics arrived, but he could have sworn he remembered her riding into Pascagoula with him in the ambulance, holding his hand and talking to him. Maybe he'd been mistaken about that, too.

"I don't kill easy."

"That's a very good thing."

"You have any trouble with the sheriff here?"

"Surprisingly little. I was afraid they wouldn't believe me, especially not about McKey, but when they found Diane's body inside the house and that rifle—engraved with his name, by the way—beside his, it was clear he'd been involved."

"I never even knew he had a place out there."

"I don't think he used it anymore. Not since he'd gotten so wealthy. It was pretty primitive. But then, according to the sheriff here, he had owned it for a long time."

"I wonder if that's where he met Richard."

"Wherever that rendezvous was supposed to be, it's possible Adams stopped Richard before he reached it. Even in a situation like that, on the run and essentially in hiding, I think Richard would still have responded to flashing lights coming up behind him. Especially with Emma in the car. He would probably have be-lieved it was one of those small-town speed traps if he'd thought anything about it."

"Wayne must have been on McKey's payroll a long time before that night. You don't just call up the local law and ask him to commit a murder for you."

He'd been lying here thinking about the possibilities. Of course, he'd had nothing else to do. Nothing except think about Susan.

"That's what the sheriff believes, too. Adams cer-tainly could have used the money, given the typical pay of rural law enforcement officers down here. And you'd be hard pressed to find a county as poor as Johnson."

"A little homegrown corruption must have been tough to resist," he said. "And I doubt McKey asked him to do anything very objectionable to begin with. I'm also sure, knowing how well off the good doctor was, that he would pay well. Probably before he knew it, Wayne was in too deep to get out."

"And Buck? You think he just inherited the job?"

"Jemison may have been in on things from the start. Or McKey may have dangled enough money in front of his nose to convince him it was to his advantage to take out his boss."

That was another conclusion he'd come to that night. It was probably Jemison who'd murdered Adams. And he was convinced it *had* been murder, designed either to keep Wayne from talking as the situation began to unravel or to punish him for screwing up seven years ago.

"It would have been so easy to do," he said aloud. "Just stand there talking to him while Wayne worked under his truck. Buck had probably done the same thing a hundred times."

"And this time he just kicked the jack out of the way?"

"I don't think we'll ever know all of it. Not for sure. But…we know enough."

She nodded. The silence that followed the natural end of that line of thinking was definitely strained. Like one between strangers who have run out of pleasantries to exchange.

"When will they have the results of the DNA match for Emma?" he asked, more to ease that tension than because he really wanted to know.

"They promised them as soon as possible."

"I won't hold my breath."

"I think, after the publicity this has generated, they really mean it."

"You're probably right. Considering McKey's involvement, I'll bet the media are all over the story."

He hadn't turned on the TV since he'd been in here. He hadn't needed it. He'd had his own fantasies going. Mooning over Susan like some lovesick kid.

"*And* considering who you are," she said, smiling again.

"*Me?* What does that mean?"

"Special Forces hero solves cold case and takes out the bad guys. I'm sorry to be the one to break the news, because I suspect you'll hate it, but you're quite the media darling."

"You're kidding, right?"

"Someone's bound to offer you a book and movie

deal for the story. Get approval for whoever plays me, please."

"Shit," he said succinctly.

If there was anything he *didn't* need right now it was some idiot trying to get a headline out of this. He could imagine what his guys would say. If they saw anything like that mock headline Susan had just spouted, he'd never hear the end of it.

"You better get used to it, Jeb," Susan said, her voice suddenly serious. "The story has already gone national. A celebrity doctor with a Fortune 500 company. Add to that a couple of unsolved murders, an abducted baby, and you, of course. All the thing needs is a little sex—" She stopped, a flush of color moving under the smooth translucence of her cheeks.

"You're the only woman I know who blushes because she made love. We're consenting adults, Susan. What we did is legal. *Even* in Mississippi."

"But...it isn't something I do lightly. I guess that makes me... Actually, I don't know what it makes me."

"Smart. Especially these days."

He had known that night was an aberration. That had been evident in everything she'd said and done. And he had also known exactly why she'd let him make love to her. It had been a way to forget, if only for a few hours, that she had no idea where her daughter was or whether she would ever see her again.

"If I was going to do something so out of character—and believe me, it was—then I'm just glad I was smart enough to pick someone like you. Someone I could trust."

He supposed that was a compliment. Again, he was

hard pressed to be grateful. "Someone like you" felt pretty generic. And *nothing* that had happened between them that night could be characterized as "generic." Not for him.

But then, he had already realized Susan didn't feel the same way. He'd walked away from his share of relationships through the years simply because the other party wanted to make them into something he didn't intend for them to be. He was the last person on earth to blame her for doing the same thing.

"I don't think I can ever express how grateful I am, Jeb. If it hadn't been for your help—"

"I don't want your gratitude." That didn't come out the way he'd intended. He sounded curt. Almost belligerent.

"That doesn't stop me from feeling it. I won't *say* it again if it makes you uncomfortable, but you *have* to know what finding Emma means to me."

"I know," he said, working to erase the anger from his voice. "I'm glad everything's worked out for the two of you. How's she doing, by the way?"

Susan's shoulders moved, not quite a shrug. "She's… a little lost, I think. We're both feeling our way. You were right about that, too. I realized it that night at the river. She had no reason to trust me. She still doesn't. I'm working on that, but I know it's going to take a long time."

"Have you told her everything?"

"She heard the hardest part that night. I wondered how much she understood, but she's very bright. Very perceptive. Do I sound as if I'm bragging?" she finished with a laugh.

"You have a right to."

"Do I? I didn't have much to do with shaping her into the kind of person she is."

"They say kids' personalities are pretty much formed by the time they're two. You had her most of that time. And you can't discount the role heredity played in who she is."

"The psychologists would have a field day with that."

"Don't give them a chance," he advised. "Take her home and just...love her."

"I will."

The few seconds of silence that followed her promise felt as strained as the previous one had. As if they were strangers.

"Take care of yourself," she said softly.

He nodded, not trusting himself to speak. She took a step toward the door before she turned and came back to the bed, much closer than she had been before. Then, just as on the night he'd killed McKey, she bent, laying her fingers along his cheek.

This time her lips were warm and very soft. And once again they trembled.

That tiny crack in this morning's cool, collected facade revealed *some* emotion she hadn't confessed, releasing the dam his anger and pride had built. He put his hand on the back of her head, pulling her to him almost roughly. He pressed his lips against hers, demanding, until they opened to his tongue.

The kiss was long and deep. Again, she was the one who broke it, leaning back to look into his eyes.

"Don't go," he said.

Her pupils dilated slightly before she blinked. He

could still see the sheen of moisture from his kiss on her bottom lip.

"What does that mean? *Exactly*," she added.

"It means whatever you want it to mean."

"That isn't an answer."

"Is this?"

He leaned forward, trying to put his mouth over hers again. She avoided the kiss by backing up a step. His hand slipped off the silk of her hair, freeing her.

"Jeb?"

He didn't respond, closing his lips, the feel of her kiss still on them. He'd made his offer. Whether or not she accepted was up to her. He damn sure wasn't going to beg.

"What did that mean?" she demanded again, her eyes searching his face.

"It meant I don't want you to go."

"*You're* going."

"*Me?* Where the hell do you think *I'm* going?"

"Back to your unit. That's what you said. That it was all you've ever wanted. You were so excited." She stopped, comprehension flooding her eyes. "Oh my God, Jeb. McKey."

He knew, as unbelievable as it seemed, that she hadn't thought what the doctor's death meant to him until now. That was hardly surprising. She'd had to deal with the authorities and the press, on top of trying to reconnect with Emma.

Besides, he was a grown man. And normally a realistic one. Even with McKey's influence, it would have been a long shot that he'd have gotten another extension.

The Army didn't work that way, especially not with Delta.

"It probably wouldn't have changed anything."

"I'm so sorry."

"Don't be," he said too harshly. He needed to say this without revealing the tangled emotions he'd already had time to come to terms with. "McKey was a murdering son of a bitch. He killed at least three people, and he would have killed you and me and Emma without giving it a second thought. He deserved to die, Susan. I'm glad I was the one who got to do it."

"And I'm glad you were there *to* do it. So don't tell me I don't have the right to be grateful."

"Except gratitude isn't what I want from you."

*You'd made it this far, and then you had to spill your guts. The question had already been asked and answered.*

"What *do* you want, Jeb?"

As open an invitation as he'd ever gotten. Except if he told her what he wanted, and she turned him down—

Then what? At least he'd have tried. And he wouldn't spend the rest of his life regretting that he hadn't. All she could do was say no.

"I want what Richard had."

The stillness after his confession stretched a long time. He could hear the faint hospital noises from the corridor outside, but they seemed to belong to another world. His had narrowed to what was taking place in this room.

"And what would that be?" Susan asked finally.

"You." *First and always.* "Emma. A place to come home to. Someone waiting for me there when I do."

"To come home from somewhere like Iraq?"

He knew what stresses the kind of life he'd lived brought to a marriage. Some didn't survive. Some grew stronger.

Now that Susan was starting to put her life back together, to rebuild the bonds with Emma that had been broken so many years ago, it wouldn't be fair to ask her to undertake that as well. Besides, he'd given it his best shot. Even with McKey's influence, it might not have worked. Without it…

Delta, and all it represented, was over for him. After that night when he'd fought for their lives, he had known he couldn't change that. For injuries as extensive as his only so much rehab was possible. He had reached that point. Maybe if he hadn't found something he loved as much as he'd loved his profession, he might feel differently. But he had. And he didn't.

"Jeb?"

She was waiting for his answer, which was more than he deserved. But not deserving it wasn't going to prevent him from reaching out and taking what he wanted. He'd never been afraid of a challenge, even one he knew he might lose.

"Not from Iraq. From Linton. Or Atlanta. From wherever you'll agree to let me call home."

"Does that mean…? What *does* that mean?"

A desk. Retirement. Things that had been unthinkable a few days ago. The only unthinkable thing now was letting Susan walk out that door and knowing he'd never see her again.

"I don't know. I've never done anything in my entire adult life except the Army. But…I'm willing to try. If you are."

"Are you asking me—" She stopped, shaking her head slowly.

"Is that a no?"

"It's not a no. This is just such a surprise."

"Yeah. To me, too. Good or bad?"

"What?"

"A good or bad surprise?"

"Just… Are you sure you know what you're doing?"

"The one thing I didn't have that night was a concussion. I, Jubal Early Bedford, being of sound mind—"

"That's for making a will."

"I think deciding to get married should require a sounder mind than making a will."

"Is that what we're doing? Deciding to get married?"

"I don't know what you're doing, but I think I decided that a pretty good while ago."

"So this has nothing to do with McKey's death. Or the fact that…"

"That I'm not going to go back to Delta?" he supplied when she hesitated. "Maybe. At least partially. But it has a whole hell of a lot more to do with how impossible it would be to watch you walk out that door and know you aren't coming back."

"I have a daughter, Jeb. An eight-year-old daughter who doesn't even know me."

"It's as easy to get to know two parents as it is one. We may as well start as we intend to go on." He laughed, remembering where he'd learned that.

"Lorena says that all the time. I never understood what it meant until now."

"What do you think it means?"

"That I intend to marry you. And that I intend to be a father to Emma. And that I intend to love you both for the rest of our lives."

"Do I have any say in any of this?" she asked with a smile.

"Only if your say is yes."

"Then…yes."

He had expected resistance. At least some hesitation. A plea for time to think. He was infinitely relieved there had been none of those. Just yes. Unquestioning and unequivocal.

"Soon," he suggested. Now that he had her agreement, he wasn't going to allow her time to have second thoughts.

"How soon is soon?"

"As soon as I'm out of here."

This was going to be one memory not tainted by starch-assed nurses and the smell of disinfectant. He hadn't had many of those during the last ten months, but this one was going to be right.

Actually, he thought as Susan took a step toward the bed, it was *all* going to be right. For the rest of their lives.

# EPILOGUE

*Eighteen months later*

"SOFTBALL, HUH?" Jeb had put down the book he'd been reading as Emma sat down on the arm of the couch beside him.

Susan never tired of watching the two of them together. And never ceased to be amazed at the effort Jeb had made to win her daughter over. An effort that no one who knew them could doubt had been successful.

"And we need a coach."

"Don't look at me. I don't know anything about softball."

"It's not that different from baseball. You know something about baseball, don't you?"

"I played a little."

"Don't worry. You don't really have to *do* anything. Not like running or hitting or anything. You just have to say who gets to play where. Like who's on first and all."

"And I don't know's on third."

"What?"

"Never mind. Old joke."

"Oh, like in *Rain Man*."

"No, like in Abbott and Costello."

"Whatever," Emma said dismissively. "Will you do it?"

Sending Emma to private school in Moss Point had been the one concession they'd made to the firestorm of gossip that had rocked the area after the truth had come out about Richard's murder. Other than that, they had tried to live their lives in Linton as normally as possible.

Susan had briefly considered returning her new family to Atlanta, but the memories there were almost more painful than the ones here. And she could send her illustrations to her publisher from anywhere.

Besides, there had also been Lorena to consider. The growing bond between the old woman and the child who had come to live in this old house was something Susan was also grateful for every day of their lives. Every child needed a grandmother, and there had never been a more loving one than Lorena.

"Who told you to ask me?"

"We talked about it."

"We who?"

"The girls. We decided you should be our coach."

"I think you should be flattered," Susan said. She folded the last of the clothes she'd taken out of the dryer and put them into the basket to take upstairs.

"Flattered because I'm being told I can take the job without having to worry about being able to run or bat?"

"Maybe they think you're too old," Susan teased.

She loved the hint of gray now mingled with the dark hair at his temples, but she would imagine that to a bunch of preteen girls that would certainly suggest old age. She would beg to differ, but then her knowledge on that particular subject was far more intimate than anyone else's.

"What do you think about that?" he asked, a gleam she recognized in his eyes.

"I think you ought to take the job."

"I didn't mean that."

"I know what you meant."

"So will you?" Emma demanded, thankfully missing the subtle undercurrent of their words.

"I'll think about it."

"But I need to know by tomorrow. We have to have uniforms and everything. Oh, and a team mother," she said, turning imploring eyes toward Susan.

Little could her daughter know how flattered she was by the suggestion. She suspected Jeb was as well, but this would be a greater commitment of time for him.

"What color are the uniforms?" Jeb asked.

"I don't know yet. We haven't decided."

"Make it khaki, and we have a deal."

"Khaki? Who wants a khaki uniform?" Emma asked, her small nose wrinkling in disgust.

"Certainly nobody around here," Jeb said, grinning at Susan. "That was just a touch of nostalgia."

"I don't understand."

"That's because you're just a little girl," Jeb teased.

Emma leaned over, putting her face very close to his. "Will you or won't you?"

"For you, princess, anything."

"Does that mean yes?"

The joy in her face would, Susan suspected, be reward enough, but when Jeb nodded, putting his forehead against Emma's, she threw her arms around his neck in a hug.

"Thank you."

"You're welcome."

Emma scrambled off the couch to head to the phone. "Oh, I forgot," she said, turning back in the doorway. "Would it be okay if I called you Daddy? That's what the other girls..." The explanation trailed, but the hope in her eyes expressed the one she hadn't quite articulated.

"I think I'd like that," Jeb said.

"Maybe just not during the games. I should probably call you Coach then."

"Good idea."

"Okay. I'll go tell them." Emma disappeared, bare feet slapping against the wooden floors of the wide front hall.

"I think I like that, too, Daddy," Susan said. "Congratulations."

"Better than oak leaves any day of the week."

"I don't think I've said thank-you lately," she said, taking Emma's place on the arm of the couch. She moved the book out of the way before she leaned down, just as her daughter had, to press a kiss against his forehead. "Thank you."

"Not that I'm opposed to a little gratuitous gratitude, but what exactly am I being thanked for here?"

"For Emma. For sharing Lorena with her. And with me." She kissed him on each eye and then on the tip of the nose as she enumerated the items. "For loving her. For loving me."

With her final kiss against his lips, Jeb pulled her into his arms, wrapping them around her so that once more she could feel his heartbeat. Slow and steady. Comforting. Dependable.

After a moment, he put his chin on the top of her head and whispered what sounded like, "'I thank whatever gods may be…'"

"What?" she asked without moving.

"Something I read once. It seemed appropriate."

"I love you, Jubal Early Bedford."

"And that, my love, in case I haven't told *you* lately, is what *I'm* grateful for."

*Turn the page for
an exciting preview
of
Gayle Wilson's
TAKE NO PRISONERS
a new
PHOENIX BROTHERHOOD
story coming from
Harlequin Intrigue in
July 2005*

*And don't forget to
watch for
Gayle Wilson's
next mainstream title from
HQN Books
DOUBLE BLIND
Available in November 2005*

"I've already told Griff I'm not interested. Several times, actually."

The deep voice on the other end of the line seemed resigned, almost amused rather than angry. Dalton Rawls knew that amusement wouldn't last.

This was a call he'd been dreading having to make ever since Griff Cabot had broached the idea. They had both agreed, however, that there was no one better suited for this mission than Landon James. And since technically it wasn't a Phoenix undertaking…

"This isn't about joining the Phoenix," Dalton said.

There was a beat of silence as the ex-CIA operative he'd just phoned digested the information. "Then what is it about?"

"A mutual acquaintance who's in trouble."

The silence this time was even more prolonged.

"If this isn't about the Phoenix, then I suppose I should assume that whoever we're talking about wasn't part of the External Security Team."

"We're talking about Grace Chancellor," Dalton said, seeing no point in making a mystery of his request. "Griff said you'd remember her."

The quality of the silence this time was different

somehow. As ridiculous as it seemed to believe he could judge something like that over the phone, Dalton knew he'd just taken the other man by surprise. A feat that had once been almost impossible to achieve.

"I remember."

Dalton couldn't quite read the tone of those two words, but he'd been right in his earlier speculation. Both the resignation *and* the amusement had disappeared.

"Tell me," Landon demanded into his continued silence.

"You know that she testified before Congress a few months ago."

"You mean when she told the Hill that their vaunted intelligence services didn't know what the hell they were doing during one of the most critical periods in this nation's history?"

"I don't believe she phrased it in exactly that way," Dalton said, making no effort to conceal his own amusement at how accurately Landon's opinion echoed those that had been expressed privately among the members of the Phoenix.

The Middle East had been Landon's area of expertise. Just as it was Grace Chancellor's. She'd been an intelligence analyst rather than an operative, but despite the fact that the two had struck sparks off one another on a number of occasions by supporting conflicting opinions about operations there, Dalton knew Landon had respected her opinions.

Whether that respect would translate into the ex-CIA agent taking action in this situation was something neither he nor Griff had been willing to predict.

Neither had they been willing to bet against it. They had agreed, however, that Landon James was their best hope.

*And Grace Chancellor's best hope as well.*

"Apparently she phrased it strongly enough that it's gotten her into trouble," Landon said. "The CIA despises whistle-blowers. Even those compelled to testify under oath."

"So much so," Dalton agreed, "that as a result of her testimony, the powers that be found Chancellor a new assignment."

"Let me guess. Reading satellite images."

"Something slightly more challenging. They put her in charge of stopping the heroin traffic out of Afghanistan."

Landon laughed, the sound short and harsh. "I'm surprised they didn't give her a spoon and a bucket and point her toward the nearest ocean."

"Grace wanted to see the extent of the problem for herself," Dalton went on, "as well as every aspect of the process by which the drugs are transported out of the country."

There was a noise from the other end of the line that sounded like derision. Unsure, Dalton decided to ignore it.

"The Army provided her with a military escort, some lieutenant colonel who was supposed to know the ropes and show her around. Chancellor probably knew more about what was going on before she arrived in country than he did after several months there."

"And knowing Chancellor," Landon said, "she didn't tell him that."

"The Kiowa they were riding in was hit by small-arms fire. Fortunately, the pilot was able to set the chopper down, but…"

"Go on," Landon urged when Dalton paused.

The voice on the other end of the line had become very soft.

"The body of the colonel's aide was found with the helicopter. Lieutenant Colonel Stern, the pilot and Grace Chancellor were not."

"Where did they go down?"

"The mountains just north of Kabul."

"Son of a bitch." The expletive was again soft, but obviously heartfelt. "How long ago?"

This was the part Dalton had most dreaded. "Nearly two weeks."

The expletive Landon uttered this time was expressive of his contempt. "And of course, no one at Langley knows who took them. Or where."

"Not a clue."

"Griff wants me to find her?"

The hesitation this time was Dalton's. "He recognizes that he has no right to ask you to do anything. He simply wanted me to make you aware of what has happened."

"Okay," Landon said. "Tell him I'm aware."